MURDER AT MADAME CHAMBON'S

LONDON LADIES IN PERIL MYSTERY
BOOK TWO

BEVERLEY OAKLEY

S A N I
PUBLISHING

ISBN: 978-0-6455868-7-9

www.beverleysbooks.com

Where danger and desire walk hand in hand...

PROLOGUE

1880

Evelina glanced out of the train window at the dusky haze of the fading afternoon and tried to temper her excitement.

The rhythmic clatter of wheels had put her maid, Mimi, to sleep, but Evelina was hurtling towards her future—at last! —with lightning speed.

Not only was she finally leaving France to return to the land of her birth, but she had all the backing needed by a young woman determined to make the most glittering marriage of the season and to secure the future *she* chose for herself.

"One scarlet and blue polonaise with blue velvet swathes and bows for Lady Gilray's ball, and the brown and green checked walking dress for the first promenade in Hyde Park..."

Mimi and she had spent hours deciding which of her vast couture wardrobe she'd wear for the events for which Lady Perry had secured an invitation for Evelina.

There'd be more to come, Evelina's mama had written, once word had spread of Evelina's beauty and accomplishments.

Not to mention, her dowry.

Then she'd wear the rose-pink princess-line polonaise with fan-shaped train to Lady Marchant's soiree...

She had hoped to have a ball or soiree lined up for every night of the week. At nearly twenty-one and with her beauty at its peak, Evelina didn't want to wait too long to find a suitable husband. In fact, she was determined to do so during her first London season. A brilliant match was what she wanted, though a good one would do if it happened sooner rather than later. She wasn't looking to fall in love. The nuns at the convent had made clear *that* was only in fairytales.

She rather thought she'd make a good political hostess in view of the education the nuns had given her, followed by her finishing school in Switzerland, complicated by her illness, which had held her back nearly two years.

But now she was in the best of health and her enthusiasm for becoming mistress of a large, impressive landholding, or similar as befitted her value, was at its zenith.

Then, for the Duchess of Kintyre's weekend house party, she'd have to take two trunks to fit—

Evelina was just doing a mental inventory of what to pack for the penultimate event of the season four weeks hence, when a bone-rattling jolt thrust her book out of her hands and sent her maid sprawling to the compartment floor.

"*Mon Dieu!* What's happening?" Evelina shielded her face as metal shrieked, the luggage from overhead tumbled to the floor, and passengers screamed in the surrounding compartments.

"Mimi! Mimi! Are you alright?"

A shuddering jolt propelled Evelina against the window with force, her head hitting the glass and her vision blurring.

She was vaguely aware of the commotion around her, but the urgency had dimmed, and suddenly everything seemed muted and very far away. She thought she could see Mimi bobbing about in the corner, and closed her eyes, for she didn't like the way her elegant French lady's maid looked right now, and—

"Miss! Madam!" The voice that jerked her into consciousness made her aware of the cold water seeping through her clothing and Evelina opened her eyes to a scene of horror, overlaid by the insistent calling of a male voice whom it took her a moment to locate.

A handsome young face loomed above her.

This seemed very odd, for she was in a train carriage on her way from Dover to London and no-one was supposed to be on the roof.

But then she realized the carriage in which she and Mimi had been traveling from the docks was on its side, the plush seats torn from the wood paneling, and water was now rising from the broken window at her feet.

"Please, miss! Quickly! Take my hand! There's not much time."

Evelina struggled to sit up, her sodden skirts heavy and confining about her ankles as she tried to regain her balance.

She realized that the face above her belonged to a young man who was crouched by the open door of the compartment which was on its side. He'd extended his arm and, judging by the look on his face and the urgency in his voice, matters were serious, and time was critical.

She managed to stand and to reach up, her hand curling around strong fingers before another violent lurch broke her grip.

With a scream, Evelina fell back against the window beneath her, and the young man's face grew distant.

"Take my wrist. I've got you!"

He hadn't, but his words were the reassurance she needed before she remembered her companion.

"Mimi?" She swung round, screaming again as she saw that the older woman's head was at an odd angle and her eyes were open and sightless.

"You can't do anything for her! Take my hand. We're running out of time!"

His urgency galvanized Evelina into action, but she had to jump to bridge the growing distance between the hand he held out as he now lay flat upon the upturned compartment which Evelina realized had slid down the embankment and into the river below.

And which was sinking fast.

He was strong. Strong enough to haul her entire body weight the distance needed before he had sufficient purchase to reach out his other hand and drag her through the broken window.

With a mighty heave, he pulled her free from the wreckage just as the carriage, burdened by its own weight and the pull of the river, slid into the water with a deafening splash.

Breathing heavily, Evelina collapsed against a pair of supporting arms and listened to the cries and screams of passengers amidst the turmoil and confusion.

But she was safe.

The thickness of her skirts and bodice had shielded her from the worst of potential injuries, though she saw her left hand was bloodied. Or perhaps it was a head wound, she wondered, as she withdrew her hand from wiping the hair from her eyes.

"Monsieur?" She cast around for her rescuer, her panic, at discovering she was alone again, increasing as she registered the carnage.

Not that she could see much until a gust of wind cleared the smoke sufficiently for her to realize that hers was one of two carriages that had derailed and slipped into the river, while the front few carriages remained on the track at the top of the embankment.

She was alone again, but alive, and all she needed to do was to negotiate the muddy climb to the top.

If she had the energy.

Evelina sank down upon the metal side of their compartment which separated her from Mimi. She wouldn't leave her friend, for Mimi had been with her since she'd gone to Switzerland. The young man would have to come back so he could get the older woman out when he'd finished saving other lives.

Her dazed thoughts were running in discombobulated loops before she was roused by the insistent screams of a woman some yards away, she saw, as the smoke once again cleared.

"William! My son William is still inside!"

Evelina sat up sharply. Then, scrunching up her skirts so she could move, she struggled through the mangled metal and mud towards the woman who was kneeling on the upturned carriage, dangling her arm through the gaping window.

"He's too small to reach! Help me! The water's rising!"

Evelina stared helplessly into the void. She couldn't see the child, but she could hear his frightened whimpers. The woman's cries grew louder in relation to Evelina's desperation.

"Please, sir! Help me!"

Evelina saw she'd thrust out her arm to grip a checked trouser leg, and she looked up into the face of the young man who had dragged her to safety a few minutes earlier. There was a cut above his eye and a smear of mud on his cheek, but nothing else marred his obvious good looks.

Unless it was the bleakness in his eye which was directed now towards the sound of the young boy in the far depths of the carriage. Even Evelina could see it was hopeless for him to help, for the distance was too great for his seeking arm to help a small child.

Unless—

"Hold me while I reach for him! You're strong enough!" Evelina burst out, unbuttoning her tight-fitting bodice, and unclasping her skirt as she spoke, closing the distance between them. The thick heavy swathes of embellishment slithered over the bustle cage which she untied with trembling fingers and tossed aside, unembarrassed as she wriggled into a sitting position with the help of the young man who hauled her into position. The glass of the window had completely fallen away, so at least no jagged edges impeded her rescue attempt.

Only the strength and willingness of the young man, but he was already gripping her wrist while she gripped his as he carefully lowered her into the compartment.

The claustrophobic darkness hit Evelina with force and momentarily dashed her bravado as she dangled helplessly into the void, completely dependent upon the strength of her rescuer. "William?" she called.

But when small fingers almost instantly tickled her palm, relief and purpose galvanized her courage once more. "William, take my hand and don't struggle!" she said, shouting back up to the light, "I've got him! Bring me up now!"

The little boy's eyes were wide with terror as he was drawn into the afternoon haze, before his mother threw herself upon him and Evelina fell back, her strength and courage drained.

"My name's William, too."

She blinked open her eyes as her handsome rescuer supported her into a sitting position, his warm, open smile revealing strong while teeth, his dark blue eyes seeming to connect to something deep inside her, causing a flowering sensation to bloom in her heart.

Then he was straightening at a distant cry for help, while a billow of smoke obscured him from view.

When Evelina tried to find him again so she could thank him properly, he'd gone.

"Miss! Are you all right?" Another team of rescuers, obviously from the nearby town, swarmed over the wreckage and Evelina was soon covered in a blanket before they carried her towards a line-up of carriages parked at the top of the embankment.

She twisted her head, searching for the young man—the older of the two Williams. But now the muddy slope and mangled carriages were overrun by strangers.

"Miss, let me tend to that nasty cut upon your forehead." They were motherly words and the soft hands of a woman who'd come to help were soothing. "Poor child, is someone looking for you? Let me clean you up so your loved ones can recognize you. Your poor mama, for a start, wouldn't begin to know who you were."

She was a farmer's wife by the look of her, and she'd seated herself next to Evelina in one of the carriages, cleaning Evelina's face as she spoke.

Evelina didn't answer. Her mama wouldn't know her, either way, for she'd not seen Evelina since her daughter was fourteen years old.

As for any other loved ones, that was why she'd come to London.

If not to love, then to establish a life.

The life she'd grown up believing was her due.

The one in which she finally would be mistress of her own destiny and no longer beholden to the mother who had farmed her off to the nuns when she was six because she'd said Evelina's wild and stubborn ways was the reason her papa had removed himself from the family home.

CHAPTER 1

LONDON ~ ONE WEEK LATER

It was business as usual at the editorial offices. The once austere back room of London's popular magazine *Manners and Morals* had been made more comfortable and in keeping with its new role: finding employment for the city's less employable.

But Lily McTavish—or Lady Bradden as she was known in society—was far from happy.

"Why the long face, my darling?" her husband asked as he lounged against the doorframe, having just stepped out from his own office. "I thought you'd be thrilled at having secured places for three girls in the past fortnight."

"But that's out of twenty girls, Hamish. And I had to offer mighty fine inducements." Lily leaned back in her chair and looked at him over her steepled fingers.

"Always so impatient," he said, his tone fond.

"I think it's reasonable to want to make up for lost time." Lily didn't usually dwell on the past. To her horror, a large tear trickled down her cheek which she dashed away, embarrassed and angry before she felt Hamish's hand on her shoulder.

"You have every reason to feel that," he said softly. "Two years stolen from you; spent in an insane asylum. But so much more than that when you consider what your late husband put you through."

"This isn't about me," Lily said, refusing to allow her beloved husband to make her feel any better. "I got more compensation than I needed or deserved when I married you, Hamish. But now I want to do what I can for these poor unfortunate women who are condemned to poverty and… and selling their bodies through no fault of their own. It pains me that people are so unwilling to employ them and so quick to condemn. They know nothing—"

"Hush, my love." Hamish stroked her hair. "Nor should you condemn my readers—and those who are merely seeking a 'good' girl to work for them—for their ignorance. Their lives are so cosseted and ordered. They will never understand life as you do. While it's all very well to educate them, it will take time. Patience," he added with a smile.

"It's hard to have patience, Hamish, when your weekly article has sparked so much interest, and women are coming here to seek a 'reformed' girl to work for them …but then they lose heart at the last moment. I have so many more girls seeking work than I do prospective employers."

"I think you mean to say that my weekly article—which, of course, is inspired, and written, by you—has sparked controversy." Hamish's tone was wry. "My father is horrified. He says we are going to lose subscribers, but I would argue the opposite. Controversy galvanizes people into voicing their opinions, which stimulates discussion. It certainly is true that our new article a week on one of London's unfortunate but deserving citizens is a grand way of getting people worked up. Now, that was an inspiration, Lily, my love."

"You inspired me to do good, Hamish. But I am failing."

"Nonsense. This is your third week of business. It takes time."

"Madam." The nervous clearing of a voice heralded Lizbeth's frightened face as the little secretary put her head around the door. "There's someone here to see you. It's regarding the position of lady's maid."

Lily heaved in a breath as she put her hand up to her fore-head. "Oh Hamish, I just don't know that I can help these women as I had hoped. So many of them who have fallen into vice now think I can find them respectable employment when the reality, I've discovered is—"

"Madam, it's a young lady who wishes to employ one of your girls."

Excited, Lily gripped Hamish's hand.

"I told you the tide would turn," Hamish murmured, straightening. Smiling at the young girl who had, herself, been a skivvy at Madame Chambon's, one of London's most notorious Houses of Assignation, before she'd been rescued by Lily, he said, "I'll leave now, Miss Whiley, so you can show my wife's new client through. Finding the right lady's maid is a difficult enough business at the best of times."

Certainly, securing a lady's maid for the young woman seated across the desk from Lily several minutes later would not be easy, Lily soon realized.

"You want her to be fluent in French?" she clarified. "But you are English?" Lily could hear the faintest trace of an accent with certain words.

"Yes, my former lady's maid, Mimi, was French. She used to prattle away in French and although it irritated me at the time, I now realize it's a comfort that I miss."

"You left her behind in France?"

"She died. She was killed." The young woman dropped

her gaze and her hands trembled. "In the train accident last week."

Lily drew in her breath, her gaze flying to the healing cut above the young woman's eye. "You were with her and you ... survived?" she surmised. "Oh, my dear Miss Tarot, I am so sorry to hear it." She sent another perceptive look across the table, adding, "And it is lonely arriving in a large city without the help of someone trusted who has been with you for so long. Of course, we want to help you find just the right lady's maid. One who is skillful in matters of dress and hair arrangement, and—in your instance—who understands the curiosities of English society, but who is also companionable." Lily drew in a breath and said expansively, "Miss Tarot, you are doing such a service by choosing us. We started our business only this last month and we rely on the goodness of people—women—like you who are willing to offer a second chance to life's more unfortunate who may not otherwise find respectable employment. The only difficulty is that there are none I know of who can speak French, either fluently or badly." Lily stopped when she saw that the young woman was looking at her oddly.

"I don't understand what you mean," replied Miss Tarot. "I was directed here when I asked for the name of an establishment that could help me find another lady's maid. My... sponsor, Lady Perry...the woman who is chaperoning me this season, posed the question in the presence of her housekeeper, who furnished her with this name. *Manners and Morals*, she said, were an exemplary magazine. She said that an associated employment agency—yours — would be a fitting place to begin my search."

Lily pondered her response. There were many she'd spoken to who lauded the concept of offering life's unfortunates a second chance. They just didn't want to do this themselves—like this young woman whose concern was entirely what she expected in such circumstances.

Clearly, Miss Tarot was not as philanthropic as Lily had thought, but she was here, and she needed a lady's maid. Now was Lily's chance to win her over.

"Perhaps it is better to have a lady's maid who does not, in fact, speak French," Lily suggested. "You have indicated you were fond of your maid. Would it not be better to have as few memories that will make you sad or have you comparing?" She would not labor the fact that the women she offered were fallen women. Best to forge ahead. "And I gather you need to find someone at the earliest opportunity since you are about to sally forth for your season."

The girl gave a cautious nod, her expression still suggesting she wasn't sure she was in the right place. "My chaperone had intended accompanying me to your office, but as I wished to find someone today, if possible, and she had a prior engagement, she walked me here and will have someone waiting for me in half an hour. Is it possible to employ someone today? You, of course, would check her credentials."

"Today." Lily nodded, her mind racing. "Yes, we can find someone today. I have several excellent candidates and will send them over to you for assessment. This evening, perhaps? Naturally, if neither was suitable, you would be free to continue your search through another employment service."

Lily certainly hoped she could find what Miss Tarot was looking for. None of the girls she had on her books were suited to employment as a lady's maid, but she knew just the kind of girl whom she believed would be ideal for this serious, ambitious young woman.

When Hamish's calm tones interrupted her reverie after

Miss Tarot had left, Lily jumped. "I take it you've notched up another success? But why so glum?"

Lily glanced up, tapping her fingers on the desktop. "I'm not sure I was as truthful as I should have been. The young lady had not realized that we take such a...charitable approach towards our employees. She assumed that the moral outlook of our employees is aligned with the readership of *Manners and Morals*."

"She is a subscriber?"

Lily shook her head, distracted. "She's lived most of her life in Paris, and it was only due to her patroness, who is a subscriber, that she was directed here. Miss Tarot seemed cautious, but then said that as long as the girl was moral and honest, that's all she cared about."

Hamish scratched his chin. "Moral? Well, that could be interpreted in various ways, I suppose. Most of these girls were brought up to be moral and upright, but were forced into immorality against their will. You'll have to find a way to navigate that one. Perhaps she's not the client for you after all, my love."

Lily shook her head energetically. "I have found a way to navigate that. I'm sending her Kitty."

"Kitty? Is there a Kitty on the books?"

Again, Lily shook her head. "No, but I intend to ask Kitty, who is Madame Chambon's maid. She's worked at the brothel for years, but she's never worked as the girls have. Too skinny and too plain, Madame would say. And Kitty would not have...done what the other girls did. She was just happy to have employment, but she told me she'd happily leave if a better position was offered. Yes, I'll send a note around to her now."

CHAPTER 2

E velina cast a critical eye at her reflection in the mirror.

Or, rather, at the young maid braiding her hair. For such a plain, skinny little creature, young Kitty was remarkably deft. Creative.

Evelina liked that. When the girl had initially appeared on her doorstep, Evelina had been inclined to decline her services on the spot. Mimi had been so stylish, so...French.

But perhaps Lady Bradden was right. Best to have someone as least like Mimi as possible so that she'd not be reminded.

She shuddered, remembering the horror of the accident, the noise, the screeching, the acrid smell of the smoke.

And the young man who had rescued her and who, in turn, had helped her to rescue the young boy. William.

Except that it was William—the man—she thought of now as she nodded her approval to Kitty, looking in the cheval glass and murmuring, "I like the combination of braids and ringlets."

"It suits yer, miss, wiv yer high cheekbones an' eyes like

almonds. The ladies I worked fer liked ter accentuate their eyes ter make 'em look like yers. Yer don't 'ave ter trouble yerself cos ye're a natural beauty."

A glow of warmth surged through Evelina. No one had ever told her that. Certainly not the disapproving nuns at the convent who had taught her in place of the mother she barely knew.

And most certainly not her fellow schoolmates, who were jealous and quarrelsome.

The first time she'd felt admired and appreciated was when the handsome young man—the mysterious William — had made it clear with his brief allusion to her bravery...and her beauty.

"Tell me more of the ladies you worked with." It was better to think of something other than the handsome young man to whom she owed her life and whom she'd most likely never see again. London was a busy, bustling, exciting city, and she'd rub shoulders with perhaps several hundred gentlemen—potential husbands—during the balls and other society events Lady Perry had lined up for Evelina. William would have to be amongst the upper few hundred to interest Lady Perry and her mama.

But William had certainly interested her. She recalled the torn coat and the streak of dirt across his handsome face, then accepted the reality.

Yes, it would be unlikely that Evelina would rub shoulders with the anonymous 'William' at any of the events to which Lady Perry had ensured Evelina was invited. Only the 'right' kind of husband would do for Evelina. It was what her mama and papa expected, of course, and it was what Evelina knew was the culmination of her education in Paris and Switzerland.

"Well, miss, there was a few—" Kitty began before stopping suddenly.

"A large contingent of sisters? No doubt there was much sibling rivalry." Evelina smiled. "I remember it well." It was strange that she was growing sentimental over memories of her school days when she'd hated them so much.

"Yer 'ad sistas, miss?"

"No, I'm referring to the school for young ladies I attended. I was sent there when I was six. Over the next twelve years, I became an expert on female jealousy, cunning, etc. There's little you can tell me about that, Kitty. I had a school full of jealous rivals. Your family of sisters can't have been that numerous."

Kitty lowered her eyes and agreed in a suitably deferential tone, "Yes, miss."

Again, that was to Evelina's liking. She didn't want to foster the familiarity that had existed between Evelina and Mimi. "There! I am ready. How do I look?" She stood up and did a twirl, her heavily draped pink skirts fanning about her.

"Oh, miss, like ye're a princess! All the gennulmen are goin' ter want ter marry yer."

"Well, I need only one."

"Then this one gennulman who sets yer 'eart on fire will definitely want ter marry yer."

Evelina swallowed down her amusement. She wasn't used to such fulsome declarations. "I haven't met him yet," she said, trying once more not to think of the mysterious William.

But perhaps tonight would be the night she would meet her future husband.

She had three months in London to enjoy the social whirl under Lady Perry's patronage. Then she'd have to accompany Lady Perry to dreary spa towns in the hopes of finding the right marital prospect. A companion might suit, but really, Evelina was more than ready to make a sensible marriage and set up her own household.

Escape and independence. That's what she'd dreamed of throughout her schoolgirl years; and, with a dowry as generous as the one her father had bestowed upon her, she knew she would have no difficulty in finding a man who'd want to make her his wife. She didn't need to love him; she just needed to assure herself she'd be satisfied being mistress of his estate and household.

Now, as she was announced in company with Lady Perry at Lady Oxenholme's ball, she felt the first real flurry of butterflies in the stomach. School life had hardened her resolve, her ambition, and her belief in herself.

But standing on the threshold of her future was suddenly daunting.

For but a moment.

She could feel the interest she garnered in so many covert —and not so covert—gazes as she made her slow progress at Lady Perry's side through the ballroom. Not surprising, for her gown was eye-catching and clearly cost a king's ransom with its thousands of tiny, hand-sewn pink beads that caught the light when she moved.

A thrill of excitement nearly made her shiver, but Evelina had learned to master such frailties of emotion.

Finally, she was here, where she'd dreamed of being.

In an English ballroom at her first ball. And the people were so…

English.

"Smile, Miss Tarot. Just a little."

Lady Perry's admonishment was soft in her ear. Evelina obeyed.

She'd learned that fear made her appear standoffish, but she'd learned to temper this. She'd learned a great many things, including how to appear cool and confident, though her insides might roil with anger or humiliation or terror.

So, she smiled, so that she did not appear haughty. She

didn't want to alienate the women or daunt the men for 'an aloof and unfriendly beauty' was what she'd overheard herself described by the girls at the convent, and learning to regulate her behavior had served her well when she'd realized there were no real friends to be had amongst them.

Now she was in a different country in an unfamiliar environment, and she knew exactly what she wanted. Needed.

The right man. The right husband with, preferably, a title.

"Lord Dunstable, may I present to you Miss Evelina Tarot?"

Evelina inclined her head. She knew a great deal about Lord Dunstable, though she pretended otherwise. Lady Perry had told her he was the gentleman her mama and papa had identified as most suitable to her requirements.

"A pleasure, Miss Tarot."

Evelina returned his smile. He was, she guessed, about ten years older. Handsome, sandy-haired, with a flourishing mustache and military bearing. His estate, in the west, boasted a rambling Queen Anne home, and a profitable tin mine, Lady Perry had told her; and the viscountcy was five generations old.

Yes, Evelina would love to dance.

She was a good dancer, too.

And Lord Dunstable was an adept conversationalist. As adept as he was on his feet.

They spoke of his large, comfortable home and his two younger sisters. His father was dead, and his doting mother's only wish was that he would marry well and bring his wife home to become mistress of the thousand acres of grazing land and manicured gardens that comprised the family estate.

Charmed by her. That's what he said as he led her off the dance floor.

But there were others who wished to make her acquaintance.

Captain Blackheath, raven-haired with a devilish smile and a chipped tooth that curiously added to his reckless charm that was unaccountably attractive after Lord Dunstable's restrained gentlemanliness.

Evelina enjoyed their energetic whirl and the wicked glint in his eye as he warned, "Don't trust a charmer like dried-up old Dunstable when you'd be infinitely more entertained by a man who knows how to enjoy life, like me."

But when she compared the two men in the uncomfortable intimacy of her carriage ride home with Lady Perry, the older woman gave a disdainful laugh and said, "Captain Blackheath has a crumbling pile in the desolate Norfolk marshes and needs a wife with a dowry like yours, Evelina. Lord Dunstable wants a consort to grace his beautiful Queen Anne estate in a county where the sun shines more than it does over the rest of the British Isles."

So, there was every reason for Evelina to smile as she seated herself at her dressing table at the end of the evening while Kitty removed the pins from her hair and asked her about the ball.

"I met some very charming gentlemen, Kitty. Yes, one in particular. Is it too early to divulge his name?" She demurred a moment and then allowed unfettered license to her smile, for indeed, Evelina felt quite triumphant. "Lord Dunstable."

CHAPTER 3

The ball was declared a triumph. Evelina received more invitations. Her social calendar was full.

"An' 'ow shall I dress yer 'air terday, miss? Are yer goin' ter see yer gennulman? Lord Dunstable?"

"Please don't call him 'my gentleman'," Evelina said. "It sounds…cheap."

Kitty looked chastened. "Yes, miss." Then, undaunted. "Is it Lord Dunstable takin' yer ter lunch, miss?"

Evelina closed her eyes. In fact, she felt the beginnings of a megrim and wasn't sure if it was from last night's revelry or due to her fears over what lay ahead.

"I'm meeting my mother, Kitty."

"That's nice, miss."

"I'm not so sure, Kitty."

"An' why is that, miss?"

Evelina wasn't sure it was wise to pursue this. She hadn't been going to tell Kitty but now she was nervous and wanted someone to talk to.

"I haven't seen my mother for nearly seven years. In fact, since the age of six, I've only seen her on three occasions."

"An' are yer afeared that yer will disappoint yer mama or that she will disappoint yer, miss?"

Evelina gave a short laugh. "I don't know. Both, I suppose."

"Where will yer meet? At 'er 'ome? Why are yer not livin' wiv 'er now that ye're in London?"

"Do you always ask so many questions, Kitty?"

"The girls called me a chatterbox, miss. But they liked it. Made 'em feel better ter 'ave someone ter talk ter, they said, after the gennulmen—" She stopped abruptly.

"My, Kitty, you talk about the girls as if there were dozens of them. How many sisters were there in this family of obviously popular young ladies? You're forever referring to their gentlemen callers."

"Am I, miss?" Kitty bit her lip.

"Indeed, you are." Fearing she'd been too harsh, Evelina asked, more kindly, "No doubt, in such a large family, there was much call upon your attentions. Tell me about the most difficult of these girls." Evelina had been called difficult on many an occasion.

"Miss Celeste," replied Kitty without hesitation and Evelina laughed. "You didn't have to think one second before you replied, Kitty. Why was she so difficult?"

But Kitty's expression suddenly became shuttered, and Evelina had to coax her to respond.

"Celeste was the most beautiful," the young maid replied with a sigh. "She were also the most demanding an' 'aughty an' the gennulmen liked her best out o' all o' them."

"Well, bravo to Celeste. I admire a woman who isn't afraid of making it clear what she wants. No doubt she married well."

Evelina glanced up when she saw Kitty's expression in the looking glass and that tears were welling in her eyes. "She didn't? I'm sorry to hear that. But…where there's life, there's hope." Evelina thought of her own mama and papa and her hope that they might one day be reunited. It was what she'd hoped for throughout her young life: that her papa would return from the gold mine he owned in Africa and buy a big house where she and Mama would live. He was back in England now, but, apart from two treasured letters he'd written when she was six and eight, she'd not heard from him.

"'Cept there ain't even that fer Miss Celeste is dead now. Murdered."

"Dear God!" Evelina crossed herself instinctively.

"It ain't a story fer yer ears, miss, an' I oughtn't a' blurted it out. Not when tonight is anuvver grand ball an' yer should be so 'appy. Tell me 'bout yer mama. Six years is a lon' time. She'll see a fine youn' lady an' not a wee girl when yer meet. My, but she'll be right proud o' such a beauty, miss."

"You think so, Kitty? That's kind of you to say it."

"Now, wot shall I lay out fer yer ter wear, miss? If ye're ter take luncheon together, I think the pink silk is lovely. 'Specially if yer aven't seen yer mama in such an age. Pink is fer young girls an' youn' ladies, an' yer'll b both ter 'er."

Evelina smiled. "I like that way of thinking, Kitty." She nodded at the lovely ensemble Kitty had fetched and now held up for her. "Lady Durham has invited both of us to luncheon at her home in Mayfair. Mama has traveled into London to see me and doesn't wish me to be seen in a public place. I fear—" She stopped, then continued at Kitty's enquiring look, "I fear that Mama is a woman of exacting morals and that my independent streak may not be to her liking. It has been a topic discussed during our correspondence over the years when the Mother Superior of the convent where I went to school was critical of my dress or manners on certain occasions."

Kitty's eyes were wide. "Lady Durham? Why, to be sure

Lady Durham will be a fine person fer seein' that yer morals an' manners do not run afoul o'...of the establishment."

"You know Lady Durham, then?"

"Yes...no, no, I 'ave neva met Lady Durham."

"But you know of her?"

"Indeed, I do. I mean, afore she became Lady Durham. She was one o' the nicest girls—I mean, she's a woman greatly thought o' 'avin' made a respectable marriage none o' us could countenance at the time."

"Kitty, do stop talking in riddles. What do you know of Lady Durham? It would help me to school my behaviour, as I'd like to make the most favorable impression on both Mama and her friend. Perhaps she sought out Lady Durham to aid my entry into society here in London.

Evelina caught Kitty's dubious look and was troubled. "Do you think Lady Durham will disapprove of me?"

"No, no, miss, no' that, o'course! Now, let me 'elp yer inta yer lovely gown an' then I will finish brushin' yer ringlets inta place."

EVELINA WAS a bundle of nerves by the time the carriage drew up in front of Lady Durham's London townhouse. Her mama had proudly claimed credit for Lady Durham's elevation from lowly governess to viscountess, but Evelina wasn't sure what to believe. Her mother had always been one to gild the lily.

After being helped to alight, she stopped on the pavement to tweak her skirts and quell her anxiety. For the first time in six years, she was to see her mama.

The weekly letters she received from her, laying out Mrs. Tarot's expectations, had accorded oddly with the woman Evelina remembered from when she was fourteen.

Her mother, dressed in severe black, had had memorably vivid red hair. Evelina would never forget the color, not having seen quite such a shade of red on anyone she had ever met.

But her mama's lofty bearing and the way she'd delivered her expectations for Evelina had been almost military.

"Careful, miss, or you'll get run down!"

Evelina stepped back as a carriage drawn by four handsome bays passed them and, as she locked eyes briefly with the occupant, recognition hit her like a physical blow.

Surely that was William?

A surge of excitement made her dizzy, and she had to cling to the handle to steady herself. She'd remember the shape of his jaw and those piercing blue eyes beneath curling dark blonde hair anywhere.

But perhaps not. This man was in a handsome carriage whereas the 'William' she'd met had been coatless, his face and shirt streaked with dirt. Yes, he'd spoken like a gentleman when they'd both rescued the child, but she'd not expected to see him again.

She watched as the carriage disappeared around the corner, and the moment was gone.

Still trying to compose herself, Evelina shook out her skirts and took the first step.

And her heart, which was already beating much faster than usual on account of her suspected sighting of the man who had saved her life, now went into double time as the door opened and the parlor maid greeted her with, "Good morning, Miss Tarot. Lady Durham and Mrs. Tarot are waiting for you in the drawing room."

CHAPTER 4

S o, this was her mother.

Six years older, her hair was not the same eye-catching shade of red, though it was certainly brighter than Evelina had expected of a woman of her mother's years.

Now, it was fashionably styled with curled bangs at the front, and a braid-wrapped chignon beneath a pert little hat upon which perched a turtledove, its feathers dyed to match her gown.

The neckline of Mrs. Tarot's emerald silk polonaise was demure, but the abundance of accessories was troubling. There were too many of them, from the mauve gloves to the enamel chatelaine watch and the garnet necklace, bracelet and earrings, all in shades to match the dyed feathers of the turtledove atop Mrs. Tarot's headdress.

"Evelina, my dear, come and greet your mama!"

Evelina stepped forward, deliberating whether to kiss Mrs. Tarot on the cheek or offer her hand.

The decision was made for her when she was drawn into a brief but not unaffectionate hug before her mama set her away from her and, after some pontification, declared, "You are every bit the beauty I had hoped."

Cautiously, Evelina sat opposite the two ladies.

Lady Durham was a slender, delicate, and composed beauty who spoke in soft, modulated accents.

Evelina's mother, by contrast, was a force to be reckoned with. Statuesque, with features that hinted at the beauty she must have been, her voice was her most confusing feature. She sounded like an Englishwoman trying to sound French. And Evelina, having lived the past twelve years in Paris, should know.

Furthermore, while Evelina had never enjoyed an easy familiarity with her mother, she now felt she was staring at a stranger.

Her mama's laugh was like a deep bark, her voice harsh and her tone emphatic.

Evelina had remembered her as a forceful and dominating person; and she was still. But there was something... somehow coarse about her. She hated to admit this even to herself, and now she was glad she was meeting her in the privacy of Lady Durham's drawing room.

But she would not criticize, not even silently. Evelina was dependent on her mother's goodwill and satisfaction, as she would do well to remember.

"Evelina, in three days, you have accomplished more than I hoped for. You have secured the interest of Lord Dunstable, and now you must work hard to draw him in."

Evelina must have revealed her shock, for her mother leaned forward, shaking her head as if Evelina had already objected.

"Your father has provided you a fine dowry, my dear. Lord Dunstable has a grand estate, a title, and everything for which a girl like you could hope. You do not want to become the prey of fortune hunters."

"But Mama, I have attended but one ball. Lord Dunstable was pleasant enough, but I barely know him. I hope I shall have many suitors from which to choose."

Although Evelina could envisage marriage to a man such as Lord Dunstable, she had to assert a modicum of independence, she realized, in the face of her mother's dominance.

"You have a few short weeks and there is no time to dilly-dally, my girl. You're already older than I would like. It was most unfortunate that you fell ill when you did, but you are recovered now, and your beauty has returned. It is, in fact, in full bloom, and we can't risk it fading before you secure the right husband."

"I shall certainly encourage Lord Dunstable as I shall encourage equally suitable suitors. Lady Perry said there were many more to whom I would be introduced."

"Indeed, there are. Yes, Lord Dunstable is only one of many. Perhaps I am being hasty. I would simply hate for you to risk losing such a prime catch."

"And what does Papa think?"

A spasm of something indefinable crossed her mother's face. Then she leaned back, a smile upon her thin lips. "What do you mean, my love?" Her tone was like syrup. "He has no real interest in you, if that's what you're asking. He wanted a son. However, he has done what any good father must do, and he has provided you with a fine dowry. You are a lucky girl."

Evelina didn't feel lucky. She suddenly felt friendless and something of a commodity. She'd hoped that her reunion with her mother would feel less transactional. When she'd been fourteen, her mother had been more concerned with her education and her deportment and elocution lessons. The two of them had visited the couturier, Madame Lemarche, who had created a magnificent collection of clothes that Evelina wore whenever she was not required to wear the drab sack-like convent dresses. Her clothes were far finer than those worn by the other girls, which had set up resentment, though there'd been nothing Evelina could do about that.

She'd always been an outsider.

"And you are in London to make a fine marriage. That was agreed before you came. You are English and you will marry an Englishman."

"Yes, Mama, it is what I want."

"And you like Lord Dunstable?"

"Yes, Mama, though I like Captain Blackheath equally."

She thought she heard her mother gasp and asked with a frown, "Do you know Captain Blackheath?"

"I have met the gentleman. Not that I would call him a gentleman. No, Evelina, he is not the man for you. For a start, he has no title. He is also looking for a rich wife so he can restore his crumbling house and fortunes."

Evelina studied Lady Durham while they waited for the maid to bring in the tea tray. "You are kind to have allowed Mama and me to meet here, Lady Durham."

"Your mother has been good to me over the years. It was the least I could have done."

Evelina opened her mouth to ask what form this kindness had taken and then changed her mind. The look the pair had exchanged sent a charge of foreboding through her, and she suddenly didn't want to know the specifics.

A portrait of Lady Durham hung upon the wall opposite Evelina. Full length, it dominated the room, a testament to a husband's love for his wife.

"I sat for Henry Scott Tuke," Lady Faith said, following her gaze. "My husband commissioned it the year we married. He is a friend of Lord Dunstable's," she added.

"A fine catch," her mama said again. She turned to Evelina. "I should be well satisfied if you made a match with

Lord Dunstable. Then I need worry no more about anything."

"Except losing good staff," Lady Durham said with a smile, causing Mrs. Tarot to harrumph. "What have I done wrong, Lady Durham?" she demanded. "I have lost three girls these past four weeks. And now my best worker has joined them. Where is loyalty when I rescued them from the gutter and gave them everything they needed?"

"They are still grateful. They are just looking for different opportunities," Lady Durham murmured. "Please don't chide yourself when there's nothing you can do."

"I can stop this woman from poaching my girls. In fact, I've a mind to go over there this afternoon. She should be grateful too since I housed her under my roof for six months before she herself made a fine match herself."

"Hush, now, Mrs. Tarot, there's no need for that," said Lady Durham, sending a look of mild anxiety at Evelina. "Would you like more tea, my dear?"

CHAPTER 5

A throaty sigh prefaced the arrival into Lily's office of the woman she expected would soon visit her.

"Madame Chambon." Lily rose with a smile, though her heart was racing for Madame would not take kindly to Lily having poached Kitty.

Madame Chambon had a particularly soft spot for Kitty, whom she used like a galley slave, but to whom she was also surprisingly indulgent on occasion. Kitty would never graduate to become one of Madame Chambon's girls. Not without the lush sensuality, culture, or beauty that was required. But she was earnest and conscientious and also very kind. Lily remembered her kindness—a stark contract with Celeste's — just as she remembered Madame Chambon's ruthlessness which was, admittedly, interspersed with unexpected acts of compassion, for Madame had her favorites amongst the girls and to these young women she would bend over backwards to ensure they got their happily-ever-after outside the brothel.

"You had no right to take Kitty, Lady Bradden." Madame Chambon came right to the point before she'd even sat down. "Kitty has been with me since I rescued her from the gutter—literally—as a six-year-old."

"And after more than ten years, she has exercised her free will to make a change. I'm sure she's more than grateful to you, Madame, and will always be."

"Kitty is the fifth girl you have enticed away from me. And not because you can offer them any more than I can. Why, Victoria could have married a prince if she'd been allowed to develop as I had planned. Instead, you now have her working for a pittance as a companion to some dreary old woman in Park Lane."

"With all due respect, Madame Chambon, you cannot make the girls' choices for them," Lily objected mildly. "I am simply offering them an alternative. None of your girls chose the life they live under your roof. You do recall that I, too, lived for years denied the ability to make choices—first in a lunatic asylum near Brussels, and then as Mr. Montpelier's so-called spiritualist. Now I can make decisions of my own. It's a liberating feeling. Tea, Madame?"

"I have tea coming out of my ears! Lady Maxwell, my former protégé, has just had me for tea. Now there's someone who shows gratitude for my offering her a chance when she had none. Ruined she was, and in the streets, bartering her body for coins to keep her alive until she landed on my doorstep, and I molded the broken little former governess—"

"Vicar's daughter. She was never a governess," Lily interrupted, for she remembered the girl well.

"What does it matter? She was never going to marry a nobleman unless I set her up for it."

Lily shook her head. "Faith, Lady Maxwell, married the nobleman who had asked her two years before she disappeared, having been ruined by another man in the meantime. Yes, you might have supplied a roof over her head, but she hated what you required her to do in order to survive. Kitty is happy in her new position."

"And what and where is her new position?"

"I'm afraid I can't tell you that. Now, since you have declined tea, I hope you will excuse me, as my husband's photographer has a question to ask."

Relieved to finally dispatch Madame Chambon, who'd spent another five minutes grumbling but who'd gleaned nothing about the location of the girls Lily had re-situated, Lily waved in Archie Benedict, her husband's intrepid photographer.

"Mornin' m'lady," the stocky little man greeted her, grinning broadly as he dumped a canvas bag onto Lily's desk. "I got a parcel o' photographs ter run by yer afore yer 'usband returns to 'is office. Yer 'ave the eye, but I can't tell that ter Mr. McTavish, obviously."

"He knows it and he's happy to leave this to me," Lily said with a wink as he took a seat and spilled half a dozen photographic plates before her.

Lily loved her role, writing an advice column in her husband's newspaper and having editorial control of 'Lost Souls', a weekly segment dedicated to showcasing someone deserving who might win support to improve their lot in life through exposure in *Manners and Morals*.

Though the magazine continued to be of an upstanding, educational nature, readership had increased rapidly since these inclusions, and life had become busy for Lily who had to juggle her responsibilities to the newspaper and with the employment agency besides being the doting mother of an infant, not to mention loving wife and her husband's hostess.

But she had all the help she needed to ensure nothing was neglected. And so far, everyone was happy, especially Hamish, who often commented on the bloom in her cheeks which she declared she got from doing something worthwhile in her life.

One exception was Hamish's exacting father, who owned the magazine and, though he never complained at the increase in readership and revenue, had his own ideas on Lily having any role other than that of wife and mother.

As Lily pored over which photograph to select for the Lost Souls column, Archie asked, "Me Gracie misses 'er friend Kitty wot's now workin' fer this Frenchie girl, new in town."

"Miss Tarot is Paris-educated and very English," Lily corrected him. "And Kitty is very happy in her employment, though it has been only a few days. Miss Tarot offers nothing but praise for her ability to prepare her for each engagement."

"Anuvver carefree beauty 'ere ter snare a duke or a wealthy viscount. Talkin' o' wealthy viscounts, I 'ear Lord Dunstable 'as made a wager that e'll be married afore the end of the season."

"Your sources are correct," Lily said with a twinkle in her eye. "I believe, in fact, that he is the wealthy viscount Miss Tarot will indeed snare. But you knew that, didn't you?"

Archie scratched his nose. There was little he didn't glean in the course of his work, scouring the back alleys for potential candidates for Lily's Lost Souls column, or London's drawing rooms for society beauties to grace the magazine's society pages; or when visiting his sweetheart at Madame Chambon's. It wasn't uncommon that some of the gentlemen visitors to Madame's House of Assignation were those he encountered in the grand drawing rooms of the rich and titled.

But only Archie would notice. He had a spectacular ability to slip beneath notice in most situations, if he wished. With his sweetheart, Gracie, and her friends working in the basements of London's great homes, and his photographic work taking him into the grand saloons and drawing rooms of London's upper class, he was a marvelous resource for gossip.

Not that Lily sought gossip, but it did help to know which society matron was in need of staff or where some of Madame Chambon's girls may have come to grief—just as Lily had, having once been married to a baronet before being discovered and reunited with her real father, Lord Lambton.

Since their touching reunion the previous year, a firm bond had grown between Lily and her father, and she was now a frequent visitor to his London townhouse in Cadogan Square.

Just as she was a frequent visitor to Covent Garden, where she mixed with the flower sellers, hat makers, and dancers who earned a precarious living.

It was a photograph Archie had taken of one of these girls that had caught her interest for the next Lost Souls column. For while Archie photographed people from all walks of life on his own, he often did so at Lily's behest if she'd had a particularly illuminating conversation with someone whom she felt deserving of a mention in the magazine.

"I'm impressed with Liza Frith," she said, pointing to a photographic plate of a dark-haired girl with impossibly large eyes and an almost imperceptible smile that managed to hint at a wealth of knowledge. "She's brought up ten brothers and sisters on a milliner's pittance without having to resort to what Madame Chambon can offer her. I want to print her story as a message of hope. She's resourceful and organized, and it's because she has the respect of her four brothers, she's able to operate the family unit like a business so that all resources are pooled for the common good. It's quite remarkable, really."

"Not if yer consider that the bruvvers don't drink an'

actually listen ter a girl." Archie looked at the photo with a frown. "Don't reckon it's quite natural, if yer ask me."

"Considering the girls in the family earn less than half of what the boys earn yet they work twice as hard, I'd say it was a testament to Liza's ability to make them dream of a future beyond drudgery and poverty." Lily's tone was warning, and Archie looked suitably chastened. "Liza is a force to be reckoned with. She's an inspiration to the working classes. A young lady who knows what she wants."

"Like Miss Tarot," said Archie. "She's bin in London less than a week an' already she's linked wiv Lord Dunstable, though Kitty were tellin' me Gracie she also fancied a feller by the name o' Captain Blackheath."

"Well, good on Miss Tarot," said Lily, distracted as she selected photographs. "Just as long as she doesn't rush into anything, though she seemed a very level-headed young lady when I met her last week." Having put aside three, she sat back, saying with a wink over steepled fingers, "So, have I perhaps secured Kitty a position as a lady's maid to the future Lady Dunstable? Now that would be a fine elevation for a young maid-of-all-work at a brothel, don't you think?" Lily could say that word now without feeling her face flaming. The six months she'd spent at Madame Chambon's being nourished for Mr. Montpelier when she'd escaped as mere skin and bone from the lunatic asylum had been illuminating. Fortunately, she'd never been physically threatened.

Most of the young women at the brothel lived for the day they could forge a better life. And for all her faults, Madame Chambon was not averse to them securing an alternative as mistress or in some rare cases, wife to a man of rank or wealth—though not without a sizeable kickback to herself.

The young woman with whom Lily had shared at the brothel, Celeste, had been one of these. Quiet and mysterious, Celeste's past had never been revealed. Not even by the police who'd investigated her murder under Madame Chambon's very roof, though the perpetrator had since been apprehended and was now serving his sentence.

Although Lily had never been close to Celeste, Celeste had been a catalyst in Lily's desire to offer a different future to as many of the girls forced to work there as she could.

"Maybe there'll be wedding bells afore we know it," Archie said, gathering his parcel of photographs as he rose. "I shoulda put a bet on it when the odds were better."

"Does there have to be a wager on everything?" Lily asked with a sigh.

Archie looked at her as if she were mad. "Reckon yer don't know 'ow the world works 'alf the time, beggin' yer pardon, m'lady," he said.

"Well, I don't think it would have been a wise investment since I'd remind you that Miss Tarot has met the gentleman but once and hardly has a gauge on whether he'd make a good husband."

"It's the title wot's important," Archie said as he slung his bag over his shoulder.

"Not that a title is any guarantee of happiness, though I wish her good luck," Lily said.

No, a title was no guarantee of either security *or* happiness, as Lily knew to her cost.

Her new role as Mrs. McTavish, wife to a successful newspaper mogul who was kind and invested in her happiness suited her far better than when she'd been Lady Bradden, wife of a domineering baronet who'd been prepared to see her thrown to her death over the white cliffs of Dover in order to wed the mistress who was carrying his child.

No, while a girl could expect security with a rich husband, it was certainly no guarantee of happiness.

Liza Frith's enigmatic smile from the photograph on her desk caught her eye once more, as it did Archie's, who held it up to the light, saying, "So this is yer gel fer the week? Would yer like me ter tell 'er yer'll be stopping by for a chat? She'll want ter 'ave on 'er Sunday best, I reckon. An' yer will want me ter take anuvver photo, o'course. But in them rags, she do look jest the part as will warm the cockles o' the public's heart an' set a light ter their conscience."

"And will make them put their hands in their pockets to support my fledgling cause," Lily added. It had taken Hamish's father some persuasion to allow the column to go to print with a line at the end encouraging charitable donations to Lady Bradden's: *"Protect the Morals of Young Working Girls in London"* fund.

Liza Frith would remind their readers that honest young women who toiled hard could house and feed large extended families, but Lily's ideas for future columns were more daring.

She was hopeful her new employment bureau would see some of the 'fallen women' forge new lives that would make the readers of *Manners and Morals* finally question their hard-held beliefs about what constituted a good and moral woman.

CHAPTER 6

I t had been the busiest ten days of her life, and Evelina was exhausted.

But she was elated, too, and with Kitty's help, the sparkle in her eyes remained undimmed by shadows of fatigue.

For what was happening now was the pinnacle of her ambition.

After less than ten days, during which they'd seen each other five times, Lord Dunstable had just proposed, and the satisfaction and relief that Evelina was not going to be on the shelf when she turned one and twenty was enormous.

"My father has already given you his blessing? How...did you approach him?" The fact that reclusive Mr. Tarot had even been in communication with Lord Dunstable was even more surprising than Lord Dunstable's proposal.

During the past few days, she'd been apprised by Lady Perry of her future husband's Cornish interests and properties and where they'd live, and the lifestyle to which she'd soon become accustomed.

What had not been mentioned was Evelina's father, despite her heavy hints.

So, sitting on a sofa in Lady Perry's drawing room, between two glass domes containing stuffed animals and a large aspidistra, Evelina tried to contain her impatience for detail.

Lord Dunstable patted her hand. "I wrote to him and we discussed the matter before he gave his agreement. Of course, it was too onerous to make the journey from Aberdeen all the way to London for a man in his situation."

"But he's not going back to Africa, is he?" Evelina asked anxiously.

"My dear, your father is very secretive about his movements. I have no idea what his plans are. You will have to ask him that."

"Of course," Evelina agreed, as if she had even an inkling as to how she would manage that when her mother refused to tell her how to contact him.

"But my dear Evelina, I hope to make you the happiest woman in the world," his lordship now said, brushing away any possibility Evelina had of gleaning the minutiae of the 'discussions' that had taken place between her future husband and her father. She presumed they involved her rather large dowry and the personal allowance Evelina would enjoy. Clothing and millinery should present no problem, for she'd be showcasing Dunstable's considerable wealth.

And he was a handsome man with a pleasant smile which was focussed on her now, as if he truly had offered for her from the heart.

"I'm sure I will be," Evelina said as both his hands closed around hers and he drew her towards him in the prelude to the kiss for which she was preparing herself.

She'd never kissed a man before and wondered if his mustache would make it uncomfortable.

But in fact, it was soft and not unpleasant, she found, though it was clear he enjoyed the experience considerably more than she did.

He was the one to break the kiss, saying as he drew back, "Good lord, Evelina, I must be careful when I am around you. You really are…quite astonishing."

The gleam in his eyes hinted at the desire of her future bridegroom for what Evelina had heard referred to as the pleasures of the marriage bed, though in truth she had little idea of what this really meant. Her convent schooling had enshrined such talk in secrecy, and she wasn't sure her mother was going to prepare her.

So, Evelina merely dipped her head, pretending shyness, because she'd found he responded well to the idea that she was less robust than she really was, even if she really was as ignorant as he believed her.

But ignorance was not a state Evelina could tolerate.

So, when Kitty attended to her later that evening, she decided the young maid would be as well placed as any to answer her questions. Kitty came from the working class where people lived in crowded conditions with little privacy. Evelina didn't know what she didn't know, but questioning Kitty would be a start. And the girl was friendly and honest.

"Well, who'd a thought I'd become lady's maid ter the future Lady Dunstable," the girl said without preamble as she ran her brush through Evelina's long dark tresses while Evelina sat at her dressing table.

"Indeed, but Kitty, this is to remain secret for now," Evelina said. "Lord Dunstable has made it clear he doesn't yet want a public notice in the newspaper, or in fact, anything to become common knowledge, before he has spoken to his own family about our marriage."

"Mum's the word. An' yer mama must be right pleased!"

"She is." Evelina paused. "I hope she will know what else to say to explain what marriage…involves."

"Involves…?" Kitty frowned at her.

"Yes." Evelina swallowed. "As in, what is expected of me?"

Kitty stared, her brush poised. "You mean…yer don't know, miss?"

"How can I know? I've not seen my mother for six years, and I've grown up in a convent. The nuns don't know what's involved in marriage, so they couldn't tell me."

"I reckon the nuns know verra well wot's involved. They just ain't about ter tell yer," said Kitty under her breath.

Evelina began to feel faintly alarmed. "It can't be that bad, surely? I must be his hostess, look after the accounts, which I'm good at. My mathematic abilities were highly praised at the convent, and I was told this would be one of my chief roles after marriage."

"That an' providin' 'is lordship wiv children. Yer do know 'bout that side 'o things, don't yer, miss?"

Evelina shrugged. Any allusion to this subject was always either skirted around, or spoken of in hushed tones, and was considered highly vulgar, which was, of course, why Evelina knew nothing about it.

But she ventured with more boldness and confidence than she felt, "Well, I know there's…kissing…" She felt her cheeks burning.

"Not always," said Kitty. "Though 'at's a good way ter start. Yer want ter get some pleasure outta it, if yer don' mind me sayin' so, miss."

"There's more than kissing?" Evelina asked before she could stop herself. What else could there possibly be? When Lord Dunstable had kissed her earlier that day, she'd felt she'd gone as far as any married woman would and that her behavior was verging on immoral.

Kitty looked at her strangely. "Yer mean yer really don't know, miss? Yer don't know wot yer'll 'ave ter do ter give 'is Lordship children?"

Evelina shook her head.

Kitty sighed. "Ain't my place ter tell yer that, miss. In fact, I reckon I'm the last person wot should tell yer wot goes on between men an' women an' wot can lead ter babies."

"It doesn't always?"

"Course not! Otherwise the world would be so filled wiv babies we wouldn't know wot ter do wiv 'em all. Why, the lengths me girls went ter in order ter stop havin' babies—" Kitty stopped abruptly and it was Evelina's turn to look at her strangely.

"Your girls? The sisters you worked for, you mean? They told you things like—" She swallowed. "After they were married, they talked about it?"

Kitty bit her lip. "An' afore," she muttered. "But that's nobody's bizness, I reckon. Ye're a young lady wot's got ter get 'erself a rich 'usband. 'Avin babies is yer job. Yer got the money ter be a good catch, an' that's yer part o' the bargain. 'Is part o' the bargain is ter treat yer nice. An' b'cause ye're a fine lady, I reckon 'e'll treat yer nice an' buy yer expensive clothes, an' then when yer've given 'im a son an' maybe anuvver jest ter be sure, 'e'll leave yer alone, an' yer both can do wot yer want. That's the way I sees it mostly happens."

Evelina stared. "Leave me alone? What are you talking about, Kitty? I'm about to marry a man who fulfills the requirements I'm after in a husband. Marriage is a contract. I know that. All I'm confused about is what is required of me so that I can...give Lord Dunstable a son. Well, I certainly hope it'll be a son. And I do know that some women don't succeed and they are forever maligned by society, but I don't intend that to be me."

Kitty put down her brush and met Evelina's eye. "'As Lord Dunstable tried ter kiss yer, miss?"

Evelina blushed as she nodded.

"An' did yer like it?"

"It wasn't unpleasant."

"That's a good start. Yer might even find yer like it when 'e takes off yer clothes an' does them things men do ter give yer a baby."

"Is it necessary to take off my clothes?" The thought made Evelina feel suddenly ill and very vulnerable. She had suspected there was more than kissing, but whenever talk strayed into avenues pertaining to relations between men and women the nuns had quickly shut it down.

This was the closest she'd ever get to anyone preparing her for her wedding night, she suddenly realized. Just as she realized that she was going to marry Lord Dunstable and would have to go beyond the realms of the comfortable. It was inevitable. She was going to spend the rest of her life with this man and yet the prospect was filled with murkiness. Suddenly, she wasn't sure she wanted to do this if it meant taking her clothes off. How was that supposed to work?

"No, yer can do it in the dark wiv yer clothes on. 'E just needs ter get 'is manly appendage ter...ter where it needs ter go."

"What manly appendage?" Evelina gasped and Kitty, looking utterly mortified, picked up her brush again and said through gritted teeth, "I reckon I can't go on, miss, since I 'and't realized quite how much yer didn't know. Mayhaps Lady Perry can tell yer."

"Perhaps Lady Perry can tell Evelina what?" came that imperious voice before the old woman swept into the room in a swish of black bombazine.

"Me mistress were askin' me 'bout weddin' nights but I

reckon I ain't the one who should be tellin' 'er," Kitty said boldly with the result that Lady Perry shrieked, "Indeed not, Kitty! I hope you've kept your mouth closed. This is definitely not talk to be had between a servant and her mistress."

Or between anyone, Evelina realized dismally as she finished dressing and accompanied Lady Perry to Lady Conway's ball a few hours later. She should be thrilled at the prospect of their impending marriage announcement, but instead she felt filled with terror.

A terror she naturally tempered as Lord Dunstable danced her around the ballroom before leading her back to a group of older ladies and gentlemen—his friends, who complimented her and questioned him slyly on the subject of possible forthcoming marriage announcements.

But he was strangely reticent. "Until certain details of the marriage contract have been finalized, it is too early to announce our marriage to the world," he explained to Evelina later, pressing her hand to his lips. With a smug smile, he raised his head and smiled. "Let people surmise as they will, but we will keep our surprise a little longer."

Despite her mixed feelings, Evelina did enjoy being squired about the room on his lordship's arm. Strangers complimented Lord Dunstable on his exquisite eye, and her beauty. They lavished praise upon her gown, the way she carried herself, the glossiness of her ringlets and braids.

Then Captain Blackheath intervened and danced a Viennese waltz with her until Evelina was breathless and laughing at his wicked asides—something that never happened with Dunstable and which the captain pointed out, saying, "You're surely not going to ally yourself with a man who has no sense of humor, are you, Miss Tarot? Not when I make you tremble like a blancmange at my mere proximity."

"Well, you're not asking, and Lord Dunstable is eminently eligible."

Captain Blackheath's nostrils quivered. "A fine set of clothes and such slick assurance may hide many flaws. On what authority would you make the assumption that he is eminently eligible?"

Evelina drew her breath in sharply as she dropped her hands before the dance music had died away. "My father is satisfied—"

"And has he done his due diligence?" Captain Blackheath's good humor had suddenly fallen away. "You'd do well to make your own enquiries, Miss Tarot. Lord Dunstable is—"

"Is the man I intend to marry, and your jealous meddling is only determining me upon it," Evelina declared before she spun on her heel and hurried back to Lady Perry, who was conversing with Dunstable.

His smile melted her indecision. For a lonely girl who'd been brought up in a convent, his attention was intoxicating. And the warmth emanating from Lord Dunstable's smart evening clothes as he held her close during their next waltz together made her feel, for the first time, valued.

When he steered her to a dim alcove just outside the ballroom and cupped her cheeks with his hands, Evelina was quite happy for what was to come next: the kiss.

His lips were soft and his mustache smooth and tickly.

"You have made me a very happy man, my dear Evelina," he murmured. "Tomorrow morning, I will discuss those finer details of the marriage contract with your papa. After that, I shall make my declaration with all the pomp and circumstance it deserves." With a smile, he gently pinched her cheek. "My dear mama is very much looking forward to meeting you."

Evelina swallowed. "And mine is very much looking forward to meeting you and your mama." She wanted to ask Lord Dunstable where he was to meet her father—but was too ashamed. All she needed was to be patient and her father would make contact.

"All in good time, dear heart." He looked fond. "My mother is so very accomplished at arranging lavish affairs. No need to trouble your dear mama."

Evelina was surprised at his words, but also relieved. There was something a little…odd…about her mother and she wasn't quite sure she did want Mrs. Tarot to be introduced to the illustrious Dowager Lady Dunstable until their marriage was upon them.

She cleared her throat and said, nervously, "My father—" She should bring up the subject now. Was her father indisposed? An invalid?

Strangely, Lord Dunstable seemed to know all about Mr. Tarot.

"All that is important is that your father has given his blessing, and we have drawn up the terms of the contract with only a minor point of contention." He contoured her face with his soft, tender fingers and Evelina felt something warm within her come to life. She wondered if this was what Kitty had been trying to tell her, for it was certainly like a thawing within herself towards his lordship. He kissed the tip of her nose, and she arched forward as he said, "There is just one…little…clause on which we need to agree."

Evelina wasn't listening. "I'm very much looking forward to meeting your mother…tomorrow?" she said, feeling happy and relieved.

"There's plenty of time for that. Now, I see some friends whom I would like you to meet." Placing her hand on his forearm, he led her towards a small group of elegantly attired ladies and gentleman near the piano. Three men were talking politics while the two women fanned themselves as they gazed about the ballroom. In their beautiful ballgowns they looked like Evelina had always aspired to look: beautiful, confident. And rich.

"Ladies. Gentlemen," Lord Dunstable began, "Allow me to introduce to you Miss Evelina Tarot."

Smiling, Evelina nodded to Lady Blaine and Mrs. Gringle. She blushed prettily as Lords Belton and Grainger sent her approving looks through their eye pieces.

And then she felt a strange lurch before something in her heart cavity seemed to thud to her feet and she had to stifle her gasp as the third man, introduced as Lord Bellingham, turned to face her properly.

For it was William.

Her rescuer, William.

CHAPTER 7

Evelina didn't know how she managed to contain her shock, but she must have, for Lord Dunstable had continued to speak in that even, equitable tone that made him seem so consummately at ease in any environment.

William, whose eyebrows had risen above a flare of recognition, also kept any surprise contained as Lord Dunstable made the introductions.

"Why, Dunstable, you dark horse, this is very unexpected," remarked Lord Blaine with a look that demanded satisfaction. But Dunstable merely smiled and said, "What arrangements have you made for Scotland? I'm not sure I will be in the country this August."

The ladies tittered and Lady Blaine said, "That's very cryptic, Dunstable."

As Evelina listened, some of the shock drained away. Lord Bellingham was no doubt safely married and unobtainable, so any disappointment she'd felt at not having properly made his acquaintance before she accepted Lord Dunstable was ill founded. Besides, she was not a lovelorn miss inclined to palpitations.

So, as Lord Bellingham continued to talk with the rest of the gathering, while Evelina quietly listened, for she was the only unmarried woman amongst them and they were all seasoned society matrons a few years older, she tempered her feelings.

Dunstable had asked her opinion on ideas for a wedding tour. He'd spoken of the home in which they would live, his large estate in Cornwall. He'd solicited her opinion on what would make an ancient Queen Anne manor house a place she would feel comfortable. What flowers might she like in the garden, and what colored papers upon the walls?

He was the perfect catch. Yes, Bellingham was no doubt married. For a split second, she'd allowed herself to be swayed by foolish daydreams.

"I'm sure Evelina would enjoy that."

She jerked her head up at her name and tried to appear as if she'd been following the conversation.

Lord Dunstable smiled. "You weren't paying attention, were you, my dear? Bellingham is leading an expedition to the zoo tomorrow with his daughter and his sister and niece. He thought we might like to join him. I have a cousin, Clara, who is very fond of the zoo. She and her older sister, Victoria, could act as chaperones…" He sent her a contemplative look. "That way, Lady Perry's services would not be required. Would you like that?"

Evelina nodded. Lord Dunstable was ever concerned to ensure that she was in accord with his wishes.

And his words had just confirmed that Lord Bellingham was married with a child.

Slowly, her heart rate returned to normal, and she could look at Lord Bellingham without the spasm of mixed emotions that had made their introduction so uncomfortable for her.

A trip to the London zoo the following afternoon would be delightful, she concurred.

THE WEATHER, however, was not delightful. Though it had started sunny and bright, dark clouds soon covered the sun, though the rain held off.

Evelina's short time in London had encompassed little more than the local environs, so the Zoological Gardens were an added thrill. She tried to ignore the pleasure that would be augmented by Lord Bellingham's company. No doubt he would bring his wife when he met them there, for certainly a man so handsome could not still be single.

So, at mid-morning, Lord Dunstable arrived in his carriage at Lady Perry's townhouse, his second cousins already ensconced when he helped Evelina into the equipage.

Though they chatted amiably after introductions, it was only when they were outdoors that Evelina observed what an odd-assorted pair they were. At sixteen, Lady Clara was still a young girl, her skirts not yet full length and her chestnut brown hair still in braids. She chattered happily while her plain, pale-faced sister, Lady Victoria, a good ten years older, was firm, to the point of bossy, though she failed to dampen Lady Clara's irrepressible spirits. Clearly there was affection between them but, Dunstable explained briefly during a moment alone, their mother had died three years previously and Lady Victoria had assumed the role of Clara's guardian with almost fervent ardor.

Lady Victoria's educational efforts, however, allowed Lord Dunstable closer proximity to Evelina, as the older cousin was at continual pains to ensure Lady Clara behaved decorously and 'not run' when she became excited.

"My dear cousin Victoria cannot abide disorder," remarked Dunstable with an eye roll as the two young women walked ahead of them. "And what about you, my dear Miss Tarot? Are you adept at bookkeeping and all those skills required by a young lady of your station to manage a household? I've heard you have a steady head on your shoulders."

"You have?" Evelina wondered where he might have heard that—her mama or papa?—but it gave her a thrill to think what might have motivated his question.

"At the convent school in Paris I attended," she replied. "Mathematics was a subject I liked more than most of the other young ladies did. I was good at it."

"Glad to hear it," said his lordship, briefly squeezing Evelina's hand as they traversed the serpentine walks, gazing in wonder at the plumage of the birds, and then the extraordinarily human-like antics of the primates.

"I could almost imagine he's trying to tell me something!" Evelina said to whom she thought was Lord Dunstable at her side as she laughed at a monkey making faces at her.

To her embarrassment, she turned to find she'd addressed Lord Bellingham. He must have just appeared around the curve of the path, as Dunstable had turned back to talk to his cousins.

With a smile, he said, "They're extremely intelligent. So I am told by a friend who traveled to the dark continent and lived there for some time with a monkey as a pet."

"I beg your pardon, I didn't realize you'd arrived, Lord Bellingham." Evelina's smile was unsteady. The churning in her breast, occasioned by this handsome gentleman, was utterly foreign and completely disconcerting.

"I'd like a monkey as a pet, Papa," said the little girl clinging to Lord Bellingham's hand. "Can I have one for my birthday? I'll be turning six soon," she told Evelina importantly.

Evelina bent down to reply. "I think the monkey might get into too much mischief for your papa's liking. Have you ever seen a monkey before?"

The little girl shook her head. "I wanted to see a monkey the most, and Papa promised he'd take me on my first visit to London."

"Do you like London?" Evelina asked.

The little girl's eyes shone. "I've never seen so many people or such big buildings or so many carriages. I think I'd like to live here, but I can't because Papa hates London."

Evelina slanted a glance up at Lord Bellingham and was caught off guard by the intensity of his look. He glanced away while Evelina forced herself to say as calmly as she could to Edwina, "Then you are lucky he wanted to come here, after all, and that he brought you."

Edwina smiled back. "He didn't want to come to London, but he said he had to find a beautiful lady."

"I think that's enough, Edwina." Lord Bellingham patted his daughter's head, then pointed to the next enclosure. "Shall we see the giraffes?" He caught Evelina's eye briefly, the connection and flare in his so fleeting she wasn't sure if she imagined it before the bland smile he offered her. "That's a giraffe, Edwina. Remember, I showed you the picture in your new book?"

But Edwina's head was still turned towards Evelina as she said, "Papa found a brave lady on a train," while her father steered her towards the giraffe enclosure, "and he said we had to come to London to find her."

Dunstable was still in conversation a little distance away as Lady Clara recounted to him a story about the goose that had chased her and her 'bosom friend' Elizabeth earlier that day.

Evelina liked the fact that her future husband could appear so interested in his young cousin's prattle as she finished with an elaborate account of Lizzie's brother Rupert and their friends' godfather, Mr. Grimshaw, coming to the rescue with waving rakes and wild banshee-like cries before the girl asked plaintively, "Really, Cousin Dunstable, you must visit us at Brockbank Manor before the end of the summer and then we can pick berries again with Lizzie and Rupert at Ravenswood Hall.

She was surprised when he shook his head and said, darkly, "I think not, Clara?" causing Clara to say entreatingly, "But all is forgiven, Cousin! You and Victoria are in charity once more, otherwise we'd not all be here. And Mr. Grimshaw and Lord Ravenswood only did what Victoria asked them to do."

"And…how was your journey here, Miss Tarot?" Bellingham asked, causing Evelina to jerk her head back to him while Edwina walked by his side, marveling at the animals she saw amid comments as to how frightened Nanny Beadle would be to see them. It was not long before the little girl returned to her theme, further embarrassing Edwina and, clearly, Lord Bellingham, who'd been unable to find anything to say after Evelina had replied that her journey had been very comfortable.

"And Papa said it was most urgent that he found this lady because he thought she was the bravest, most beautiful lady he'd ever met. Do you think you'll find her, Papa?"

When Evelina caught his gaze, he reddened. He flicked a glance at Dunstable, sent Evelina a rueful smile, and murmured, "You were very brave, Miss Tarot. I'm sorry if Edwina embarrassed you. Of course, I knew nothing about you during our brief meeting and certainly not that you and Lord Dunstable…" He hesitated, clearly not sure how to go on, before finishing, "had an understanding."

Evelina swallowed. "At the time, I had not met Lord Dunstable."

"Oh, Lord Bellingham, you've arrived!" cried Clara, breaking off her conversation with Dunstable as she turned to greet the newcomer. "Edwina told me just now her father had been a heroic rescuer and was looking for a fair damsel in distress. Did you find out who she was?"

"What young woman are you talking about?" Lord Dunstable closed up the circle with a protective hold around Evelina's waist before grasping her hand and caging it on his forearm.

"I believe Edwina was referring to the terrible train crash several weeks ago," said Lady Victoria, her sober tone a contrast to her sister's. "It was a mercy no one was killed. I'm certainly glad Lord Bellingham was not. Edwina said he was so very brave."

"There were others far braver than I," said Lord Bellingham, clearly embarrassed. He flicked a glance at Evelina and, when she remained silent, and none of the company remarked upon the fact that she had also been on the train that had derailed, he said, "So you went to school in Paris, Miss Tarot?" But not before raising his eyebrows enquiringly at her before seeming to accept tacitly that the train accident was not something with which she wished to associate herself. "But both your parents are English?"

Evelina nodded.

"Are they the Tarots of East Anglia?" asked Lady Victoria, and then, when Evelina shook her head, suggested, "Perhaps you are distantly related to the Tarots of East Anglia for they are the only Tarots I know?"

"Evelina comes from a small family far from here," remarked Dunstable. He smiled and stroked his mustache before returning his hand to Evelina's.

She stared down at it, unsure of what she felt. Triumphant? Protected?

She'd soon be Lady Dunstable.

She'd achieved her aspirations in less than a fortnight, determined to meet the expectations of the parents she'd barely known, and to prove to her schoolfellows she was every bit as worthy as the other girls whose parents lived ordinary, domestic lives under the same roof.

"Is that not true, Evelina?"

She nodded, surprised that the use of her Christian name grated, which was wrong when, of course, Lord Dunstable was negotiating her marriage contract with her father. Soon she'd be married to this man and suddenly she felt frightened and unable to breathe.

But then she realized Lord Dunstable, himself, was not the reason.

No, it was the way Lord Bellingham was looking at her. As if he'd just accepted that something he really wanted was out of reach. His daughter had said he'd been galvanized into finding the woman with whom he'd rescued a child, though she did not know all of it.

No one did.

Except Evelina and William, united forever, she realized in that act of simple bravery.

Evelina had acted too quickly in choosing a husband when she'd thought the heart did not have a place in such a decision.

Hadn't she?

CHAPTER 8

L ily rocked the crib beneath her desk as she wrote up
her ledger. She smiled.

Six girls situated within just four weeks. It was a
noteworthy achievement upon which her darling Hamish
had just congratulated her before he'd warned, "My father
may visit this afternoon."

"In which case I should make myself scarce," Lily had said
with a smile. "And take little Sebastian with me."

But now Gracie was here, and Lily was not smiling at her
news.

The long-serving maidservant from Madame Chambon's
looked pale and frightened, which was not to be wondered at
in view of the circumstances under which she'd left her
employer's house.

For Gracie had just witnessed a murder scene, though
Lily was having difficulty understanding precisely what
Gracie was trying to tell her. As the girl gulped and stumbled
over her words, Lily glanced at the doorway, unsure if
Archie's impending arrival would be helpful in calming his

sweetheart, or if it was better for her to hear everything, unfettered, from the girl's lips, first.

"Gracie, I'm going to have to ask you to go back to the beginning. Assisted, perhaps, by a nice glass of brandy to help with the nerves," Lily now said, rising. "Please stay right here, take some deep breaths, and I'll be back with the bottle. I think we both need a medicinal shot."

Hamish's office was a little down the hallway. He raised his head with his habitual adoring smile, which turned to worry when he saw her expression.

"Lord Dunstable is dead," Lily said without preamble. "His body was found in Madame Chambon's private sitting room. But that's not the worst of it."

"Dear God, it's not?" Hamish said, rising and coming towards her.

"No, it's not! Where's the brandy, my love? I need it for Gracie, who has just told me something even more shocking."

"What could be more shocking? That young Gracie killed him?" Cognizance dawned, and he said in almost a resigned, matter-of-fact tone, though with a question at the end, "But of course. It was Madame?"

Lily shrugged, her hands trembling as she took the bottle her husband held out to her. "Those are facts that cannot be ascertained right now. However, what I do find most troublesome is that the young woman who was in here barely a fortnight ago and who is betrothed to Dunstable; the young woman who hired Gracie's friend Kitty to be her lady's maid—"

Hamish frowned, recalling correctly, "Miss Evelina Tarot?"

"Yes. Miss Evelina Tarot." Lily swallowed. "I have just learned from Gracie that she is, in fact, Madame Chambon's daughter."

Hamish's eyebrows shot up. "Madame Chambon's daughter! And her betrothed…or soon-to-be…is dead in her mother's—" He looked a little gray as he added, "pleasure house." Appearing as if he would accompany Lily down the passage to her office where Gracie was waiting, no doubt, in dire need of the brandy Lily had come to fetch, but Lily shook her head.

"And why did Gracie come to see you?" His frown deepened. "Surely, no connection has been made between you and Madame Chambon?"

Lily understood his concern. Though the months Lily had spent under Madame Chambon's roof had been innocent and, to date, entirely hushed up, any whispers of Lily's association with the brothel owner could be detrimental to her reputation, not to mention that of Manners & Morals.

"I don't believe so. No, Gracie simply wanted to send word to her friend Kitty—"

"Good lord, so that's why Miss Tarot employed Kitty? The girl was recommended by her mother, Madame Chambon?" Hamish asked.

"No, Miss Tarot has no idea she's…related to Madame." Lily reddened. "To my shame, I didn't fully explain to Miss Tarot the nature of Kitty's previous employment, though at the time I had no idea of the relationship, though I'm only going by what Gracie insists is the truth. No, when Miss Tarot came to me seeking a lady's maid, I recommended Kitty saying she'd worked for a woman who had many… girls…is how I put it. But Hamish, how was I to know that Miss Tarot was Madame's daughter when Miss Tarot doesn't even know it herself?"

"Surely she must know it?"

Lily shook her head. "Gracie swears she doesn't, and that Kitty doesn't, either. Miss Tarot thinks she's the daughter of two eminently respectable parents…and certainly someone is funding her lavishly, though I have no idea who. Her gowns, alone, set her apart, and I'm led to believe her dowry is considerable."

Hamish raked a hand through his hair. "Can you be sure Lord Dunstable is dead?"

"Gracie swears he is. She said she stumbled over his body when she went to put Madame's post on her desk. Then she began to scream. She said he'd been stabbed in the neck and his eyes were wide open, and she knew he was dead because she's seen dead bodies before."

"But is she quite certain that the body is that of Lord Dunstable?" Hamish seemed more rattled than Lily, as he went on, "The same Lord Dunstable who is, supposedly about to marry Miss Tarot, who you're now telling me is Madame Chambon's secret daughter? And now Lord Dunstable has wound up dead on the old brothel-keeper's carpet?" Hamish came round from the desk and put his arm on Lily's shoulders. "My dear, this is a terrible turn of affairs."

"To be honest, everything is merely conjecture right now, however Gracie and Kitty have always been as thick as thieves so, of course, Gracie will tell Kitty, who may already know." She shrugged, feeling confused and shocked.

"And it's quite likely Lord Dunstable knew it, too, if he was thick as thieves with Madame Chambon," said Hamish thoughtfully. "Though at what point he discovered this might have a bearing on matters." Glancing through the window, he said thoughtfully, "Poor Miss Tarot. I imagine her name will be dragged through the muck as the police investigate the matter."

Lily raised the brandy bottle in acknowledgement as she made for the door. "I must return to Gracie and hear what else she has to say. It's all rather a shock and I don't think I've digested it properly yet."

Gracie was sitting on the sofa staring at the wall with a

rather dazed look on her face when Lily returned brandishing the bottle and saying, "My poor girl, you must be in such shock since it was you who found Lord Dunstable."

"It were, indeed, m'lady. I'd 'eard Madame an' Lord Dunstable shoutin' when I passed by Madame's sittin' room earlier on me way ter attend ter LuluBelle, who was seein' 'er favorite gennulman."

Lily unstoppered the bottle and poured them both a measure before sending a guilty glance at the swaddled baby in its cradle beneath the desk. But baby Sebastian was sleeping soundly, so she returned her attention to Gracie.

"What could Lord Dunstable have been doing at Madame's? How long has he been a regular, Gracie?"

Gracie thought a moment. "Not a regular, exactly. 'E came ter see Celeste but then stopped afta she were done in, God rest 'er soul. But then 'e's bin comin' more regular-like this past year. Maybe more."

"To see any of the girls, or just to see Madame?"

Gracie looked troubled. "I reckon 'e's bin 'ere more than usual in the past couple o' weeks, 'specially ter see Madame. I 'eard 'is voice soundin' loud an' so I stopped ter listen. That's when I 'eard Madame saying summat like, 'Yer leave Evelina out o' this. Me daughter knows nothin' an' I intend ter keep it that way.'" Gracie nibbled at her lip and ventured a look from beneath lowered lashes as Lily asked, "Is this why you think Miss Tarot is Madame Chambon's daughter? Because of what you overheard? Perhaps it's not the same Evelina."

"I reckon it makes sense enough when I come ter fink o' uvver fings Madame 'as said. 'Sides, why would Lord Dunstable be at Madame's talkin' 'bout any uvver Evelina when 'e's jest got engaged ter…Evelina Tarot? Course, I will ask Kitty if she knows anyfink more. But I talked ter 'er yesterday when she were pretty jolly 'bout the fact she'd be accompanyin' Miss Tarot on 'er weddin' tour. 'Cept that won't be happen' now."

There was a short knock on the door and then Archie put his head in, before pushing forward and saying, "'Scuse me, m'lady but I jest 'eard the news 'bout Lord Dunstable as I were on me way ter see me Gracie but now I found 'er 'ere." His expression softened, and he came forward saying, "An' 'ow are yer, dear girl? Reckon yer got a right shock, trippin' over a dead cove an' all. One o' the girls says Madame Chambon were wiv the police last night but they let 'er go afta questioning. Madame knows the 'ead o' the department, see," he added, looking up at Lily, his expression troubled. "'E's a regular client 'o 'ers."

"Well, that might stand her in good stead. Have you been to Madame Chambon's since this happened?" Lily asked.

"I went there ter find Gracie, who I were told were here. I need ter find out wot yer 'usband wants me ter do in the way o' a photograph. Not that a gruesome murder is wot 'is magazine wants ter print, but I'll take Gracie back ter Madame Chambon's anyways, so—"

"I doubt Lord Dunstable's body is still lying in Madame's sitting room," said Lily, looking up at Gracie's gasp. "Sorry, Gracie." Lily knew she'd seen too much in the way of violence and dead bodies while in the lunatic asylum in Belgium. She silently reminded herself to behave as was expected of Lord Lambton's gently reared daughter. Tapping her fingers on the desk, she glanced between Archie and Grace. "When should Miss Tarot be told? That is the question."

"Told wot? That 'is lordship is dead? Or that she's Madame Chambon's daughter?" Gracie asked.

"Wot's this, then?" Archie peered at them disbelievingly. "Miss Tarot, wot's bein' chaperoned by Lady Perry, is Madame Chambon's daughter?"

"Maybe it's not true," said Lily. "But Gracie overheard Lord Dunstable and Madame Chambon talking about someone called Evelina just before Dunstable was killed," she added. "Evelina is not a common name, and it seems too much of a coincidence when combined with various other hints that Gracie says she's heard." She nibbled her fingernail. If this was indeed the case, and word got out, then Miss Tarot would find her first London season suddenly curtailed. In fact, her whole future would disappear in a puff of smoke, and through no fault of her own.

Reaching down to pick up the little bundle from the cradle, Lily rose. "I'm going to see Miss Tarot now," she said decisively. "Before any word of this reaches her ears, though, I suspect I might be too late. However, it is early, still."

"Yer, ma'am?" asked Archie. "Will yer 'usband like yer getting' involved in summat that's none of yer bizness?"

"He will see the advantages, Archie, and besides, I fear that it could become my business; so it's better to steer matters in a way that might cause less harm in the future to Miss Tarot and your Kitty, don't you think?"

"I'm comin' too, then," said Archie.

CHAPTER 9

"I think I'll wear the blue this evening, thank you, Kitty." Evelina, still in her dressing gown, cast her critical eye over both ensembles her maid had laid out. What a relief that the luggage van had not been one of the carriages to derail during the accident, for Evelina's clothes had all been created by the finest Parisian seamstresses and couturiers and were essentially irreplaceable. Evelina had been aware of the envious glances sent her way by many of her fellow debutantes; first as she'd waltzed with a variety of eligible gentlemen and then in Lord Dunstable's arms.

He would escort her to Lady Glenroy's ball tonight, together with, of course, Lady Perry.

"I thought you might choose that one, miss, in view o' the complimentary words Lord Dunstable 'ad fer yer when yer last wore it. 'E reckons it matches yer eyes. I reckon 'e'll be a good 'usband, miss. Not like me sister, Janey's 'usband wot treats her summat shockin' though I oughtn't be talkin' like this. I apologise, miss. Sometimes me tongue 'as a 'abit o' runnin' away with me, miss. Now, do yer want ter sit down an' I'll brush yer 'air?"

"You do talk a great deal more than Mimi, God rest her soul, but you are a magician when you wield a hairbrush," said Evelina, smiling. At first, Kitty's endless chatter had, on occasion, irritated her. She'd been so used to Mimi's grim dedication and the general silent frostiness of her school-mates. But over the past few days, Evelina had warmed to Kitty's candor and genuine good-heartedness.

"I keep fearing one of the young ladies for whom you worked before will steal in here and kidnap you."

Kitty began to brush Evelina's hair with long, rhythmic strokes. She sighed. "Nah, they was pleased I got me a good job an' outta the place afore I was made to become one o' them."

"What do you mean?" Some of the things Kitty said were most puzzling. Evelina tried to remember the name of the large family for whom Kitty had worked. The truth was that she'd been in a bit of a daze following the train accident.

Sometimes it was as if she were suddenly back in the midst of the screeching of wheels or could feel the water rushing up to drown her. Lord Dunstable had remarked upon her occasional sudden shivers, which she'd claimed was due to his presence. Flattering him was easier than having to tell him about the accident and relive the whole awful experience.

Or perhaps it was because telling him what had happened would require telling him about William? Lord Bellingham.

She closed her eyes. Thinking about William was not conducive to whipping up the necessary excitement she needed to show with regard to her forthcoming marriage to Dunstable.

Oh, why had William shown up at the ball so late? Or at all? She could have survived either, with greater acceptance and fortitude. But to know that Lord Bellingham—her William—was both available and interested was too much.

He was, she guessed, a couple of years younger than Lord Dunstable, and he was widowed with a daughter. A sweet, pliant daughter who was seeking a mother.

Some women might not relish the prospect of being a stepmother, but Evelina liked Edwina and would not have minded taking on a child. Remembering little Edwina's hand in hers had sent warmth flowing through her.

And longing, too, as she'd locked glances with the girl's father.

But now she was to marry Lord Dunstable. She'd made her bed, the marriage contract had all but been drawn up, and she was committed.

And perhaps that was as well, for her mother had made no bones about the fact that love was an inconvenience that had no part in marriage.

The nuns had said the same thing. They just insisted she must love God.

"Will yer breakfast wiv Lady Perry this mornin', miss?" Kitty asked as Evelina stared at the ceiling, thinking thoughts she should not.

"Not this morning—"

Her words were cut short by a series of quick, sharp raps upon the door before the parlormaid put her head round, saying, "Miss Tarot, Lady Perry says yer are ter present yerself in the drawin' room at the earliest. There's someone 'ere ter see yer."

Kitty smiled. "Lord Dunstable is keen, miss, ain't 'e?"

"It's not Lord Dunstable," said the parlormaid. "It's Lady Bradden."

"Lady Bradden?" Kitty looked alarmed, and Evelina felt a frisson of concern. "Does she say why?" For people like Lady Bradden did not call on young ladies like Evelina at such an hour unless there was something of note to be conveyed.

TEN MINUTES LATER, Evelina presented herself in the drawing room, as best as she could manage under the circumstances, noting with surprise that Lady Bradden had with her a maid-servant who was holding an infant.

This was rather extraordinary, she thought, as she stilled the torrent of questions that came to her lips.

When Evelina had left her bedchamber, she'd been surprised at how distressed Kitty had been; as if the girl had been guilty of some terrible transgression in her previous employ. Was Lady Bradden on the warpath to apprise Evelina of something Kitty had done?

Now that she'd developed something of a rapport with Kitty, Evelina certainly hoped Lady Bradden hadn't come here to inform her that Kitty was a thief or worse.

She nodded at Lady Bradden, whose look was drawn and concerned as she said, "Please sit down, Miss Tarot, for you'll need to be seated to hear what I have to say."

Goodness, Lady Bradden looked as if she were about to unleash the most terrible of all news.

It was the four of them, now, for Lady Perry sat grim-faced at right angles to Lady Bradden, and a wave of fear washed over Evelina who was brought to mind of the occasions the nuns would chastise her for a transgression.

"Miss Tarot—" Lady Bradden cleared her throat and her look was suddenly deeply sympathetic. "I am so sorry to have to tell you…" She glanced at Lady Perry and then back at Evelina before she went on. "Lord Dunstable is dead."

Evelina blinked rapidly. For a moment, she could not speak.

This was not at all what she'd expected. Finally, she repeated, "Lord Dunstable is dead? How? When?"

A myriad of possibilities presented themselves. She'd

known of people to fall down dead clutching their hearts. One of the nuns had done just that in front of the schoolgirls at the convent.

"He was quite well when I saw him yesterday," she whispered as she intercepted the glance exchanged by Ladies Bradden and Perry. "Was it…apoplexy, perhaps?" It was all she could imagine.

"Miss Tarot, I don't know how else I can tell you, for you will learn the truth soon enough, and it's not for me to soften what will be a harsh blow for you." Lady Bradden fidgeted with the fabric of her skirts. "Lord Dunstable was killed with a knife late last night."

"Murdered?" Evelina gasped, clasping her chair to stop herself from falling forward. This was even worse. "How? Who?" She imagined a street brawl and poor Lord Dunstable being set upon as he walked home from his club. "Where did it happen?"

"I…I can't tell you any more, but I did feel it incumbent upon me to tell you in person since I heard it at my husband's editorial offices just now. I feared you might learn the terrible truth inadvertently. That is why I came because, of course, you must think my presence here quite out of place."

Evelina put her hand to her mouth. "What will happen now?" she asked.

And the question, really, related to so many things she didn't know where to begin.

Lady Bradden's faltering smile was kind. "I really don't know. I simply wanted to tell you before you heard it from someone else in case you'd been…forgotten."

"Because I'm not yet his wife." Evelina hitched in a breath. "And never will be," she whispered. Suddenly, he seemed the only man she'd ever wanted. His warm smile, the gentleness of his caress, the softness of his lips.

He'd promised her a future. She knew exactly what she'd wanted, and he'd appeared and offered her everything.

"My dear. I am sorry." Lady Perry offered a tiny nod, her mouth pursed. "I can't think what we should do now. Fortunately, there is no betrothal notice that will appear in the news sheets to link you with a man who has been murdered." She said it as if Lord Dunstable had been responsible for his own death.

Lady Bradden let out a soft sigh. "No, I had not thought of that." She sent Evelina a considered look. "It would be best for all if there was no mention of the engagement, don't you think? I will check with my husband that there is nothing to link Lord Dunstable with Miss Tarot. My husband's photographer is waiting outside. I shall call him and instruct him to check."

Evelina wondered why she should not be linked with Lord Dunstable. She opened her mouth and Lady Bradden said quickly, "Grief aside, you do not want to go into mourning and miss the rest of the season, my dear." She hesitated. "Not if the marriage contract hasn't explicitly made provision for you under such circumstances. Now, let me find Mr. Bentink."

Evelina was surprised that Lady Bradden's photographer should be lurking about. She remembered him vaguely, having seen him the day she'd gone to the bureau to employ a maid. The fellow was quite un-noteworthy until he spoke. He was small, with a decided swagger, but there was a twinkle in his eye that immediately put one at ease.

And Evelina needed soothing.

"Me condolences, miss," he said, bowing his head. "Terrible thing, ter be sure. So sudden! And wot a place fer it ter 'appen."

"I thought you said you didn't know where it happened,"

Evelina said, looking at Lady Bradden, realizing she sounded accusatory.

"Sorry, m'lady," said the photographer sheepishly.

"Where was Lord Dunstable found…dead?" Evelina whispered.

She heard the ticking of the clock in the awkward silence before Mr. Bentink said, "At an establishment called Madame Chambon's." He sent her a long, focused look.

"And what—or who—is Madame Chambon?" Evelina asked.

"Yer don't know?" The photographer's eyes seemed to bore into her, as if he hung on her answer. It was most odd.

"How would I know?" Evelina took umbrage at his tone. And she made this clear by pushing back her shoulders and raising her head with an expression of frosty disdain, just as she'd been taught when being schooled in the proper deportment of a lady in the company of inferiors.

"My dear Miss Tarot, I apologize for Mr. Bentink's manner," said Lady Bradden, quickly sending the photographer a quelling look.

"Who is Madame Chambon?" asked Evelina again, as a growing fear festered within her. "A married acquaintance?"

Lady Bradden nodded. "An acquaintance, yes, and no one for you to trouble yourself over. An investigation is underway. You need to be supported, and Lady Perry will do an admirable job. I shall ensure that the engagement notice does not appear in the newspapers. You do agree that is best, don't you?"

Evelina frowned and Lady Bradden went on, gently, "From a practical and pecuniary point of view, it will not help you in the immediate future since there will be no financial benefit to you as you are not yet married."

Evelina nodded.

"I understand your betrothal has been kept quiet as there were some who Lord Dunstable feared…might object."

Evelina blinked. How did Lady Bradden know so much?

"Do you know why that was?" Lady Bradden asked.

"No." Evelina fidgeted with the end of her shawl. Nothing seemed quite real. "I did not know that was the case," she added.

"My dear, until we know who was motivated to murder Lord Dunstable, and why, I think it best that you be kept out of it. Unless you do want to go into deep mourning for the rest of the season?"

Evelina shook her head a little more energetically than her grief should have allowed her.

"I thought not. In that case, I will leave now with the assurance that you will be updated. That's not to say word will not leak, but for the meantime, I think it best if you stay quietly indoors." She frowned, then added, "No, perhaps it would be better advice to continue as if you and Lord Dunstable had no understanding. After all, nothing had been announced or made public, had it?"

Evelina shook her head as Lady Bradden rose, saying on a sigh, "I'm sorry there is nothing further I can do." At the door, she hesitated. "Did Lord Dunstable have family?"

Evelina felt suddenly bereft. She didn't want Lady Bradden to leave. "He had a brother and a sister. His mother, too. I've met none of them."

"Were arrangements made for you to meet them?" Lady Bradden asked.

Evelina shrugged. "Nothing firm. Lord Dunstable said his mother was going to take it upon herself to arrange the engagement festivities." She frowned, swallowing down her humiliation before she volunteered, "Then he changed his mind and said he thought it best if we were married quietly, and that he told his mama after we returned from the wedding tour." She drew herself up, adding with the pent-up indignation she'd hidden from her husband-to-be, "He said there was some difficulty with the marriage contract he was negotiating with my father. I think he was ashamed that my parents no longer live together, but it's not as if they're...divorced!"

"I'm sure you have no need to concern yourself, my dear," said Lady Bradden kindly. "Take what time you need to digest the shock. And then I'd advise you to continue as if nothing had happened...if you think you can manage it."

Evelina rose, suddenly afraid. She didn't want Lady Bradden to leave her alone with Lady Perry. "And do I wear mourning? Full mourning or half?" She felt completely at sea with no one to guide her, for Lady Perry had been a tight-lipped chaperone who seemed only to exist to escort Evelina to the events her mother had organized.

Before Lady Bradden could respond, Evelina said suddenly, "I want to see my mother! She'll know what to advise me."

"Your mother?" Lady Bradden turned at the door. "Forgive me, but I do not recall you mentioning your mother. Only your chaperone, Lady Perry. Might I ask...who is your mother?"

"Mrs. Catherine Tarot. Perhaps you've heard of her?"

"Where does she live? Perhaps I can take you there."

Evelina lowered her eyes. "She resides with an elderly aunt who does not desire additional company, so I only see Mama when she comes here. I will send round a note."

"An' I'll take the note ter yer mama, directly," said the photographer with surprising alacrity. "It's the least I can do since I offended yer earlier, miss. An' 'cos I want ter 'elp as best I can in yer hour o' distress."

"Yes, indeed," said Lady Bradden. "We will both take the note and ensure that your mama sees you at the earliest. A young lady needs to be with her mother at such a time. We will wait while you write it."

Five minutes later, Evelina felt more bereft than she could have imagined as she stood at the drawing-room window and watched Lady Bradden and her maid, the child, and the photographer prepare to depart in Lady Bradden's carriage.

Down in the street, a footman opened the door for her ladyship, who held out her arms for the child, before the maid climbed in beside her. How very unconventional to bring a child, Evelina thought, once again.

But then, Lady Bradden seemed a very unconventional woman.

And then, to her surprise, she saw Kitty emerge, having climbed the stairs from the servants' entrance below street level.

Her maid began talking in animated fashion to the photographer whose name Evelina had forgotten, and Evelina was about to leave the window when Kitty reached into her skirt pocket and drew out what appeared to be a piece of paper, which she handed to the man.

He took it, and Kitty raised her hand to cup the man's cheek. It was a brief but telling gesture.

One that surprised Evelina more than she could say.

EVELINA TRAILED off to her bedchamber and took a seat by the window, staring into the street until she became aware of another presence in the room.

The clock chimed, and she realized that nearly an hour had passed.

"Kitty?" She blinked, startled out of her reverie, then put her head in her hands and sighed. "I want to see Mama. There hasn't been word from her, has there?"

Kitty stopped in the midst of folding a pile of petticoats to put into Evelina's wardrobe. "Yer mama will come as soon as she is able. Would yer like me ter do yer 'air, miss? You'll find it soothin'."

Lily nodded. It was soothing.

"Did you tell her the reason I wished her to come?" Evelina asked tightly as she dropped her head back and closed her eyes. "

"Oh, yes, miss, an' she were ever so sorry, as yer can imagine! She wanted ter be wiv yer on this very shockin' occasion. An' she will be soon enough. It's jest she was—"

Evelina opened her eyes. "She was what?"

Kitty shrugged. "Uvverwise engaged, miss. Oh no, miss, wot are yer doin'?"

"I'm going to see her." Evelina had risen sharply. "Where's the address?" she asked, squinting at the unfamiliar location which she'd passed on to Lady Bradden. "There's no need to come with me, Kitty, if that's what you think you're doing."

"Yer can't go out alone, miss. That's if yer think this is such a good idea."

"To see my mother? In my hour of need?"

"Then take a few minutes ter calm yerself, miss. An' ter dress. I'll 'elp yer. But first, give me jest a moment. I…must dash out fer a minute. I'll be back. Call o' nature."

Without waiting for Evelina to respond, Kitty rushed out of the room.

Evelina sank down upon the bed. She'd felt strangely numb before. Shock, she supposed. But now she had a focus for her anger.

How could her mama not have time to see her daughter immediately in her hour of need?

Still, Kitty was right. She couldn't go out and about in a city she did not know, much less, alone.

When, finally, Kitty did return, she was feeling a little more amenable to direction.

So, when the maid said, "I jest 'eard back from yer mama who can't meet yer at the address yer 'ave fer 'er as the lady wot she lives wiv is poorly. 'Owever, I'm ter take yer ter where yer dear mama can give yer the comfort an' advice that a young lady in yer terrible situation must need. 'Ere, let me 'elp yer wiv yer bonnet. We can go directly, but we may 'ave ter wait fer 'er when we get there. Yer mama is tryin' as 'ard as she can ter get ter yer, miss."

CHAPTER 10

Meanwhile, Lily, who had just received Kitty's note regarding Miss Tarot's determination to locate her mother, was facing Madame Chambon across the woman's study. The very room in which Lord Dunstable had apparently met his death.

Lily had sent Archie and the nursemaid back home with the baby, and now she was having a difficult time not succumbing to the skin-prickling horror she felt at once more being in this strange, oppressive house.

Madame Chambon's House of Assignation was just as she remembered it. The swathes of rich red velvet fringed with gold, the gilded cherubs and large canvasses of women in various states of nudity, made her shudder.

It had been an awkward reunion. Lily was now a scion of respectability and her confrontation with Madame Chambon was a strange power reversal.

The fact that Lily had learned that Evelina—who had been well received in London drawing rooms and whose carefully constructed background had been believed—was

Madame's daughter had caused an initial apoplexy, but now Madame was fully recovered.

And she was defending herself in any way she could.

"How could I possibly see my daughter so soon after being falsely accused of a terrible, terrible crime?" Lady Chambon paced before the fire, her flaming hair contrasting with the glowing coals.

"Were accusations made, and if so, were they false, and do you not think your daughter is in just as much a predicament as you are, Madame?" Lily asked as calmly as she could, sinking into a chair. She'd had a hurried conversation with one of the young women who'd been questioned by the police, which had shored up her information. It was always best to have the upper hand with Madame, if possible.

"Do you have the temerity to suggest that I am actually guilty of Lord Dunstable's murder?" Madame snapped before adding in a more conciliatory tone, "Forgive me, Lady Bradden. Sometimes it is difficult to remember you are not the street urchin who fled into this house after stealing a woman's hat."

"My husband's sister's hat, yes," conceded Lily. "And I was a street urchin before my story was at last believed, and I was reunited with my father. I do owe you some small gratitude for housing me and feeding me without coercing me into the way of life that sustains the poor creatures who live beneath this roof—"

"Not all of themselves consider themselves poor creatures. Some have made fine arrangements, brokered by me."

"Indeed." Lily dipped her head. "But that is not why I am here. You need to see your daughter and give her the comfort she needs and a mother's advice for going forward."

"How can I do that when I am in the situation I'm in?" For the first time, Madame Chambon sounded querulous before the armor-plated demeanor was back in place. "I am innocent, yet there was one policeman who had the temerity to suggest I be locked up. Fortunately, I was able to remind the police inspector of where he was when Lord Dunstable met his untimely end. Not that Dunstable didn't deserve it," she added under her breath.

Lily inferred that more than just the police inspector had been visiting the girls in their rooms upstairs and said, "I'm surprised you weren't brought in since Lord Dunstable was found in your sitting room. Dead." Lily reminded her. "And I've heard reports that some of your girls told the police they'd heard the pair of you arguing." She wasn't going to mince her words. She was Lady Bradden, not the virtual beggar she'd been when Madame had housed her. The power balance had shifted.

"How quickly gossip makes its way to eager ears." Madame had lost some of her fire. She stared into the grate, which had been reduced to a few burning coals and now gave out little heat in the chill room. "We had argued, it is true." She sighed. "And I had left the room in anger after he —" She stopped. "Well, never mind the detail. Suffice to say that I left Lord Dunstable in my study to fetch something he was demanding of me and when I returned—there he was. Dead on the carpet and Gracie screaming like a banshee." She shook her head. "There was no sign of a struggle, no noise. Quite simply, someone had driven my paper knife straight through his neck in a single, lethal stroke." Her eyes hardened as she turned to face Lily. "But the truth is that I had nothing to do with his death and no idea who did."

"What were you arguing about?" Lily asked. Madame had not invited her to sit, and they now faced each other like adversaries across the plush Aubusson carpet where, Lily presumed, Lord Dunstable's body had been discovered just hours before. "Your Evelina?" she surmised, for, of course, Lord Dunstable must have had some arrangement with

Madame Chambon. No doubt money— namely Evelina's handsome dowry—was at the heart of it and underpinned his decision to marry the girl with as little public fanfare as possible to avoid the inevitable scrutiny of her background.

"Yes, Evelina."

"And is that all, Madame? Apparently, Lord Dunstable mentioned another name, and it was regarding this girl that you left your office to fetch something. Can you tell me who it was?"

Madame looked evasive. "Celeste," she said in barely a whisper.

"You argued with Lord Dunstable over Celeste?" gasped Lily, everything else forgotten. "But Celeste is dead."

Madame Chambon turned, raising her eyebrows. "Yes, Celeste is dead, which is why Celeste, and who she was, is no longer important. It is Evelina who must be protected at all costs. She cannot ever be associated with this house, much less be seen with me in public. I have sacrificed everything to ensure that she was brought up a lady. She's attended the convent school since she was six years old. Then I sent her to Switzerland, where she learned the art of being a lady. She can play the piano, sing, dance, speak French and English like an aristocrat, she understands the Greek philosophers, can discuss Plato. And she is beautiful. I imagined her married to a diplomat, perhaps. A diplomat would take her away from this country and keep her safe from any gossip that might associate her with me." The look she focussed on Lily was imploring. "She is a lady. I cannot see all of this wasted and my poor Evelina's reputation destroyed if there is an investigation into me, following Lord Dunstable's death."

Lily frowned as she tried to read between the lines. "So, you planned Evelina's education so she could make a fine match. But then Lord Dunstable appeared on the scene. And he proved more than acceptable to you?" Lily tried to puzzle it out. "But why—if he was a man who also frequented a place like this?" She encompassed the room with a sweep of her arm.

Madame Chambon did not respond, and Lily did not press it. Of course, it was not to have been a simple love match. But now she highlighted the most important point. "Evelina needs her mother's love and support," Lily said softly. "The man she was to have married is now dead. Murdered."

Madame Chambon was silent. Then she muttered, "I hardly think the girl is brokenhearted and grieving."

Lily hesitated, then tried again. "But...you brokered Evelina's marriage with Lord Dunstable? Why?"

Madame nodded, her eyes glazed as she stared into the fireplace. "Lord Dunstable wanted her dowry, of course. Isn't it always about money?"

"You didn't have to agree if you thought he wouldn't make your daughter happy."

Madame turned and her lip curled as she said, "Lord Dunstable first came to this house several years ago. Somehow, he learned I had a daughter. And then he learned she had a sizeable dowry. He said a marriage between them was the ideal plan because he would ensure no one ever knew her real origins. But then, when I demurred, not liking the fact that Evelina's money was so much more important than the happiness of my daughter, I saw the ugly side of him. He said that if I refused—or if Evelina backed out of the marriage—he would make it known, far and wide, that my beautiful, innocent Evelina was the daughter of London's most infamous brothel madam."

Lily could understand this to an extent. "Still, the money you provided as Evelina's dowry was really due to the labor of the girls who work for you."

"It was not!" Madame bit back as she focused a haughty

stare upon Lily. "That dowry is from Evelina's father. Not that he intends to be openly associated with her, given that I am her mother. But he has visited her in Paris several times when she has not known his identity. He was pleased with what he saw. And proud. When she was fifteen years old, he drew up a contract with very generous provision for Evelina. Lord Dunstable knew of it. I don't know how. Apart from Celeste, that's what we were arguing about."

Lily hesitated. "Did Lord Dunstable ever fear Lily might choose to wed another?"

Madame Chambon examined her painted nails but did not respond.

"But…he *was* blackmailing you to pressure Evelina to marry him. Is that true?"

Reluctantly, Madame Chambon nodded.

"Then, if this becomes known," Lily said slowly, "the police will think you had a very good motive to kill Lord Dunstable."

Madame Chambon passed a trembling hand over her brow, then shrugged. "Well, Lady Bradden, I did not kill him. You know how many people come and go in a house like this. Given the man's nature, many other gentlemen here might have had a grudge against his lordship? His late lordship."

"How many of the girls might have wished him harm?" Lily added with a frown. "Since you said he did frequent this establishment from time to time."

"None of my girls would commit such a heinous crime and nor would I allow my daughter to wed a man who was prone to violence!"

Lily inclined her head before making her way to the door. There was nothing more to be said except to repeat the reason she had come. "Please, will you see Evelina? Remember that she knows nothing of this; however, her fiancé has just been murdered, and regardless of what she felt about him, she will be feeling very alone and very frightened." Putting her hand on the knob, she added over her shoulder, "I promise I will say nothing about Evelina's... background. Since I know what it's like to have one's reputation slandered, I would be the last person to allow the same to happen to her, if it were in my power. It's the least I can do."

"It is not!"

Lily, who'd been about to see herself out, was surprised by Madame's vehemence, much less her next words.

"It's not the least you can do. If you really have any sympathy for my daughter, there is something you are uniquely positioned to do that will help her. Something that I cannot do."

Lily dropped her hand, shaking her head. "Madame, Evelina has a perfectly presentable chaperone and sponsor in Lady Perry—"

"I'm not asking that of you. Lady Bradden, I'm asking you to help discover who did murder Lord Dunstable, and their motive, so that I can mitigate any potential damage to Evelina's reputation."

Lily narrowed her eyes. "Do you really not have your own suspicions, Madame?" she asked, but Madame Chambon shook her head.

"Well, that is the role of the police," Lily responded with a sigh. "How can I possibly discover who murdered Lord Dunstable when I wasn't here, and I didn't even know the man?"

With surprising speed and grace, Madame crossed the carpet towards her. "Your husband is in the newspaper business, Lady Bradden. His photographer is as comfortable above stairs as he is below, as well as in a place like this. You rub shoulders with aristocrats but can don a disguise and roam the alleyways where people speak honestly to you. You know what it is to struggle to survive, and you have a natural instinct for chasing the truth rather than allow yourself to be misled by false leads. The police won't know where to start looking. And the chief inspector isn't motivated to learn the truth about a murder that happened under his nose when he was literally yards away, on top of...one of my girls. He'll find some scapegoat. No, it won't be me, but it also won't be the real murderer. Lady Bradden, I appeal to your honesty and integrity. Find the truth! Find out who murdered Lord Dunstable. And, more importantly...why?"

CHAPTER 11

F ive minutes after dutifully greeting her with a kiss
upon her violet-scented cheek, a dull-eyed Evelina
dabbed at her eyes as she sat on the sofa in Lady
Perry's drawing room and agreed that she would neither
curtail her social engagements nor seek out Lord Dunstable's
family.

"My dear, he has not yet introduced you to the world as
his future bride," her mother was saying, "and there has been
no official announcement of an engagement between you. It
means you are free to go forth as an unattached debutante
looking for a match."

Evelina could barely believe her mother's flinty attitude.
Was she really telling Evelina how fortunate it was that Lord
Dunstable's death had occurred before he'd announced their
engagement in the newspapers?

"Of course, you are overwrought and grief stricken, but
you must not show this in public," her mother went on.

Well, this was where Evelina began to feel flint-hearted.

She didn't feel grief stricken. She'd hardly known Lord

Dunstable and the more time passed—although it was only a few hours—the more she felt relieved that she did not have a lifetime to look forward to being his wife. He'd been pleasant enough, but he'd not caused her heart to flutter like …

Well, like William's presence had.

"I shall try, Mama," Evelina said. She wondered if she should mention that she'd spent the afternoon with several people who had known of her betrothal. Or rather, her likely impending betrothal.

Her mother held her teacup poised above her purple-clad lap but did not drink. She appeared to be thinking. "No, my dear, there is every reason to consider this terrible event in a more favorable light. There had been…whispers…that Lord Dunstable was not the heroic gentleman you might have thought him." She put down her cup.

Evelina hadn't considered Lord Dunstable heroic, but she nodded.

"In fact, he was known to frequent certain establishments that…"

Evelina waited. The pursed mouth was ominous. Her mama was not given to smiling at the best of times. Finally, Mrs. Tarot said, "Certain establishments that gentlemen visit when their wives do not give them the satisfaction they are looking for."

"When they are bored," said Evelina. "Yes, Lord Dunstable appeared to have a short attention span. Do you mean his club?"

"Well, a club of sorts. Not strictly a gentleman's club. A club, in fact, where there were a lot of women."

Evelina raised her eyebrows. "He did?"

"Yes, and rumors may come to your ears that he, in fact, died in one, since I understand that you have not been furnished with the particulars as to where, in fact, he did…

"Get murdered."

Her mother looked surprised. "Yes, indeed, my dear. If you wish to speak plainly."

"I prefer to speak plainly."

"Well. Good. Then we shall."

"Mama, I should tell you I spent yesterday afternoon at the zoological gardens with his cousins and... another gentleman...and talk of our impending marriage was discussed."

Her mother looked dismayed. "Oh, I did not know. That is unfortunate."

"What should I do?"

Her mother bit her lip. "Ignore the fact anything was said. If they bring it up, refute the fact there was an understanding between you since the engagement was not made official. You must continue with your London season as if nothing has happened." Her Mama drew in a breath, adding, "Though perhaps you should resign yourself to a husband from a lower rank."

The now-familiar sense of confusion and indignation reasserted itself as Evelina smoothed her green silk skirts, which, she could not forget, had been fashioned by the finest Parisian dressmaker. "I came to London to make a fine marriage. It is what I've been brought up for, Mama. Papa has provided me with a handsome dowry. Lord Dunstable is —was—just the kind of husband I was supposed to marry. I believe there was some hold-up due to a clause in the contract, but that is all." She felt her lip trembling, but forced herself to remain calm. "Why should I resign myself to marrying someone who is not an aristocrat? I want to speak to Papa. Why will Papa not see me?"

She thought of William. Lord Bellingham. He was the man she wanted to marry. And why should she not? Lord Dunstable's death had surely cleared the path to their union.

He'd all but said in as many words that he'd come to London especially to seek her out. Her. Evelina.

Opening her mouth, she was about to tell her mama then realized it was too soon with Dunstable dead only a few hours.

"Your father is a reclusive man. Do not expect to hear from him, my dear."

Evelina clasped her hands together and gathered the courage to ask her mother where her father now lived.

She needed to find her father so she could ask him, herself, why he was being—as Dunstable had led her to believe—ticklish over that certain clause in the marriage contract.

Then she wondered if, perhaps, her father had objected to Lord Dunstable as a bridegroom.

Perhaps he would be entirely amenable if it were someone else.

Someone like William. Lord Bellingham.

She drew in a deep breath and prepared to ask her mother to furnish her with the details of her father's location.

But her mother was looking at her as if she somehow understood this was what Evelina intended to ask.

And Mrs. Tarot's expression was so severe that Evelina lost courage.

THE CARRIAGE RIDE LILY SHARED with her husband that evening as they journeyed to Lord Lambton's residence where they were to dine with Lily's father was a little tense.

Lily knew she'd been underhanded in taking baby Sebastian with her to the office, and not mentioning to her husband that she'd visited that den of vice, Madame Chambon's. But she'd been wearing a hat with a particularly thick spotted veil that day which she'd drawn down. She'd not been recognized.

However, she suspected that Hamish, though such a champion of freedom for women, would feel that his own wife had possibly run the risk of compromising her reputation and, consequently that of the very conservative magazine he ran for his father, with her antics.

After some silence in the dimly lit carriage as it bumped over the cobbles, she finally asked, "What should I expect when I open up Manners & Morals at breakfast tomorrow, Hamish?" Her mood since her afternoon's meeting with Evelina Tarot had grown darker. "Will Lord Dunstable's photograph be plastered over the front page?"

While Hamish had sent a reporter to cover the story, he'd intervened editorially and, as he reassured his wife, toned down its speculative and sensationalist tone.

"His photograph, yes. We have a duty to our readers to report Lord Dunstable's death, and while I might ordinarily not have stripped Albert Wilson's narrative of its more colorful tones, I do not think it serves our newspaper to include the fact Lord Dunstable's body was discovered in a brothel."

Lily leaned back against the squabs and closed her eyes. "I'm glad to hear it."

Her husband squeezed her hand. "I'm sure the matter will be concluded soon, and your young lady can go about her business of finding a suitable husband— though perhaps not of Lord Dunstable's caliber." Hamish finished this with a frown. For what Lily hadn't told him, Archie had, embellishing the details, as Lily had discovered when she and Hamish discussed the matter briefly while preparing to dine at Lord Lambton's several hours earlier. Hamish had, naturally, stayed later than usual at the office on account of this piece of breaking news.

"And why not of Lord Dunstable's caliber?" Lily asked.

"What aristocrat—or true gentleman—would ally himself with the daughter of a brothel madam?" Hamish looked fondly into his wife's eyes. "I don't make society's rules, my dear, and I certainly don't endorse many of them, but it's the way of the world."

"But Hamish, what you just said is predicated on the fact that Evelina Tarot's real identity will now be revealed to the world? Why can it not remain hidden? Lord Dunstable was prepared to marry her. Why not someone else of his wealth and social standing?" While Lily had initially been of Hamish's thinking, she'd changed her mind. Why did the woman always bear the greatest brunt of any scandal? Miss Tarot had been brought up believing herself a noblewoman. She'd pass muster in the most exacting dowager duchess's drawing room. Why was it not possible to continue the charade?

"Lily, I—"

"And surely Lord Dunstable would have known the truth about Miss Tarot's origins? Or at least some of it. No doubt that's why he wished to avoid making the marriage public until after the fact. If he was a regular at Madame Chambon's and knew Miss Tarot was Madame Chambon's daughter, obviously Miss Tarot's true lineage was less important than her dowry. It must have been sufficiently large that he was willing to turn a blind eye and, indeed, keep the marriage secret until after the fact so that there'd be no scrutiny of her origins."

In the weak lamplight, Hamish looked at her with new interest. "You clearly know a great deal more about this case than you led me to believe."

"I've barely had five minutes to talk to you about it,

Hamish. That's why I'm doing so now. My father will know more about Lord Dunstable and his family that might throw light on Dunstable's motives for contracting the marriage."

Hamish chuckled. "You're a clever woman, Lily. Perhaps you can even solve the murder—"

She hesitated, wavering between telling him that's what Madame had asked of her, then deciding, again, that he wasn't ready to hear that she'd visited the woman at her premises that afternoon. "I just want to ensure Miss Tarot comes out of this unscathed. Her reputation, at any rate, though I don't believe she was in love with him."

"Good Lord, Lily, what don't you know about all this?"

"Lord Dunstable's real motivation in marrying a brothel-madam's daughter—though I imagine that, of course, it would be money." She paused. "And, of course, the identity of the killer." For a long time, she stared out of the window at the passing landscape: the darkened buildings, the ragged children who darted around street corners and into alleys. "And I believe if we could confirm the answer to the first part of this—since Madame seems to have been coerced into agreeing, despite the fact Lord Dunstable had all the right credentials—it might shine a light on the second. I certainly don't believe Madame Chambon killed the man who offered her daughter what she's always wanted: respectability for her progeny. Yet she is, as will no doubt be splashed about the papers tomorrow, the prime suspect. And I fear what it will do to Miss Tarot to learn of her lineage this way. Thank goodness the pair have never been seen in public."

Hamish considered this. "It's possible a photograph of Madame Chambon does not exist in the public domain. But it won't be long before it does."

"Then it must be kept away from Miss Tarot."

Hamish frowned, but his tone was fond. "You've decided to champion the young woman?"

A shudder went through Lily as she recalled Madame's beseeching tone when she made her request of Lily. "I know the excoriating feeling of having one's character stained when one is blameless. I know what it is to fall so far you can't fall any farther. That young woman has been brought up believing she's the daughter of two respectable, estranged parents, her father an aristocrat. She expects to make a glittering marriage. And perhaps she still can if the truth does not emerge. That is what I hope to prevent."

"The truth coming out?" Hamish shook his head. "How can it not, as the investigation proceeds?" He took her hand. "My dear, your motives are honorable, and I understand your sense of injustice and your hope that what you experienced will not be visited upon innocent Miss Tarot. But there is one great difference between you, and I fear that is what will condemn Miss Tarot's marital dreams to the dustbin."

Lily looked at him enquiringly and he answered: "The truth. You were—in truth—the daughter of an aristocrat and then the wife of an aristocrat." He shook his head, his expression sympathetic. "Miss Tarot is not."

As they sat across the dining table with her father, Lord Lambton, later that evening, Lily and Hamish found him surprisingly well informed.

"Terrible business," he said as the dessert was put in front of them. "In a house of assignation, no less. A good thing he has no wife to consider. The man was a blackguard, no doubt about it." Lord Lambton put down his wineglass and leveled a beetling look at his daughter and son-in-law.

"What did you know of him, Papa?" Lily asked.

"More than I needed. He'd run through his inheritance.

Was no doubt looking for a rich wife. Lucky no woman succumbed to his lures, is all I can say."

Lily exchanged a glance with her husband. Although her father wasn't up with all the latest gossip, it was a comfort to know that Lord Dunstable's betrothal was not common knowledge.

"Did you know Lord Dunstable well?" Lily asked. It was only during the past eighteen months that she herself had discovered her real father and there was still so much to learn about him.

"He went to my club. Didn't know him well, though. Only the whispers about him. About the gambling…the women. But let's change the subject, shall we, since his murder is gruesome, and you have no interest in the man."

Lily was relieved when Hamish interjected, "Ah, now you've said the very thing to whip up the interest of a news-paperman." His smile hid the deep curiosity Lily knew he felt. "Secrets? Everyone wants to learn secrets, especially if the man who holds them has just been murdered. Perhaps those secrets point to the identity of the murderer."

"I thought the murderer had already been charged."

Lily leaned forward. "And who might that be?" she asked without thinking, for her father's expression closed over and he glanced at Hamish. Of course, her father would not speak of a brothel madam in his daughter's presence.

"I think it's time I left you gentlemen to your port," she said, rising, nodding to her father. "I have some needlework waiting for me in the drawing room."

Hamish would have to quiz Lord Lambton like the professional he was. Of course, Lord Lambton knew the boundaries of what could be spoken about in front of gently reared women, and although he knew of Lily's spiritualist phase, as it was what had united them, he certainly did not know she'd been housed by Madame Chambon.

Nor, of course, did he know that Lord Dunstable had become betrothed to Madame Chambon's daughter.

Although his reunion with Lily had been the greatest joy of his life, following the death of what he believed was his only daughter, there were some things, Lily knew, that he could never reconcile.

And the full truth was one of them.

CHAPTER 12

W illiam had never woken with such feelings of hope and expectation.

He had found the woman of his dreams.

No, he had been reunited with the woman of his dreams. Shocking and terrible though the train crash had been, divine intervention had been at play—if one believed in such a thing.

Admittedly, he'd been cast low by the knowledge that Miss Tarot was all but engaged to Lord Dunstable.

But that had not been made public and perhaps never would if the feelings he suspected Miss Tarot harbored for William could be coaxed into a more robust affirmation that he, William, Lord Bellingham, was the husband for her. Not Lord Dunstable.

"Morning, m'lord. Yer newspaper."

William looked up from his morning coffee and scrambled eggs as his butler placed it on the white tablecloth.

"Ah, yes. I'll read it later," he said, distracted. It seemed all he could think about these days was Miss Tarot.

Had she, too, experienced the same extraordinary

connection he had felt when they'd danced together? Talked together?

Why, they'd saved a child. Only because the two of them had joined forces had it been possible to whisk the young boy from the jaws of certain death.

That was no small matter. They had saved the life of the child. And as they'd exchanged, in that one look immediately afterwards, the knowledge that this would forever unite them, William had also known that Miss Tarot was the one woman, above all others, he would wed.

Everything had crystallized as, last night, he'd gone over his intended approach. Not once, but a hundred times as he'd calculated how he could navigate the disentanglement of Miss Tarot from any understanding that may have been forged between her and Dunstable.

No, Miss Tarot and William belonged together. They had already proved the strength of their union when saving the child, William, and together they would have children of their own.

If William had any doubts about where Miss Tarot's heart belonged, he had only to recall the look in her eyes when they'd rediscovered one another.

All his own desires, feelings, passions had been reflected there.

Usually, William's butler simply dropped the newspaper and left but now he hovered, uncertainly, before saying, "Yer might want ter read it when yer still sittin' down, m'lord."

William glanced at him, surprised, then pulled the newspaper towards him, nearly spilling his coffee, so great was his shock.

What was all this? Dunstable's name was splashed across the front page?

Then the headline, which he'd finally forced himself to

read, penetrated his brain. "Good God!" he spluttered, knocking his coffee cup so that it nearly overturned.

Dunstable was dead? Murdered?

Minutes before, he'd wished for a good reason to see Dunstable out of the running when it came to whom Miss Tarot would choose for her husband.

Murder had not been one of them.

He skimmed the article, searching for details, but though the commentary was florid, the facts were sparse. It did, however, allude to the fact Dunstable may have been in a dubious location.

Madame Chambon's?

William rolled his eyes. He could well imagine Dunstable a habitual visitor to that den of iniquity. Miss Tarot did not deserve the blackguard whereas William…

Carefully, William re-read the piece. There was no mention of Dunstable's impending nuptials. Nor had there been any public announcement.

For a few minutes, William stared blankly at the front page while the newsprint blurred before his eyes, his mind actively engaged on a wild ride of supposition in the absence of fact, but ultimately, relief that Miss Tarot's name did not appear.

Of course, he should feel nothing but horror at poor Dunstable's fate, but what other contender for a woman's affections wouldn't carry a hopeful flame in their heart?

Certainly, William and Dunstable had shared a friendship of sorts, but William had no real affinity with the man. He'd only suggested the visit to the zoological gardens because he had the excuse at hand after Dunstable had vaguely mentioned he'd promised his cousin Clara a visit.

In such a situation, William thought as he rose and tossed his napkin onto the table, it was entirely proper to rush to offer Miss Tarot his assistance, support…and a reaffirmation of his romantic feelings in the guise of condolences.

Thus, an hour later, he was being shown into Lady Perry's drawing room, a black armband tied around his elbow, bowing his head as lovely Miss Tarot made her entrance.

She was dressed soberly in hues of pale mauve.

Not mourning, then.

"Lord Bellingham." She offered him a half smile as she waved him to a seat, sinking down on a chair a little to his right while Lady Perry perched on one on his other side. "It was good of you to come." She hesitated. "I confess, too, to being surprised."

"And why would that be when you know—" He stopped. He was not the kind of man to blurt out declarations and was astonished he'd nearly done so. But visions of Miss Tarot had consumed him since their first meeting.

Her words, however, gave him pause.

Was it possible she may not have spared William a thought?

Perhaps she really was mourning Dunstable, for William had to remember the talk of impending nuptials during the afternoon he'd spent with them at the zoological gardens. That was why he was here.

That was why Lady Perry was as somber as Miss Tarot, having no doubt helped broker the marriage. Yet no mention was made of any understanding between Miss Tarot and Lord Dunstable during their sober, stilted conversation.

In the corner, Lady Perry's knitting needles clicked, her head bent as William and Miss Tarot stared at one another.

He remembered the way she'd looked at him when she'd seen him for the first time after the train crash. The flare of surprise…and delight.

Yes, and longing. The same look she'd failed to completely conceal just now.

But with Lady Perry sitting in on their conversation, there was little of what was truly in his heart that could be said.

When the requisite condolences and offers of assistance had been made, William rose.

"Evelina," said Lady Perry without looking up, "why don't you see Lord Bellingham out?"

To his relief, he saw she liked the idea. Perhaps even more telling was the way she tried to hide the fact.

"Of course, Lady Perry."

Oh, she was good. Miss Tarot naturally had to restrain her true feelings. It was what any well-bred young woman was trained to do, especially under such circumstances.

Her composure only reinforced her suitability for being his bride. A man forging a career in politics needed a wife who could keep her passions in check while projecting the veneer required by the polite society she would navigate.

She was a woman of infinite resources—he had already discovered that—and, he suspected, she was quick to passion —he wanted to discover this to be equally true.

Yet she could subdue her true feelings when necessary.

He stopped in the passage outside the drawing room, far enough away to be out of earshot of Lady Perry. "I saw no notices of your forthcoming engagement in the newspapers, Miss Tarot. I wonder if that means I can look forward to your presence at forthcoming entertainments this season? Perhaps at Lady Gilray's ball tonight?"

He glanced at her hands, clasped demurely in front of her, the fingers pale and slender. Bare and vulnerable, like her expression as she offered an almost imperceptible nod.

"I would like to offer you the time you need to mourn, Miss Tarot, so—"

"I would thank you not to tell others of the...understand-ing...Lord Dunstable and I had at the time of his tragic death," she interrupted.

William nodded, trying for the restraint she'd managed. Otherwise, he'd have whisked her into his arms and kissed her there and then. "Of course not. Tragic though his death is, an association with Lord Dunstable, murdered in such a brutal manner, would hinder your chances of making another match."

She winced at the words and murmured, "Who could have done such a thing?"

And William realized that the question had not even occurred to him. He'd been interested only in establishing his own claim to her attentions and regard.

Surely this visit, today, would make clear to her he viewed her as a potential wife? Little Edwina's words at the zoo had made this clear—embarrassing though they'd been at the time—but with Dunstable's death, there was no impediment to William courting her.

"I hope he will be apprehended directly," he said.

To his delight, Miss Tarot now brought up his daughter as she asked, "Little Edwina is well? What a sweet child she is. I take it she is no longer in London?"

"Her nursemaid took her back to my home, Cransley, in Essex yesterday." He smiled, glancing at Miss Tarot's clasped hands, wishing he could clasp them to his breast, as he added, "Edwina liked you very much. She asked if you would be visiting us at Cransley."

"I should like that very much."

"You would?" He realised with a rush of delight that it really was this easy. The events of several weeks ago had established Miss Tarot as a woman of valor beneath her beauty. Dunstable's betrothal had established that she had the credentials to be a worthy nobleman's bride.

No association had been made public of Lord Dunstable and Miss Tarot's relationship.

And the way Miss Tarot was looking at him made clear that Miss Tarot's feelings matched his own.

A wave of euphoria made him step forward, but he hesitated as she brought her hands up to her cheeks and a small furrow appeared upon her brow.

William was suddenly embarrassed. Was he reading too much into what was conveyed by her eyes? For she certainly had said nothing to indicate a reciprocation of his feelings.

Perhaps, in fact, she didn't really return the feelings of his heart?

And then she took a half step forward. She gripped his hands, her pale, slender fingers squeezing his for but a fraction of a second before she released him; a contact long enough to spear him with the most potent desire as she whispered with what he could only describe as fierce longing, "I can't tell you how welcome your visit has been, Lord Bellingham."

And then she was turning towards the front door, murmuring platitudes about the weather while the little parlormaid appeared from nowhere to fetch his hat and coat, and open the front door onto the suddenly bright, bustling street.

Like William's heart filled with energy and a multitude of possibilities.

EVELINA ENTERED her bedchamber with her hands on her cheeks and her heart pounding.

Kitty, who'd been tidying her dressing table, looked up. "Wot's 'appened, miss? Was it that gellulman wot was 'ere? The nice Lord Bellingham? Did 'e bring yer news of wot 'appened ter poor Lord Dunstable? 'Ave they found the murderer?"

Kitty dropped her feather duster and glided over to Evelina, who'd sat down on the bed and was clasping a pillow to her chest.

"Yer don't look like one whose 'eart is broke so I am glad yer 'adn't set yer mind on marryin' 'is poor dead lordship. There are plenty o' other nice gennelmun with titles an' fat pocketbooks who'll fit the bill an' please yer dear mama."

"You know my mama better than I thought you did," said Evelina, and was surprised to see Kitty blush. But she went on, "And Lord Bellingham knows nothing of what happened to poor Lord Dunstable. In fact, Lord Dunstable's death was barely mentioned."

"Well, it's best ter put 'im right behind yer, fer there's Lady Gilray's ball t'night. 'Ere, let's take out yer 'airpins so I can brush that beautiful dark 'air o' yers an' 'elp get yer ready. I've laid out yer gown an' yer'll be as pretty as a picture, as me old gran used ter say."

Evelina submitted obediently, her reservations fast receding, even as she asked, "Should I really attend Lady Gilray's ball when the man I was to have married died only last night?"

"Did nice Lord Bellingham, who was 'ere jest now, ask if yer'd be at Lady Gilray's ball?" Kitty asked shrewdly, and Evelina nodded.

"Then yer should go. Who else knows yer were ter be married? No one is wot I 'eard. Well then, if yer like Lord Bellingham as much as I fink yer do, then yer want ter make 'im yer 'usband as quick as yer can. Afore someone else does. That's wot these balls are fer, an' I know fer a fact that London debutantes are a connivin' lot. Maybe in France young ladies are less forward, but me advice is ter reel in yer nice Lord Bellingham as quick as yer can so yer can please yer mama, an' rest easy cos yer future's all taken care o'."

Evelina smiled. "You know a lot about debutantes. But then, you've looked after so many of them."

Kitty nodded, serious as she drew the boar-bristle brush through Evelina's unbound tresses. "All sorts they were too, miss. Reckon I know wot's what when it comes ter young ladies an' their desires. An' if yer desire is ter find yerself a 'usband, wot'll give yer the security yer need, but that'll make yer 'eart flutter, then yer no different from all the rest."

CHAPTER 13

Lady Gilray's ball was a lavish affair. Lily rarely attended such august occasions but Hamish had been invited by Lord Gilray, who attended his club and who was championing a reformist bill which Hamish was covering in his newspaper.

Rather than discuss the matter in his office or at Whites, the plush ballroom at Lord and Lady Gilray's Grosvenor Square residence sounded much more conducive to such a conversation.

It had been a long time since Lily had appeared in a ball-room. As a new, inexperienced bride, she'd dreamed of visits to the capital, but Lord Bradden had never followed through on his promises.

The London she had seen after she'd been kidnapped by Mr. Montpelier from the lunatic asylum in Belgium had offered her a very different experience. First, there were the months she'd spent hiding at Madame Chambon's while she'd regained the lush looks from the nourishment provided.

Now, as she gazed about the ballroom, she saw many of

the aristocratic men and women who had crowded into the small, dingy drawing room in St James' Wood where she'd worked as a spiritualist pretending to commune with the dead. She'd been given no choice in her occupation, but she'd also brought solace to some, and although her past was dark with shame, the acceptance of many here tonight had surprised her.

"My dear Lady Bradden, I read the terrible news of poor Lord Dunstable in your husband's newspaper. I'm sure Mr. McTavish knows more than he's allowed to say."

It was Her Grace, the Dowager Duchess of Dalrymple sniffing out gossip with the same prurient interest she'd displayed when she'd attended Lily's seances.

The Duchess put her hand on Lily's arm and whispered, "Who did it? You can tell me."

Lily smiled. "If only someone knew, Your Grace. The police are investigating."

"I heard he was found in a place we ladies should have no idea exists..." The Duchess narrowed her eyes, leaving Lily to infer her meaning.

"I believe the details of the circumstances have not been made public."

"Not by your husband's newspaper, no." The Duchess hesitated. "I saw his cousin, Lady Victoria, looking red-eyed during a walk by the serpentine, and little wonder. The gel wanted him for years and now he's dead."

"Lady Victoria and Lord Dunstable?" Lily was surprised.

"There was talk they were to be affianced, but nothing came of it. Lady Victoria turned her attention to taking the place of their poor mama after she died, looking after her young sister, and Lord Dunstable turned to pursuits less noble than looking for the perfect wife. That is, until there were whispers, he was about to pledge his troth to an unknown. In fact, to that young lady over there." The

Duchess stabbed her finger in the direction of the dance floor and Lily saw with a start, that she was referring to Evelina Tarot.

This turned to surprise when she saw Miss Tarot in the arms of Lord Bellingham.

"That's the gel. An unknown from Paris, but no doubt with a very large dowry if Dunstable was sniffing around. He needs funds, don't you know?"

"Where do you get your information, Ma'am?" Lily tried to appear as if she knew nothing and was genuinely curious.

"Nobody notices an old woman, especially when their tongues are loosened. I pick up a tidbit here and there and put things together." The Duchess looked pleased with herself. Lily had wondered at her motivations in telling her all this and now suspected it was for the fact she had the satisfaction of telling the newspaper mogul's wife what even her husband did not know.

"Goodness, what else have you gleaned—or suspect — about what might have happened to Lord Dunstable? It sounds like the metropolitan police should be talking to you."

"I'm sure I wouldn't tell them how to do their jobs." The Duchess sniffed, though there was a satisfied gleam in her eye. "But I do know he died at a notorious house of assignation because I heard the gentlemen talk about who else was there that night." After another suspenseful pause, she added, "And that included a gentleman who was mightily out of charity with our poor late lordship."

"And which gentleman might that be?" Lily asked in as measured a tone as possible.

"I'm not sure the epithet gentleman necessarily applies. Captain Blackheath. A dark fellow indeed. Always scrounging a penny if he can't borrow a pound. Mostly so he can spend it on the low pleasures he enjoys at Madame's, though that's as explicit as I'm prepared to be."

Lily gazed at the dance floor while her thoughts ran in circles. Miss Tarot was now partnering Lord Miles. She'd set her sights high then, and why not? If Lord Dunstable had been prepared to wed her, then she would naturally consider herself acceptable to any other equally highborn gentleman here.

She had the grace and beauty, together with a very large dowry, to ensure a successful season, but what would happen when investigations into her background were conducted as they surely would be? Lord Dunstable had discovered the truth, but her money had been more important.

With growing dismay, Lily registered the hope and innocence on the young girl's face. What future did Miss Tarot have? Lily doubted her lineage would bear up to scrutiny a second time.

Yet, the poor girl had no idea.

The Duchess was still eyeing Miss Tarot with singular interest. "It is curious that so little is known of Miss Tarot's family," she said as if she'd been reading Lily's thoughts. Her gaze had returned to the dance floor where Evelina Tarot was once again being partnered by Lord Bellingham.

The Duchess sniffed. "Mrs. Everard Fairfield believes her daughter, Cassandra, has caught the eye of Lord Bellingham on account of their unity of thought during a house party they attended some months ago. She plans on making enquiries and I suspect that, lovely though Miss Tarot is, her background may not bear up to scrutiny. The Tarots of Norfolk? Never heard of them!" she scoffed. "And Lord Bellingham? Why, he doesn't need blunt. He needs a wife with impeccable credentials. Cassandra Fairfield has both."

Lily's concern increased. Scanning the room, her eye lit upon Mr. John Farnley, the eldest son of Sir Walter Farnley, a baronet from Norfolk with a crumbling manor house and five daughters. The old gentleman was more interested in ensuring his offspring were comfortably placed than illustriously connected, and his son, Mr. John Farnley, was mild-mannered and not too displeasing of face, though he did have a tendency towards monologues regarding his potato growing experiments. Perhaps that was due to shyness. The main criteria was that he was perfectly presentable and perhaps Lily should engineer an introduction. The sight of Miss Tarot in the arms of someone as patently unsuitable as Lord Bellingham made her feel ill with dismay.

The Duchess was right. Neither William, Lord Bellingham, nor Lord Miles, were gentlemen whose families would countenance a bride such as Miss Tarot when the truth came out.

She straightened, prepared to do battle on Miss Tarot's account—not to facilitate a union with Lord Bellingham, which was unworkable. Speed was of the essence. She really had to avert a disaster before Evelina Tarot fell in love with either gentlemen. A series of judicious conversations with Sir Walter Farnley, who knew her husband quite well, might be a means of ensuring Miss Tarot's past remained where it should be: in the past.

"What do I get for solving the mystery, Lady Bradden?"

Lily's head snapped up as it always did when she was addressed by the name she had before she married Hamish. She far preferred people call her Mrs. McTavish however a lady who married 'down' retained her title after marriage in circles such as these.

"I am impressed, Ma'am," she said, not willing to confess her mind had wandered after she'd dismissed Lord Blackheath as a likely suspect in Lord Dunstable's murder. What did The Duchessknow, after all? She was not there and everything she'd repeated was pure hearsay or had already been reported by some newspapers.

"So, you are accusing Captain Blackheath?" the Duchess asked.

Lily appeared to be listening when she was more interested in watching Evelina. "What else have you heard?"

The Duchesssounded sly. "Ah, so you want to glean from me what your newspaper husband needs to sell his news sheet? It's not just for the homilies and Christian advice that his subscribers snatch up their copies of *Manners and Morals*, is it? Why would we want to read about poor Daisy Cooper and Liza Frith when we can learn what really happened to Lord Dunstable before the police send Madame Chambon to the gallows? For she is the woman I'd wager who did it. The pair of them were heard arguing." She hesitated, as if weighing up whether to continue before she added, "And my information is that Lord Dunstable had become a visitor several years before when his roving eye had alighted upon the charming Celeste who also met her maker at the notorious Madame Chambon's."

Lily jerked her head around to stare at the old dowager duchess. After a quick glance about her, she took a half step closer. The Duchess truly did have a grasp on the background of the case. More than Lily, in fact.

But was she inferring that she knew Lily had once shared a room with Celeste in the months before the young woman had been murdered by the Russian diplomat convicted of the crime? Was this why she'd mentioned Celeste?

It was information that Lily most definitely did not want made public. That and her brief association with Madame Chambon, for while she's skated clear of outright opprobrium for her work as a spiritualist, spiritualism had taken society by storm at all levels of society.

None of the elite here tonight, however, would think the same of her if they knew she'd spent months in a brothel.

"You believe they will hang Madame?" she asked, her tone

more skeptical as she added, "On the basis of an argument and when he was a regular at her premises? When there were many others that night who had equal opportunity—and greater motive?" She had no love of Madame Chambon, but the woman had not been unkind, and she was Miss Tarot's mother.

Furthermore, when all was said and done, Lily believed Madame Chambon when she claimed innocence.

"I hear Lord Dunstable's family desires a speedy resolution to the case." The Duchess finished her drink with a practiced flick of the arm and Lily realized with a start there was far more to the seemingly feeble creature she'd thought her. "His cousin, Lady Victoria—who obviously knows nothing of the delicate matter of where he was murdered—is demanding the police find the culprit at the earliest. Don't be fooled by her apparent fragility. She is on the warpath for justice. And I know for a fact, she has the ear of the man in charge of bringing Lord Dunstable's killer to justice with, let us say, unusually generous inducements. I suspect the convenience of charging Madame Chambon with Lord Dunstable's murder will come at the cost of true justice." The Duchess shrugged. "And perhaps that doesn't matter when she is guilty of robbing so many of the women here in this room of the domestic felicity they deserve."

It was time, Lily decided, to leave the Duchess to her sleuthing so that Lily could find Hamish and solicit his help in ensuring there were no developments in the budding relationship between Lord Bellingham and Miss Tarot.

CHAPTER 14

The feel of Miss Tarot in his arms was more sensually charged than William had expected.

Miss Tarot not only looked like an angel, she danced like an angel. The Viennese waltz was fast, but she was light on her feet; a consummate dancer, as was he, and when he caught her eye, the exhilaration she clearly felt matched his.

The pupils of her dark eyes were dilated and her ivory skin glowed, setting off the glossy ringlets and plaits of her coiffure, as superb as a raven's wing.

When he led her off the dance floor and fetched her a glass of champagne, he was infused with the desire to learn everything about her.

Dunstable was dead. He should feel more angst over that.

But William had been given a second chance with the woman who was to have married his friend.

Miss Tarot had barely known Dunstable. A few conversations, perhaps? She'd not reciprocated the depth of feeling she clearly felt for him.

No, he and Miss Tarot were destined to be together.

William, back in the country after three years abroad, was fired up on multiple fronts. He'd seen so much during his travels that made him believe he could fix through his new role in parliament.

And meeting Miss Tarot under such circumstances had convinced him that she was 'the one'.

She was beautiful and intelligent The consummate society hostess, she'd win the hearts of his political friends and foes alike. She was still very young, but she had a consciousness that transcended age. She was fearless and driven to do right and good.

Her heroism during the train rescue indicated how much her impulses were driven by the heart. And what a good heart that was.

She'd saved a child. A little boy called William.

And her acceptance of his eventual offer was going to be the making William the man.

William could think of no other reason for what had happened. Their meeting truly was destiny.

"You look beautiful this evening." In her gown of pink, adorned with cream swathes and pink bows, with pearls sparkling in her hair, he'd seen no one more beautiful. It was the first opportunity he had of being with her in a setting where an understanding between them could be properly established.

The train crash had been urgent and adrenaline-fueling, but it had brought them together.

Their meeting once more at the zoological gardens had ignited the fire in both their hearts. It had made clear the level of her interest in him and her disappointment that she'd allied herself too peremptorily with Dunstable.

Surely this had been borne out by his visit to her following Dunstable's death?

And tonight was the night he would act on this, regardless of any lack of tact or delicacy due to the fact Dunstable had only just been murdered.

"Thank you."

Dimples appeared in her cheeks. He hadn't noticed them before. Perhaps because she was of a more serious demeanor. Or perhaps he'd mistaken a natural gravity for the inevitable disappointment she'd felt at having been steered in Dunstable's direction before realizing that William was just as eligible and surely even more eager.

However, William was not going to allude to the horror of Dunstable's death when nothing formal between Miss Tarot and Lord Dunstable had been made public.

She was free to marry whomever she chose.

And she was smiling at him with such warmth, he truly had every expectation that he was that lucky man.

"What are your plans for the next week, Miss Tarot?" he asked, as he led her to a secluded alcove. He didn't care that his interest would be observed. Lady Perry was doing her duty as chaperone nearby, but she was gossiping with another old woman in somber hues. Their nearness did not cast a blight on his ability to make the most of this moment. He was too happy for anything to cast a blight on what he believed was the beginning of the rest of his life.

"I—"

She'd started with a smile that was quickly wiped from her lips. "Lord Dunstable had invited me to the opera tomorrow night," she whispered as if she'd only just remembered, and William cursed himself for the question. Of course, she'd have had a social calendar that revolved around Dunstable.

"You could accompany me to the opera tomorrow night instead," he said quickly. His expression was somber, but he was not going to offer words of sympathy he did not feel.

She inclined her head. "I should like that."

"Your mama... or papa... would not object so soon after —?" He had to ask. Dunstable's presence was everywhere, as he supposed it would be, considering what he had been to this young woman. The man to whom she was about to become engaged, though she'd carefully not said it in so many words.

"I don't think so." She shook her head.

"Your family hails from Norfolk, I believe?" He realized how little he knew of her background though he understood they were a solid, respectable family. They would have to be for Miss Tarot to be accepted here.

"My mother is from Norfolk and my father from further north. I haven't seen my father since..." She frowned as she toyed with the drink he'd handed her. Concern clouded her eyes, and she did not look at him as she said, "Not since I was a child."

"But he is in London now?" William needed to know where to find the man to ask the question he would inevitably ask before the next few weeks were over. He wanted to marry Evelina. It was as simple as that.

"No. Mama and Papa don't get along very well, but Papa has always been very ... generous."

William felt the first stirring of disquiet. Her parents were estranged?

Then he relaxed. Two individuals who'd chosen to live separately while sparing no expense on their child was not uncommon. Clearly Mr. Tarot was maintaining wife and daughter and there was no suggestion of scandal. No divorce ... no public indiscretion.

"Where is your father now?" Regardless of where the man was, William still needed to ask him for his daughter's hand in marriage.

He saw the color flood her cheeks before she turned away. The glass she held trembled, and she looked suddenly desperate to find somewhere to deposit it. William took it from her, wishing he'd not asked her something that clearly caused her such pain. "He's at home in—" She hesitated. "He has a house in Scotland. Aberdeenshire."

"Aberdeenshire." William smiled, anxious to put her at ease. "A remote but ... a beautiful part of the country."

"I have not visited," she said softly, dropping her head so that her neck resembled that of a dispirited swan. She took a deep breath then suddenly raised her head to look at him as she said, "Papa left Mama and me when I was a baby and I've had no contact with him since. Just his financial support." Her eyes swam with tears and her shoulders rose, then fell as she whispered, "You are entering politics, Lord Bellingham, are you not?" She glanced about the room, then said, "I think I should not dance with you again."

Her seeming realization of the delicacy of the situation galvanized his determination. "Why would you say that?" he challenged, gripping her wrist gently, as if she might take to her heels.

"I'm not good enough for you. My mother is not ... in the same mold as yours." He released his grip, but she did not flee. "Your mama would wish you to be dancing with someone else," she added.

William glanced about the room. Then, caging her hand upon his forearm as if he were merely leading her off the dance floor, he skirted Lady Perry, still deep in conversation, and adroitly maneuvered Evelina through a doorway at the judicious moment a knot of guests entered from the passageway.

She went with him willingly, not questioning or resisting as he hurried her around a corner into the gloom of a back passage.

When they reached the sanctuary of a storeroom that opened off a servant's passage, she fell into his arms, as eager as he to cement their unspoken feelings by this mark of mutual hunger.

She raised her head and his lips met hers, soft and yielding as his arms went about her, and the strains of the orchestra drifted from afar.

The delicate, floral fragrance that had tantalized him on the dance floor sent a rush through him as he breathed her in, and the eagerness with which she kissed him back made him hard with desire.

"I want you, Evelina. What does the state of your parents' union matter? The fact you're accepted in these circles is enough for me," he ground out between kisses. "Regardless of anything, that you are a guest here means you are as worthy as any female in this room."

She was delirious with happiness when they broke apart, for her eyes shone with unshed tears as she cupped his cheeks and asked softly, "Do you feel what I feel here, William?" as she touched her breast. "It's only been two weeks since the train crash but when I wake up with the horror of it—" She stopped before adding, softly, "Seeing poor Mimi, my maid, dead on the floor, and hearing the people screaming and the water rising...suddenly I'm reminded of you and how you saved my life."

"And how little William's life was only saved because of your bravery, Evelina." He gripped her hands tightly as he touched his forehead to hers. "I realized in that moment that I had met a very remarkable young woman. You didn't wail and succumb to hysterics. Your instinct was to do everything in your power to do good. Why, Evelina, without giving a thought to the proprieties, you were intent only on rescuing that little boy and you knew exactly what was required. You removed your hampering gown and you put your life in my hands when I lowered you into the train carriage."

He drew in a shuddering breath. "What if I had allowed

you to slip from my grasp? What if I'd not been strong enough to hold you, much less both you and that little boy? You'd have fallen into the darkness just as the carriage became submerged? That's what wakes me in the night. The thought of your trust in me—a stranger—and how easily I might have been responsible for your death."

She smiled as she raised her hand to touch his cheek. "I knew that would never happen," she said simply. "I did not hesitate to let you lower me into the carriage because from the first instance I just knew you were a man to trust."

"But when I found you again, you were to wed Dunstable?" He had to confront the elephant in the room.

"I presumed such a fine, handsome man like you was either married or not a man I could marry." She wasn't embarrassed to say it. "And you were married, Lord Bellingham. With a very sweet daughter who quite entranced me when I met her."

"You liked Edwina?" He felt a sudden overflowing of love, not just for his child, but the fact this beautiful woman had brought Edwina up in such fond terms. "She's a sweet, playful little girl, and she clearly liked you." He hesitated. "Her mother died in childbirth after a long illness. We'd only wed nine months before and had met a few weeks before that. Our parents approved, and the match was suitable to us both. But I feel I never properly knew Margaret. I wanted to mourn her properly and to say I'd loved her…" He stopped, surprised at his candor, for he'd not spoken his true feelings to anyone. They shamed him. And such unburdening was perhaps not appropriate here.

But she raised both hands to rest on his shoulders once more and said, "It is a burden when one's obligations of the heart experience conflict." Perhaps seeing the flare of confusion in his eye, she went on quickly, "I've seen my mother only a few times in my life, for she sent me to Paris to be educated by the nuns when I was six years old. Now I see her through the eyes of an adult and … the truth is … I am ashamed of … being ashamed of what you might think of her…when you meet."

"I don't care about your parents," he assured her quickly. "It's you I'm interested in. You that I love. And yes," he added, his conviction now cemented, "I know that I love you, Evelina, and that I want to be with you every minute of every hour. But these are early days and I don't want my family to claim that I am acting in haste. Just know that is the reason for any delay in declarations, my darling Evelina."

Her joy echoed his—he could feel it—as he kissed her again. To everyone else, this was the first ball they'd both attended, at which they'd apparently met. No one would suspect the depth of their feelings for one another, nor would they understand the extraordinary circumstances of their meeting.

Finally, conscious of the time they'd spent away from the ballroom and Lady Perry, William reluctantly put her away from him. The dark little cupboard would open onto the corridor where an injudicious exit might have grave repercussions for Evelina's reputation.

It didn't matter that from the moment this brave, bold, yet shy, young woman had burst into his life, he'd known she was the one for him. There was still her good name to protect, and now he felt remorseful.

Though not when he thought of how these few moments together had made clear that she felt as he did.

"What is it, William?"

He loved that she used his given name, as he had hers. As if it was foolish to pretend they were not on a Christian name basis after all that had happened.

"I'm going to slip into the passage and lurk there until someone trustworthy can escort you back to the ballroom," he replied. "It was rash of me to whisk you here. Please forgive me."

"Oh William, there's nothing to forgive," she said with a laugh as he carefully closed the door behind him and then, within barely seconds, encountered Lady Clara laughing as she tripped along the corridor with an equally jolly female companion.

"Oh, Bellingham!" cried Clara. "How lovely to see you. Let me introduce you to my friend, Lady Elizabeth Craddock. What are you doing here? Are you surprised to see me? Victoria relented when Elizabeth asked particularly persuasively if I could accompany her family to Lady Glenroy's ball tonight, since Lady Glenroy is my godmother and also Lizzie's."

Divine intervention, thought William as he matched his jovial tone to young Clara's, detaining them further when it appeared they were about to continue to the ballroom.

"I gather you've just been to the—"

"Ladies' mending room," supplied Lady Elizabeth, smiling brightly at him. The two girls were of a similar age. Perhaps only seventeen or eighteen, and clearly only just 'out' though William knew that Lady Victoria considered her younger sister still too young.

But if Clara acted younger than her years, she was also of just the right temperament to happily accede to a request such as the one William now put to them. The girl answered that she'd be happy to escort William's friend back to the ballroom.

Whisking Evelina out of the tiny cupboard and into the corridor, William felt enormously and suddenly unburdened by his duty towards Evelina, and Lady Clara had just uttered, "Why, it's Miss Tarot! What a surprise!" when her older sister rounded the corner and William had the sudden sense that he'd miscalculated.

"Lady Victoria, I'm so sorry for your loss," he managed, taking in her half mourning and not quite sure how to continue, for it would be clear to her—as perhaps it had not to the younger girls—that William had been consorting with Evelina without a chaperone.

With a quick glance at Evelina, Lady Victoria turned back to William, saying, "Dunstable's death was a terrible blow, of course, and we are agitating for a speedy conviction. I am here on sufferance and because, despite everything, Lady Glenroy insisted that Clara be allowed to witness the dancing until ten o' clock, after which she and her friend, Lady Elizabeth, will return home. To be truthful, I couldn't abide the idea of remaining at home like a dormouse because, here, I may learn more about the fateful night through an unwitting remark by one of the guests. I find it extraordinary how people think a female does not pay attention to what others may unwittingly divulge. Having neither the beauty of Miss Tarot or Elizabeth, nor the girlish charm of my sister, Clara, people are remarkably careless around me, and I have gleaned a few facts which certainly have not found their way into the newspapers, and which may have been overlooked by the police."

"You are quite the sleuth, Lady Victoria." William wasn't sure whether to be admiring or rattled. "Maybe you will be the one to crack the case of who was responsible for poor Dunstable's death."

"I'm more interested in *why* Dunstable was murdered." Lady Victoria's nostrils quivered. "Now, let me take pretty Miss Tarot under my wing as we return to the ballroom. You may count on my discretion, Lord Bellingham. I shall look after her as if she were my own dear cousin."

William remained in the passage, smiling as Evelina looked over her shoulder to nod a farewell. She was beautiful and innocent, and he wanted her for his bride. The faint misgivings regarding her potential suitability he'd experienced earlier were nothing.

What did it matter that her parents might not be from the upper ten thousand? The upper four hundred? That she might not be the 'perfect' wife for a man of his standing on the brink of a political career where being supported by the 'right' hostess counted for so much. His mama had drummed that into him enough times. But William was twenty-seven years old and would make his own decisions.

Evelina was being sponsored by Lady Perry, and she had the backing of a large fortune. Sensibilities had progressed a great deal in the past decade. Money now spoke louder than respectability. Lord, he'd not even asked her about her father's situation. Yet if Mr. Tarot had made his fortune selling chestnut conkers, what would it matter? Evelina was an heiress and there were many penniless peers who'd make no distinction when it came to how a man acquired his fortune. Just so long as he provided his daughter with a handsome dowry to sweeten the marriage contract.

When she reached the doorway into the ballroom, she turned to look at him once more, causing his whole body to riot with want and need.

Miss Evelina Tarot was going to be his wife.

No one else would do, and nothing was going to stop him from forging ahead with this union.

Miss Evelina's parents might not pass muster with his exacting mama, but what did that matter?

It was hardly as if he'd chosen for his wife a brothel-keeper's daughter.

CHAPTER 15

L ily glanced up at a knock on her office door. She'd not intended to come to Hamish's editorial offices today, but the baby was sleeping so peacefully at home and the nursemaid was in full control. It had been a spur-of-the-moment decision to leave their leafy house in the suburbs in order to enjoy the hustle and bustle of London.

There was also the fact that home was the most unlikely place Lily could add to the dossier she'd started on Lord Dunstable. The police investigation was, of course, continuing, but there had still been no mention in the newspapers of the precise location of Lord Dunstable's death, nor the name of Madame Chambon. Of course, it was only a matter of time, but Lily found the matter curious.

It wasn't long after settling herself behind her desk and pulling out the file of young girls without a 'character' desperate to find work that she learned the answer to what had been puzzling her.

"'Appens that it were more 'n one of our esteemed

madame's girls who were entertaining the copper wot's 'eading this operation," Archie cheerfully informed her, putting his head around the door and clearly angling for an invitation to enlarge upon the matter. "There was, in fact, three of them—and photographs to boot! Girls wearin' the coppers' headware, no less! And wiv not a stitch o' clothing besides. Now, wouldn't that make a good front page?"

Lily was glad Hamish was ensconced in his office with the door closed. He'd not consider Lily's interest in Dunstable's murder necessary, ladylike, or likely to yield answers.

"Good lord, how do you know that, Archie?" Lily asked, waving him to the seat across from her. Then she gave a short laugh, for nothing embarrassed her these days. She felt as comfortable in Archie's company as she did in Hamish's. And, perhaps more so when Hamish was joined by his friends, for of course Lily, with her colorful background, was more than just a curiosity. She verged on being on the other side of that indelible but savagely scored line between 'respectable' and 'not respectable'.

"I presume it was Gracie who told you," she said, dipping her pen in the inkwell and adding with a grin, "I daresay there's not much she misses, flitting from room to room to serve the girls—or, rather—their... gentlemen admirers." She sent another quick glance towards the door, suddenly embarrassed by such vulgarity. No lady ought to know what Lily had learned during her time sharing a roof with the fallen unfortunates at Madame's.

Archie settled himself comfortably in the chair on the other side of the desk and laced his hands over his belly. "Not that Gracie's been asked by the police to furnish them wiv the answers to the questions wot they ought to be asking." He looked a little smug, but Lily was scandalized.

"Of course, Gracie has a duty to tell the constabulary

everything that might be of interest or help discover Lord Dunstable's killer."

"Not when it might compromise the girls. Or breach a trust." Archie raised his hands, palms out. "Gracie reckons her duty is to the girls before it is to Lord Dunstable—cos he's dead, so nothing ain't goin' to bring him back. And since 'is lordship weren't liked by the girls at Madame's—specially not Miss LuLubelle—Gracie reckons it's the right thing to keep mum."

Lily put down her pen and leaned forward. "Archie, do you know exactly how many times Lord Dunstable visited Madame Chambon's? Does Gracie have any thoughts on why someone would want to kill Lord Dunstable—other than Madame Chambon, since he was blackmailing her? Who else was there at the house at the same time as of his visits? Maybe Gracie knows. Could you ask her?"

"I know that already. You jest got to ask me the questions, m'lady, and Archie'll find the answers. Lord Dunstable first visited Madame Chambon's about two years ago. Just occasionally, like, in the beginning. Then suddenly he started to visit more and more, not just to see the girls but to talk business to Madame." Archie began to clean beneath his fingernails with a pocket knife and Lily bit her tongue. She'd rather know whatever he could tell her than risk his deciding to leave if she pointed out the impropriety of a personal manicure in her presence.

"So, Lord Dunstable was … unkind to LuLubelle?" Lily shuddered, though it didn't surprise her. In fact, it was almost a relief to confirm that Miss Tarot had had a lucky escape.

"Yes. 'Cos she wouldn't tell him where Miss Celeste's particulars were kept. Cos he were with Miss Celeste the first time he came to Madame's an' he learned LuLubelle shared a room with Celeste, so he reckoned LuLubelle would know. That's why he came back to make her tell him, but she wouldn't. And that's why he came back to see Madame. To make Madame force LuLubelle to hand over the papers or whatever it was wot proved who Celeste really were."

Lily tried to breathe evenly. Celeste again—even though this was about Lord Dunstable with the most likely reason he was killed revolving around what he knew about Evelina Tarot's relationship to Madame.

But could the murderer's motive, in fact, be what Dunstable knew about Celeste?

Could someone who knew the mysterious Celeste's background have a reason for killing Dunstable so that he wouldn't reveal what he perhaps had discovered?

The very first time Lily had rushed into Madame Chambon's establishment two years before, having jumped from Mr. Montpelier's carriage after he'd kidnapped her from the lunatic asylum to which her late husband had confined her, she'd been confronted by Celeste, Madame Chambon's most beautiful 'fair cyprian'.

Later, Lily had shared a room with Celeste after Mr. Montpelier had made an agreement with Madame to feed and house Lily for the months it would take to nourish her in order for Lily's beauty to return.

Like so many of the girls at Madame's, poise, grace, and charm, together with a knowledge of the arts, had been a pre-requisite. But Lily had always sensed Celeste was not simply pretending to be a lady.

Many of Madame's girls adopted pretensions but, as Lily knew, having been born into the upper classes, there was always some small oversight that gave them away. Celeste had never made a single misstep in the months Lily had known her.

But after Celeste had been murdered, her identity had remained shrouded in mystery.

And although the case had been sensationalized when the Russian diplomat Ivor Novichov was convicted of murdering a woman in a brothel, Celeste's identity as a supposed prostitute seemed to have been of little importance.

Or rather, it had been eclipsed by Lily's sudden celebrity status when it was learned that the spiritualist who had taken London by storm was, in fact, the natural-born daughter of Lord Lambton.

Yet it had been Celeste who had alerted Hamish to the threat that Novichov posed to Lily.

It was Celeste who had paid the price, and Lily would feel forever bound to the unfortunate young woman.

Now Celeste's name had resurfaced, this time in relation to Dunstable, who had visited Madame Chambon's, been entertained by Celeste, then returned, and, later, blackmailed Madame Chambon over material that would identify the young woman?

As a prostitute, Celeste had gone unrecognized and unmourned. A fallen woman deserved her fate, or so that's what much of the public would appear to believe.

Lily tapped her fingers on the desk while she thought feverishly.

"Are you suggesting Lord Dunstable blackmailed Celeste because he knew who she really was? And that he wanted to find proof so he could blackmail her family after she was murdered?"

Archie shrugged. "You got it in one, m'lady." He put down his pocketknife. "In fact, you're a step ahead of me." He pursed his lips and squinted. "I didn't think of blackmail, but that'd be why Dunstable got Madame to crack in the end, and why she went off to fetch Celeste's things just before Dunstable were done for."

"Is that what Gracie said?"

Archie nodded.

"But if Madame Chambon was being blackmailed, then Madame would have just the motivation for killing his lordship?"

"'Cept she didn't." Archie sounded very sure about this.

"Yes, that's what she told me, too. But why do you think she didn't?"

"Cos Gracie says she saw Madame checking in on the copper wot's leading the investigation, just as one of the girls said she heard a cry from Madame's study before someone ran out into the passageway. And that it weren't Madame Chambon cos she was upstairs wiv this copper chappie."

Lily gave a lopsided smile. "So, Miss Tarot won't see her mama go to the gallows and have her reputation dragged through the mud. She does have some chance of contracting a decent marriage. I am relieved about that, at least."

"That's if Lord Bellingham don't mind who her ma is," said Archie rising, but Lily waved him back into his seat saying sharply, "She can't marry Lord Bellingham and there's an end to it. However, Mr. John Farnley danced with her twice at Lady Gilray's's ball after I introduced them. He seemed very taken."

Archie pulled out his pocketknife once more and began to fiddle with it. "Farnley's wasting his time, if you'll beg me pardon, m'lady... an' so are you. Fact is, Miss Tarot's heart is set on Lord Bellingham."

Lily was not going to accept this. Of course, Miss Tarot would hope that a young man of Lord Bellingham's caliber would offer for her, but a little digging and her reputation would be in tatters. "Lord Bellingham is very dashing and gallant, but he is far too above her for a match between them to be possible. He has a future in politics. He needs a wife of impeccable lineage and, believe me, Miss Tarot's background will be scrutinized to the nth degree. Mr. Farnley just needs money and would be more than happy to overlook Miss

Tarot's lineage, besides which, he's a very sweet young man. Not like Lord Dunstable, who clearly blackmailed Madame into agreeing to the match and would no doubt have soon shown his true colors to Miss Tarot. But no, Lord Bellingham can't risk marrying Miss Tarot. We must prevent it. For the sake of both their happiness."

Archie frowned. "Neither of 'em know wot you and me know, m'lady. An' I reckon you're too late. My Gracie says the words Lord Bellingham wrote to invite Miss Tarot to the opera made Kitty's heart fair melt after Kitty recited what his lordship had written to her. Now me Gracie wants me to be a poet like 'im but it ain't necessary when Gracie knows how I feel about her."

"Does she?" Lily asked, distracted, before bursting out, "How did it get this far so quickly? I thought they only met at Lady Gilray's ball last night? Or at least, they surely have only danced a couple of dances." She clasped her hands together, the photographs on her desk forgotten. "Miss Tarot must simply return Mr. Farnley's regard and all will be well." She nibbled her little fingernail while anxiety churned. "I shall speak to Hamish. He'll know what to do." When the photographer merely sent her a skeptical look, Lily made another appeal. "Do you understand what I'm saying, Archie? Miss Tarot's sensibility is that of a lady. I don't know she'd survive the discovery of who and what her mother really is? Worse, how would she feel knowing that Dunstable more than likely blackmailed her mama into marrying her? He knew Evelina Tarot came with a very handsome dowry and he was prepared to overlook everything else in order to claim it. Plus, no doubt, he knew Madame would prove a lucrative ongoing source of revenue as he continued to blackmail her while married to her daughter."

"You ought to be leadin' this investigation, m'lady," Archie said admiringly. "I never thought o' that, but it makes perfect sense. Well, maybe Miss Tarot's papa will double her dowry and then it really won't matter to Lord Bellingham. That's if he doesn't care about apolitical career., He can then take her off to far distant oceans where 'er troublesome reputation won't be a bit 'o bother."

Lily tightened her clasped fingers to control her agitation. "That's if we knew who Miss Tarot's father was. We know her mama is Madame Chambon, and that's bad enough. But what if her father is a felon who stole a fortune which he secreted away, and who's now languishing in Newgate Prison? I don't suppose that's something your darling Gracie or her friend Kitty might know?"

Archie sighed and shrugged his shoulders before asking in a resigned tone, "So what do you want me to do about all this, m'lady?"

Lily gazed at the photographs on the table before her. There was the Princess of Wales, regal and elegant, flanked by her philandering husband, also known by the moniker Dirty Bertie. As a royal, Bertie could get away with little short of murder and he'd still be received anywhere.

But Lily knew how lonely and painful it was to be shunned by society.

And that's what Miss Tarot had been reared to believe was her ... tribe; the people amongst whom she belonged.

If her past was laid bare and it became known that her mother was a brothel madam and her father... what? ... a criminal, murderer, or, just as bad, simply anyone who refused to acknowledge her, then she would live her life friendless.

Lily rose. "I must go home now, but Hamish will be in the office with you until late this evening, I know." She reached for her cape and bonnet, putting them on as she added, "Just tell my husband that if he sees Lord Bellingham at his club tonight, he must do what he can to dilute his Lordship's interest in Miss Tarot. Matters cannot have gone too far since they've met only once or twice. But, please, tell Hamish that even if it's a white lie, Lord Bellingham must be made to understand that his association with Miss Tarot is too risky to continue for a man who is about to launch a career in politics."

CHAPTER 16

Evelina was intensely aware of William's closeness on her left as they sat in the stalls and watched the performance onstage. Lady Perry sat on her right, quiet and crow-like, poring over the program, occasionally making some remark to Evelina.

This was all for show. Lady Perry had little real interest in Evelina. She'd been hired by her mother to adhere to the protocol.

Evelina didn't mind. She was totally in thrall to Lord Bellingham.

William.

Her William.

The orchestra began tuning their instruments in the pits, and the audience stirred.

It should have been a source of intense excitement to see a Crystal Palace Saturday Concert in the lofty concert hall.

Evelina had never been to the theater or a concert of any kind in such a large and public arena. And certainly, to nothing public in male company. Lord Dunstable was to have taken her, though she'd been more excited at the prospect of the program that featured Beethoven, Wagner and Mozart than his actual company.

Now it was the company that gave her the greatest thrill.

In fact, when she tried to recall what Lord Dunstable looked like and what he made her feel, everything faded into insignificance compared with the tumult brought on by the man next to her.

The indistinct murmur of the audience as the orchestra tuned the instruments provided the perfect foil for Evelina and William to build on the intimacy that had received such a boost in the broom cupboard near Lady Gilray's ballroom.

William turned his head and smiled. "I hope you enjoy the program. I think Mozart will never sound sweeter than when I hear it with you."

"He's my favorite composer," said Evelina. "I've always enjoyed music and never minded practicing, unlike the other girls."

"And I can't wait to hear you play. I'd wager you were the most gifted of students." William squeezed her hand and Evelina smiled at the warmth that washed through her, though she said, "I don't know how I'll feel when I'm put to the test. It's been a while since I was at the pianoforte."

"You'll not be found wanting, just as you weren't when speed and urgency were required. You know how to rise to the occasion, my love." He was serious now. "What's more, you put your faith in my hands without a second thought so I could lower you into the train carriage to rescue that child. That took courage. I knew then that I'd met someone incomparable."

As the lights went down, Evelina clung to his fingers, the clandestine thrill sending tingles up and down her spine as she kept her gaze deliberately on the stage so as not to excite rumors.

She responded in a whisper. "When I saw how single-minded and commanding you were, helping people who needed help, my admiration was immense. After I was hustled away by some well-meaning people to tend to my scratches, I wanted to leap out of the carriage and search for you. I thought I'd never see you again."

"But here we are. It's fate that you should cross my orbit. God knows, I wouldn't have wished ill upon Dunstable, but nothing now stands between us—"

At his hesitation, she glanced at him and saw in the gloom that his expression was tense, almost nervous, as he continued, "—getting to know each other properly."

The music launched into the first overture as the curtain rose and the audience clapped.

Conversation was effectively halted, but Evelina imagined what she might have said in response. Another warm glow suffused her as she continued to grip William's hand under the cover of darkness.

She'd never been happier.

And as she and Lady Perry waited in the foyer for William to fetch them refreshments during the interval, the warm glow of happiness remained undimmed in his absence. For William had declared himself hers. For the first time in her twenty years, Evelina had a companion, a like-minded friend, and a stalwart champion. He was going to ask her to marry him, and she had no hesitation in saying yes for now she knew what her heart was supposed to feel for so important a matter as a lifelong union.

"Oh, I beg your pardon! Why… it's you!"

Evelina was at first dismayed to find she'd stepped on the train of another young woman who'd turned around but was now suddenly smiling with recognition before she extricated herself from the two older women and a gentleman who continued conversing near the stairs.

"I must thank you again for the other evening," said Lily,

suddenly feeling nervous before realizing by the guileless look on the girl's pretty face, she was not of the nature to trade upon Evelina's disadvantage.

"Oh, it was nothing and a pleasure." The young lady dimpled. "I can imagine the distress of finding your chaperone had deserted you when you came back from the ladies mending room and getting lost in the corridor before that other nice gentleman happened upon you and of course, he could not have accompanied you back to the ball alone."

She said all this as if she truly believed William and Evelina's deception.

Whether this was because she was young—perhaps still seventeen and only just out—or that she was happy to obfuscate a more savvy understanding didn't matter at this moment. Evelina was simply happy to make the acquaintance of another London debutante. "And did you enjoy Lady Gilrays's ball?" she asked.

The girl rolled her eyes. "Mama and I have different opinions on what constitutes a nice young man." She lowered her voice as she indicated the tall, stately woman nearby who was speaking to a handsome gentleman, his dark blond hair flecked with silver, and an older, stouter gentleman with grizzled gray hair and mutton-chop whiskers whose back was to them. "My decorum is being scrutinized by my parents and godfather, who would all have me dance with such dull fellows when I like a man with a sense of humor."

"Elizabeth!"

At a command from her mama, Miss Elizabeth rolled her eyes once again. "The voice of authority must be obeyed," she whispered. "Nice to have made your acquaintance more properly, Miss...?"

"Miss Tarot," Evelina supplied. "And the pleasure, as I said, is all mine, Lady Elizabeth Craddock, if I recall correctly?"

"Lizzie to you, since you are a friend of Clara. Ooh, this is so unconventional. I do hope we meet again."

And then she was back in the fold of her family, just as William arrived with refreshments.

Evelina felt the tingle of connection once more as he touched her hand when giving her the glass, his fingers lingering a second longer than necessary. She smiled into his eyes, seeing her feelings reflected there.

At last, in the busy metropolis where she'd initially felt such a stranger, Evelina was finally finding a place of warmth and comfort with friendship ... and love.

Only the sudden memory of Lord Dunstable's murder of a few evenings before could blight the dawning joyous wonder she felt. But how could she feel guilt at her lack of sorrow when she'd hardly known her former husband-to-be?

And when she'd been spared making what would have been the biggest mistake of her life?

EVELINA WAS STILL LIGHTHEADED with love when she stepped over the threshold into Lady Perry's drawing room, giving a brief squeal of alarm when her mother rose unexpectedly from the shadows and remarked, "A good evening was had by all, it would appear? A music recital, I believe?"

"Mama, I didn't know you'd be calling." Evelina felt guilty that she was not as pleased to see her mother as she ought to be, considering she saw too rarely as it was.

"A mother does not have to make an appointment to see her own daughter." Mrs. Tarot smiled but was clearly not delighted by her lukewarm reception. "And who invited you without telling me, pray tell? Lady Perry?" She glanced at the old companion who merely shrugged and said, "A gentleman whom any mama would be delighted to welcome into the family, Mrs. Tarot. I think you will not be disappointed to learn that Lord Bellingham appears to have developed quite an interest in your daughter."

Evelina smiled at her mother. She couldn't help it. Everything made her smile these days. But to her surprise, her mother was frowning.

"Lord Bellingham?" Her mother's clear dismay did not indicate the delight with which Evelina imagined she would have received this news. "He is in politics, my dear, is he not? A vastly demanding and scrutinized position."

"I do not know very much about that, but he has political ambitions, yes, Mama." Evelina was puzzled by the disapproval in her mother's voice as she followed her to a seat in the drawing room and sat down at right angles to her. Lady Perry took her usual seat in the corner and picked up her knitting.

The fire had been tended in their absence, casting a soft glow in the dim room, for the lamp had been turned down. Mrs. Tarot's face was in shadow, but her tone conveyed a disapproval that made Evelina tremble. She'd so hoped to please her mama with her announcement of William's interest.

"I understand Mr. John Farley took a great liking to you during Lady Gilray's ball on Thursday?"

"He asked me to dance twice, Mama, but I do not like him as I like Lord Bellingham." Evelina hesitated. "Lord Bellingham has a title and a fortune and an estate in Hampshire, Mama. I thought that was the kind of fine marriage that would please you. Mr. Farnley is little more than a gentleman farmer of modest means."

"Mr. Farley is a solid young man who is dependable and will not lead you on, Evelina."

Evelina gasped. "Are you suggesting Lord Bellingham is

merely playing with my affections and has no intention of following through with a marriage offer?"

"I do hope it has not gone as far as that, Evelina."

Evelina found it hard to suppress her trembling as she tried to remain calm. Tears sprang to her eyes. "I believe Lord Bellingham is going to ask me to be his wife," she said quietly. "And I intend to say yes."

Her mother shook her head. "Lord Dunstable is barely cold in the ground, Evelina."

"And he was nothing to me!" Evelina burst out. "Besides, you said yourself that since he'd not publicly declared our engagement, I was free to engage in the activities that underpin my whole reason for being here. To make the most advantageous marriage possible. The fact that Lord Bellingham is so eminently eligible, and I love him should have pleased you enormously, I'd have thought."

Her mother put a hand to her lacquered hair. Her chest rose. "Mr. Farnley has invited us both to the London Museum on Thursday, Evelina.

Evelina shook her head. "That is the day of Lord Dunstable's funeral. Lord Bellingham felt it was only right that we should pay our respects—"

"You were not married to Lord Dunstable, and you will not be marrying Lord Bellingham!" Her mother's anger was like a lash. "No, Evelina, you will not be attending Lord Dunstable's funeral on Thursday, and you will certainly not accompany Lord Bellingham there or even meet him there."

For a long second, Evelina stared mutinously at her mother. It was the first time she could remember such an altercation, but suddenly the past returned, and she was the feisty six-year-old her mother had pushed into the hands of her governess, saying, "Take this wicked child from me. She is going to school across the sea to learn some manners!" It had been several years before Evelina had seen her mother again. And then she'd been so desperate to please her mama, she'd never spoken a word out of turn.

Until now.

"And what if I decide I want to go anyway, Mama?" she said in a low voice. "I love Lord Bellingham and if I want to go to Lord Dunstable's funeral with him rather than attend the museum with dull Mr. Farnley, I will. You can't stop me."

There was a curious glint in her mother's eye.

"Perhaps I can't, Evelina." Her large bosom rose, and she appeared to find it difficult to speak. "But you will find life very different when you suddenly don't have fine, fashionable clothes to wear. And perhaps your Lord Bellingham won't be quite so attentive when he learns your dowry is not as magnificent as he'd been led to believe."

Evelina gasped. "You're threatening me?" She leaned forward, conscious of the click-clack of Lady Perry's knitting needles, the only sound made by the other old woman clearly listening from the corner. "You think Lord Bellingham wants me only for my dowry?"

"I can't imagine why else he'd want you, my dear?" her mother sniffed. "London is stuffed right now with girls seeking glittering marriages, and Lord Bellingham is spoiled for choice. Granted, you have a pretty face, but so do many other debutantes who also have ten thousand to entice a potential husband."

"Bellingham would marry me if I had nothing!" Evelina declared. And the fact she honestly believed this gave her the courage to go on. "I love him! We love each other! Perhaps you've never experienced what it feels like here—" she touched her heart—"to know that love is pure and honest and not...not based on money. You always make it about money, Mama! Is that why Papa left you? Is that why he keeps away from me? Because he suspects I'm too much like you? Venal and grasping? Why, if you had an ounce of kindness, you'd tell me how to find him so that at least I had the chance to know my own father... and let him decide for himself if he wants to know me. But you've always wanted to control everything, haven't you, Mama? Even my heart! Well, you know what?" She rose, shaking, seeking the words to match her mama's. "You can't control my mind. I will do what I want, and I will decide my own destiny. Good night, Mama!"

CHAPTER 17

William was a man in love. The stars shimmered above him, casting a romantic glow over the bustling streets of the Haymarket.

Gas-lit lanterns illuminated the path, elegant women and smartly dressed men passed by, their conversations blending with the distant sounds of carriages and the clip-clop of horses' hooves.

But as William made his way through the crowd, all he could think of was Evelina.

The moon hung low in the sky, larger and brighter than usual. Or so it seemed; mirroring the intensity of his emotions.

But beneath the surface of his infatuation, unease gnawed at him.

Why would Evelina suddenly declare herself not good enough for him? Who was her father, a man she claimed to barely know?

Had he made his fortune in trade—for undoubtedly, he had made a fortune? The size of her dowry and the fact

Dunstable was a man in need of funds was something William had heard whispered at Whites.

Was Evelina perhaps embarrassed by this possible connection to trade? Certainly, ten years ago this might have been a consideration—for an aristocrat—but it was nothing now.

The vibrant energy of the Haymarket swirled around him: theatergoers like himself but also the less savory characters of the night. Prostitutes, painted and brazen, thrust out their hands and, yes, he was not totally insensible to their plight but the idea of paying for sex repulsed him.

Clearly, Dunstable had had no such reservations, and although visiting a brothel hardly warranted the fate that had been visited upon him, the thought that the man had almost married his innocent and perfect Evelina sent shivers down William's spine.

Turning a corner into Fleet Street, William was passing beneath an awning, momentarily shielded from the busy street, when the doors of a nearby shop swung open and two gentlemen emerged, causing William to sidestep to avoid a collision. Apologies were exchanged, and then recognition dawned.

"Lord Bellingham!" exclaimed Hamish McTavish, the editor of *Manners and Morals*, and husband to the beautiful Lady Bradden. The city had been abuzz with the story of Lady Bradden's reunion with her long-lost father eighteen months prior. William had briefly met McTavish at a Christmas gathering, and now he nodded in acknowledgment, about to continue on his way.

"Are we talkin' Lord Bellingham wot went to a concert with Miss Tarot this evenin'?" a little man beside McTavish interjected, lacking in manners but not in boldness. William wasn't sure if he should dignify such rudeness with a response. His personal affairs were no one else's concern.

McTavish, clearly embarrassed by his companion's impertinence, cleared his throat. "Forgive my photographer's lack of finesse. This is Archie Benedict. We've been working late to get the latest magazine to print. Lady Bradden learned from Miss Tarot that she was attending a concert with you, and I happened to mention it to Benedict. Lady Bradden wanted me to offer her regards to Miss Tarot and inquire if she needs a friend in the capital." He glanced around cautiously, almost as if afraid of being overheard.

William couldn't comprehend why these two near-strangers were discussing Miss Tarot with him. It felt like an invasion of his privacy, as if he were being spied upon.

"After all, she is new to England," McTavish added.

"She is an Englishwoman, and her family is very English," William replied. "I'm sure she would appreciate Lady Bradden's kindness, though she may not lack the friends your wife imagines. Good day to you, gentlemen."

"Do you have a moment, Lord Bellingham?" McTavish's hand lightly touched the sleeve of William's coat. He gestured toward his office with a nod of his head. "It's a matter of delicacy that cannot be discussed in the street. Our meeting is opportune."

Uncertain of what to expect, William reluctantly acquiesced. The little man, Archie Benedict, followed them inside, locking the door behind them, and a sense of foreboding settled over him as William ascended the stairs to McTavish's office.

"McTavish, I fail to see why you employ such cloak-and-dagger tactics to speak with me," he protested as McTavish retrieved a bottle of brandy and uncorked it. "I would have willingly engaged in conversation if you had asked."

"It's about Dunstable's murder," McTavish began, almost uncertainly. "The police have asked me to keep certain details out of the newspaper at the same time as passing on to them anything that might have a bearing on the case." His eyes flicked to the amber liquid in his cut-glass tumbler which he raised a few inches from the desktop. Then he sent an incisive look at William, saying, "I stumbled upon some information that may be of interest to *you*. It concerns Miss Evelina Tarot."

William's heart skipped a beat. Cautiously, he asked, "What about her? What could she possibly have to do with Dunstable's murder?"

"Not Miss Tarot, personally, of course. But... do you know Captain Blackheath?"

Surprised, William replied, "I served with the blackguard in the army many years ago, but I certainly did not call him friend."

"Blackheath was in the same house at the time Dunstable was murdered. Do you know where that was?"

"I heard it was at that vile Soho pleasure house, Madame Chambon's, but I've not seen it reported in the newspapers." Lord Bellingham scowled. "But what has this got to do with me? I was nowhere near the place."

"No, which is why you are not a suspect. But Blackheath is," said Mr. McTavish. "You see, I have been asked by certain people high up the chain to keep the matter as discreet as possible, and out of the newspapers, while also being furnished with certain particulars in the hopes of, in fact, discovering the killer." A look of discomfort crossed McTavish's face as he seated himself opposite. The photographer remained standing by the table.

"Some of these particulars that have been unearthed during the investigation," he went on, "while not directly associated with Dunstable's murder, may have consequences that could cause difficulties for *you*, my lord." McTavish drained his brandy. "That is, if you have an interest in Miss Tarot."

"Good God, sir, what has Dunstable's murder got to do with Miss Tarot? And what business is my private life of yours?"

"None, whatsoever," the newspaper man replied hastily. "However, my wife, who has taken Miss Tarot's happiness greatly to heart on account of her own trials leading up to her reunion with her father, Lord Lambton, has begged me to furnish you with information that—she believes—is necessary to safeguard the happiness of both you and Miss Tarot. Or rather, that may spare you both unnecessary pain if..."

"If, what?" William knew he spoke too harshly, but this was not a subject to be trifled with. If matters progressed too far."

"Good God, sir, what is it to you whether I make Miss Tarot my bride or not? She is a creature beyond reproach, and I object to your insinuations that she is involved in any wrongdoing—"

"Not willingly," the photographer interjected. "But this Blackheath who is a murder suspect... Why, he and Miss Tarot—"

"Are you suggesting something inappropriate in the relationship between Blackheath and Miss Tarot?" Revulsion swept over William. "She danced with him, it is true. But other than that..." He trailed off, not sure what to think as McTavish and the photographer exchanged glances. "Besides, what concern is Miss Tarot's conduct to you? I thought you said your wife was anxious to safeguard her happiness?" Anger was easier than dismay. These men were slandering his angel, and he had to take them to task. "What has Miss Tarot done that she should have such shabby treatment rained upon her? How dare you malign the woman I love?"

"Please, Lord Bellingham!" McTavish held up his hand for calm, though it appeared he was struggling for calm himself.

"There was no intention of maligning anyone. "I merely am passing on concerns regarding Miss Tarot's... background... that you may wish to factor into any decisions regarding your future in view of your... political aspirations. But, of course, any question regarding Miss Tarot is neither here nor there, as you correctly pointed out, since she can have had nothing to do with Lord Dunstable's death, though it was suggested to me that since Miss Tarot was in both Lord Dunstable's company, as well as Captain Blackheath's, on several occasions in the days before Dunstable was murdered, Miss Tarot might have—" He reddened, took another swig of his brandy, then added, "mentioned to you something that could have a bearing on the matter."

William rose, slamming his whisky onto the table. "Speak plainly, sir! Are you telling me Miss Tarot's relationship with Captain Blackheath has been inappropriate, either now or in the past? Or *are* you suggesting that Miss Tarot was involved in Dunstable's murder?"

To his relief, both men shook their heads.

"Then, are you suggesting Miss Tarot is guilty of any wrongdoing, either now or in the past?"

Again, both men were quick to shake their heads.

"Then that is all I need to satisfy myself that Miss Tarot remains worthy to be my bride. If no slander can attach to her—which, it appears, it cannot—then London will be hearing wedding bells to celebrate our nuptials in the coming weeks."

With a decisive nod at both men, William rose.

He could hardly believe it when the photographer put himself between him and the door saying, urgently, "You're a man with a career in politics ahead of him, and a man in love —I get that, m'lord. All we're sayin' is that wiv the information we've gleaned in the course of the police investigagin' this case, you'd be wise to check Miss Tarot's background."

Evelina, Lady Bellingham.

That's who she was going to be.

Evelina stared at herself in the mirror, frowning as she alternated between memories of William's sweet kisses and her mother's scowls.

Well, regardless of her mama's unexpected opposition the previous night, and their terrible fight, nothing was going to stop Evelina from achieving her heart's desire.

She'd gone to bed, seething with fury and uncertain what the new day would bring.

Apart from a tension headache, she'd been at her dressing table when Kitty had handed her a note. Believing it to be from William, she'd been dismayed to recognize her mother's handwriting, but the few words had made her feel better. If not exactly an apology, they were enough to make her feel that her mother was not about to completely cut her off. Neither was her father.

"We were both not at our best last night, Evelina, and I regret some of what was said," her mother had written.

"I do have one stipulation, however, and that is that you do not attend Lord Dunstable's funeral."

Kitty was as cheerful as ever as she twisted a curl and pinned it into place. "Is everything all right, miss?" she asked. "Lord Bellingham is still wantin' to go walkin' wiv yer?"

"He's said nothing to the contrary," replied Evelina. "And as my mama has not outright objected, then I shall go."

Evelina was just glad her mama did not live under the same roof as she preened in front of the mirror. This was her favorite walking ensemble, and she remembered the excitement she'd felt when her French seamstress had consulted with her on colors, fabric and drapery, utilizing skirt tiebacks to achieve the long, slightly scandalous, fashionable lean silhouette. Kitty now helped Evelina fluff out her second petticoat, which went over her corset before Evelina stepped into the green check wool fan skirt trimmed with contrasting brown velvet.

"Why, miss, you look a sight for sore eyes," Kitty marveled as she stepped back to admire her mistress. "If Lord Bellingham don't go down on bended knee the moment he sees you walk into Hyde Park, I'll eat me hat. Yer mama is goin' to be right delighted when the pair of you make a match."

Evelina's smile disappeared. "Mama disapproves of Lord Bellingham. She says he's only interested in my dowry."

"Same as Lord Dunstable then? Nah, that can't be right." Kitty frowned. "I'm sure you've got it wrong. Madame... I mean, your mama wants only for you to marry a rich, handsome feller like Lord Bellingham. And he don't need your dowry. Specially not if he loves yer."

Evelina nodded energetically. "That's what I told her," she replied, pulling on her gloves. "I'm sure Mama will come round. She's probably still sad about Lord Dunstable's death, for I believe they've been acquainted for a long time. She'd not have been so keen on marriage between us if she hadn't thought he'd make me a kind husband." Evelina bit her lip. "And I do feel very guilty for not missing him like I should, but really, Kitty, I hardly knew him. Yet I feel like I've known William forever." She smiled as she touched her heart before making for the door. "William and I have a connection that goes so much deeper than the things Mama cares about, like money and appearances. Why," she declared in a burst of feeling as she patted her jaunty little green hat with its single egret feather, "I'd run away with him tomorrow and give up everything if it meant we could be together."

Kitty nodded, "And I reckon he'd do the same, if you don't mind me sayin', Miss."

"Oh, not at all, Kitty." Evelina smiled, happy beyond measure and glad to put last night's unpleasantness behind her as she prepared to embrace a future with William while remaining in her mother's good graces.

As satisfied as she was by her appearance, she was also satisfied by the admiration on William's face when he saw her coming towards him, Lady Perry trailing a little behind her, though she was concerned by his gravity immediately afterwards.

"Is everything all right?" she asked, noting his frown as she tucked her hand into the crook of his arm as if it were the most natural thing in the world. But she barely attended to his answer, so busy was she imagining herself promenading with William every day when they were newlyweds. Then his words sank in and a frisson of alarm made her jerk her head around as she repeated, "You've been quizzed about Lord Dunstable's murder? What would *you* know about that?"

"Nothing, of course," he said quickly, his smile reassuring. "Certainly, I was nowhere near where it happened, but I do know someone who was. The police have enquired as to whether…"

She glanced up at his pause, frowning as he went on, "Captain Blackheath was apparently in the vicinity. And because I attended Lady Gilray's ball which Captain Blackheath also attended, I've been asked if the captain said anything to me."

"Did he?" Evelina bit her lip, then asked in a rush, "Do the police still have no idea who… who killed the poor man?"

For a long moment, William pondered the answer to this. Then he shook his head before saying, in a rush, "Evelina, you… don't know *anything* that might be important, do you?"

"Goodness, what do you mean, William?"

"Dunstable didn't say anything to you the last time you

spoke that might have suggested he was … meeting someone, for example?"

Evelina was taken aback by his uncharacteristic urgency. While Dunstable's murder had naturally horrified William, he'd had seemed to accept the consensus put out by the newspapers that the perpetrator was a vengeful rival of Dunstable's who'd quickly be charged.

Now William was asking Evelina if she knew anything.

Evelina tried to think back to their last meeting. "Why, William, you were with me the last time I saw Lord Dunstable. It was at the Zoological Gardens." She smiled suddenly. "I think my heart was beating so fast as being there with *you* that I barely attended to a word Dunstable said. But he talked about his plans to take me to the opera." Lapsing into silence, she wished she could be more helpful, if only to shake William out of the blue devils. Someone must have said something to upset him the previous night, after he'd taken her home from the concert. Perhaps Captain Blackheath was more of a friend than Evelina had supposed, and William was concerned for him. Trying to be helpful, she added, "Of course, he may have mentioned plans to his cousins, Lady Victoria or Clara. I wonder if the police have quizzed *them*. Perhaps they knew where he was going the night he was murdered."

She was surprised at the lop-sided grin he gave her, and his tone of voice as he replied, "I very much doubt it. However, there were a few people at the house where it happened, and they have all been interviewed by the police."

"Where did it happen?" Evelina asked. "I can't find any mention in the newspapers. Everyone's speculating, but for once the newspapers haven't sensationalized the story like they usually do."

He hesitated. "It happened in a sort of club. A place that was quite busy that night."

"A gentleman's club? Yes, that's what I heard. So, it was obviously only a gathering of men and one of his so-called friends turned on him."

"Not exactly. There were some women there, too."

Evelina considered this. "Dunstable was sociable, though, really, I barely knew him. I cannot believe I'd agreed to—" She put her hand to her mouth. "I mustn't speak of it. Oh, William, I ought to be ashamed of myself for switching allegiance like I have. Lord Dunstable didn't deserve what happened to him."

William didn't reply immediately. Finally, he asked, "What does your father think, Evelina? He agreed to the contract drawn up between you and Dunstable. Have you told him about... me?" He stopped to put his hands on Evelina's shoulders, and she gazed up at him, and then over his shoulder at the Serpentine glistening in the distance.

Warmth washed over her and she hoped he didn't notice her fierce blushes. "I don't know how I would refer to you, William" she murmured. "Certainly, so soon after Lord Dunstable's death, it wouldn't be quite right to call you my..."

She trailed off and he supplied, "Admirer? I am more than that, Evelina, and you know it." Gently, he touched her face, his gaze meeting hers. "And I would very much like to meet your parents. Do you think you could arrange that?"

Evelina drew in her breath. How could she explain to William that she didn't think she could? Her mother would embarrass her, and her father was uncontactable. Even more disturbingly, would her father create some difficulty over her dowry like he had with Lord Dunstable?

He seemed to sense her conflicted thoughts for he said, "I know your father does not reside in London. I understand the problem. But...I would very much like to know a little more about your father."

"He owns a gold mine in Africa and hasn't been in England these past years," Evelina said quickly.

William smiled. "A gold mine? He sounds an intrepid adventurer. As you know, I've spent the past three years seeing the world. I'd like to meet him and share stories of our travels." He touched her nose. "Though, mostly, I'd like to impress him, so he'd think me a fine match for his daughter. Yes, I want to speak to your father on more serious matters than travel, Evelina."

Evelina drank in her beloved's words, shivering with pleasure as they rippled through her. She could barely wait for the day her father and William met to discuss marriage.

Then the memory of her mother's hard stare and ominous words ate away at her fleeting joy.

Why would Mrs. Tarot not think Lord Bellingham an infinitely finer match than a lowly baronet?

"Mama suggested Mr. John Farnley would make me a fine husband. I don't know why, for I've only just met him. And besides, I love you." She put her hand up to touch his face, adding, "You don't have any dark skeletons in the closet, do you?"

He gripped her hand as he stared down into her face.

Evelina waited for him to speak as he opened his mouth, about to respond.

But when he just shook his head, Evelina smiled. "Well, that's a relief," she said. "I was worried by the look in your eyes that you were about to tell me something dreadful about yourself."

CHAPTER 18

Seven bright faces watched Archie as he poured collodion —a syrupy mixture of guncotton dissolved in a combination of ether—onto the glass plate he'd just cleaned before immersing it in a solution of silver nitrate to make it sensitive to light. Loading it into the camera, he disappeared beneath a black cloth.

"That's right, Miss Liza. Keep looking this way. And pull your little bruvver closer to yer. And the other one. You boys at the back, don't move and…."

Lily watched Archie, half hidden by the large camera on a tripod he was operating, bark directions at Liza and her brothers and sisters, clustered together in the cobbled slum lane, the three girls wearing the fancy hats and bonnets they'd made for their most esteemed clients that week.

"Finished! You can relax, now!"

The family group broke apart while Archie emerged from beneath the black cloth, hurrying to quickly transfer the plate to his portable darkroom for development.

"Very good work, all of you!" Lily clapped her hands, then pulled the thick, woolen muffler up around her lower face as she prepared to return to the thronged streets. "You're a remarkable family and you have a remarkable sister, don't you, boys? Thank you, Liza," she added as the boys scuffed their leather boots on the cobbles and the little girls smiled shyly.

It had been an illuminating afternoon, interviewing Liza, whose tale of success in this poverty-stricken part of London would serve as a reminder of what was possible to readers in the next edition of Manners & Morals.

Archie finished packing away his equipment, meeting his employer at the end of the laneway. "Reckon that'll get the subscribers opening their pocketbooks, m'lady. What a grand idea for 'em to contribute to your fund to pay for a better education for one of them younger girls."

Lily smiled happily. "Even old Mr. McTavish wasn't dead against the idea by the time Hamish had explained the benefits of appealing to the godly and altruistic inclination of his readers. And Liza does have the right blend of innocence and industry in the way you've been able to portray her." Then some of her enthusiasm drained away. "Sadly, it's the girls who are not blessed with charm or loveliness, but who work just as hard who fare worse in this cruel world. Not all of the equally deserving poor have Liza's pretty face," she said.

"Violets for a ha'penny!" cried a nearby street vendor. "Oo'll buy me sweet violets!"

Squashing her old bonnet onto her head so that it covered as much of her face as possible, Lily hurried to keep pace with Archie, who struggled with his equipment through the dense push of bodies weaving through Covent Garden. "What did you think, Archie?" Liza felt her old energy returning and wanted his opinion. "Old Mr. McTavish will only allow this column if it's a story of hope and inspiration for our more fortunate readers who too readily dismiss the concerns of the poor and write them off as lazy. But I want our subscribers to read between the lines and realize that even the most hardworking poor females of this world—unless they have brothers who contribute to the household expenses—are barely able to survive on their wages."

"Reckon that be right, m'lady." Archie had stopped, waiting for her to keep up. He flashed his wry, iconic smile at her over his shoulder. "That Miss Liza is very lucky she has three obedient big bruvvers wot's sworn off drink and that the little 'uns are the girls. Ain't no way the young woman wouldna 'ad to sell more 'n just her bonnets if she didn't have bruvvers helping to pay the bills."

Lily sighed as they continued in lock step. "Hamish says the public are not yet ready for the stories I want to tell, but that I must be patient. While his father is still alive and owns the magazine, he has to tread carefully, and I understand that."

Archie was panting with the exertion of lugging his equipment when they reached the pavement opposite her husband's editorial offices.

"I won't come in, of course," said Lily, indicating her dress, which was that of a poor woman. It served as a disguise and a protection, but she knew Hamish was concerned about his father's reaction if the old man discovered Lily participated in researching their stories.

She craned her neck to look up at the three-storied building that housed the magazine. Hamish would be upstairs, but it was possible his father might have dropped by.

She was about to turn away to hire a hackney to take her home when Archie said suddenly, "That's Lord Bellingham on the pavement, looking like he don't know whether to open the door and go up the stairs. He's turning back, ma'am. You might want to talk to 'im—" He broke off suddenly, adding with a note of embarrassment, "Me an' yer 'usband 'ad a word with him last night to put him off ideas of marryin' Miss Tarot. It's possible we might have done it a bit brown."

"What?"

"Or made a hash of it, come to that."

"Good Lord, Archie, you didn't make her out to be a consorting with a den of thieves, I hope. Remember, it's her reputation I'm trying to protect, not destroy."

"Course m'lady. But no man likes to be told to look into his beloved's past or origins like we 'ad to tell him to do. Gets 'em a bit hot under the collar and defensive-like—"

Lily cut him off. "Lord Bellingham!" she hailed him with a wave and a smile as she crossed the road. "What a pleasant surprise."

For a moment he stared at her in bemusement and Lily realized that, speaking in her cultured tones, she must have appeared an anomaly in her garb of patched cotton skirts she'd bought at a secondhand barrow, and her faded blouse and old muffler.

In fact, he clearly didn't recognize her until she introduced herself and then his eyes widened, and a blush suffused his face.

"Lady Bradden."

As he seemed not to know what else to say, Lily seized the advantage. "You are here to see my husband? He spoke to you last night, I believe. I'm not sure if he's in his office, but perhaps I could assist. Allow me to apologize for my state of dress. I've been with Archie, our photographer, interviewing a young bonnet maker in Seven Dials whom I didn't want to overwhelm with silks and laces." She smiled wryly, nevertheless feeling a twinge of trepidation as to what Hamish and Archie might have told the gloomy looking young man before her.

Archie's words had discomposed her. Hamish was

compassionate and discreet. Lily had no concerns that he'd not done his job well but if Lord Bellingham was back here to take issue with what had been said, then perhaps Archie had gone overboard in fulfilling his directive to dissuade Lord Bellingham from pursuing his interest in Miss Tarot.

For a long moment, the young man regarded Lily before transferring his gaze to Archie, whom he now addressed.

"Surely you could not imagine that I'd not be back?" he demanded. There was a look of pain about his eyes. "Mr. McTavish told me everything he needed to ... to make me champion the woman I love." Swinging round to look at Lily, he added, "I beg your pardon, Lady Bradden." Then, taking another clearly painful breath, he added, "You were kind enough to hope Miss Tarot had sufficient friends since she's so recently in London. Well, I am her greatest friend, and admirer. If there is something you think I need to know, please tell me plainly. Otherwise, I plan to make ours the grandest wedding of the season."

Lily's mouth dropped open. She started to speak, but stopped as Archie, hunched over by the weight of his photographic equipment, sent her a sidelong look then slunk off through the door and up the stairs to the editorial offices.

Lord Bellingham sucked in a breath, saying softly, "So, there *is* something?"

Lily ran the tip of her tongue over her top lip. "Lord Bellingham, nothing would give me greater pleasure than to secure Miss Tarot's happiness. And yours, for that matter." Running a hand over her darned, threadbare skirts, she said, "I must be the most fortunate woman in London... yet, had my father, Lord Lambton, not acknowledged me, my fate would have been very different." She hesitated, then asked, "Do you understand me?"

And, because Lord Bellingham could not be ignorant of

the sensational tale of Lily's past, he nodded, and let her go on.

"Yes, because Lord Lambton accepted me, so did society. Recently, I learned something about Miss Tarot's background. Something not even *she* knows. And, thinking that you and she had only just met, and therefore that you would not be considering marriage at this stage, I hoped I could just … let it be."

"Let it be?" Lord Bellingham repeated. "Lady Bradden, you are speaking in riddles. What would Evelina not know about her past that *you* do?"

Lily put her hands to her muffler, which was making her feel stifled and over-heated. She swallowed, feeling more and more on the back foot as his eyes bored into hers, though his expression was more quizzical than accusing now.

Then, in a burst of bravery, she said, "Lord Bellingham, Miss Tarot's parents are not the respectable people the world thinks them."

His eyes narrowed, and he looked about to speak but she had to continue. "My motivations were pure, Lord Bellingham! The scrutiny Miss Tarot will face as the bride of a man of status and influence could ruin her. However, a less notable union would enable her to slip quietly—and, I would hope, happily — into obscurity."

When he simply stared at Lily as if she had set out to blight his life, she said impatiently, "Lord Bellingham, you have the power to ruin her—"

"I also have the power to make her feel the most loved and cherished woman in the world—"

"And would you want to do that—and *could* you do that— if it was proved that Miss Tarot is really the daughter of Madame Chambon, the brothel keeper of London's most notorious pleasure house?"

CHAPTER 19

Lily watched him deflate with shock.

She's seen this reaction before when, as London's most sensationalist spiritualist, she'd supposedly conjured the dead from the 'other side' during the seances organized by Mr. Montpelier.

Lily had hated trading on other people's hopes and misery, and she hated it now.

But the truth was needed to orient Lord Bellingham.

If he truly loved Evelina Tarot, he would survive this.

If his love was built on shaky foundations, then it was better that he let her go now.

"I don't believe you."

Lily smiled for what else could he say? Lord Bellingham was defending his true love in the only way he knew how.

"Then perhaps you should go to Madame Chambon's and learn the truth for yourself," she said.

Archie, emerging through the doors of the editorial office, stepped onto the pavement beside them. "I can take you right now."

"Madame Chambon's?" Lord Bellingham recoiled. "I can't

step over the threshold of that den of iniquity! What would—"

"What would Miss Tarot think of you, if she were to find out?" Lily supplied for him in a gentler tone. "Miss Tarot has never heard of Madame Chambon's. I told you, earlier. She has no idea who her parents really are. She truly believes her father has settled a fortune on her and that her mother is from respectable Norfolk stock."

The young man's eyes were wild. He raked his hand through his dark hair. "Madame Chambon is Evelina's mother? But... how? Is Evelina a *foundling*? Adopted? For she surely cannot be the natural born child of a creature so steeped in sin and vice."

Lily turned at Archie's loud exhalation. "Then jest as well you found out now, m'lord. Else you could never a' looked at the poor girlie the same way." He straightened his cap and nodded as if he were about to leave. "Guess you won't be needin' to come to Madame Chambon's after all, since the visit would be... academic, as they say in your circles. You'll jest have to let her down, gently, won't you? She'll be disappointed but, lucky she has money and looks. She'll find her way in the world, and Lady Bradden will help her, I've no doubt, jest as m'lady helps so many unfortunates born wivout the right markers wot makes 'em respectable."

"No!"

Lily frowned. "No, what, Lord Bellingham? Is there something else you wished to know?" She paused, giving him time to collect his thoughts, then said, more gently, "I don't know everything, but I'll answer as best I can."

He made his decision quickly, flinging back his head while he covered his face briefly with his hands before saying, with a clear attempt at calm, "I'll come with you to the... brothel. I can't be recognized, but I need to hear the truth for myself. If what you say is true, then I'll need to speak to Madame."

Lily's admiration grew. Maybe he did love Evelina more than her money.

"Archie can run upstairs and find you something to wear that'll disguise the fact you're a gentleman," she said, waving the photographer away. "That'll help. But there is something else, Lord Bellingham," she added as Archie left to do her bidding.

He was silent, waiting for her to go on.

"We will take you to Madame Chambon's, because there you will learn the truth." Lily spoke kindly, with the sympathy she thought he deserved, though he still seemed in shock. "But there are also several girls I want to speak to in relation to Lord Dunstable's murder. I know the police have interviewed everyone there, however Miss Tarot's maid, who used to work at Madame Chambon's, tells me they haven't asked all the right questions."

"*Kitty?*" Lord Bellingham exclaimed.

"Yes, Kitty," said Archie, returning with a muffler and cap to replace Lord Bellingham's topper and cashmere scarf. "Kitty's the bosom buddy of me sweetheart, Gracie, wot works at Madame Chambon's. Gracie'll find us somewhere discreet to wait so you won't feel everyone's having a squiz at yer, don't you worry. We'll just have a look see and ask a few questions. You'll learn everything you need to know, m'lord."

The twinge of amusement Lily felt to see Archie's friendly attempts to put Lord Bellingham at ease was a welcome contrast to the sickly concern that had needled her until now. For at least Lord Bellingham seemed to have become more pliable and accepting. She'd feared he'd reject the truth outright.

"Shall we go?" she asked, leading the way, but saying over her shoulder, "I must warn you, Lord Bellingham, that I know more than a few people at Madame Chambon's, both through my work finding alternative employment for some of the establishment's fallen women, but also because Madame Chambon—" It was easier not to look him in the eye when she thought of the shame she knew Hamish would feel to hear her lay her past bare like this. "What I mean to say is that I lived—blamelessly and innocently—under Madame's roof for a few months after I escaped from the insane asylum where my husband had had me incarcerated. I just needed to explain that because you will hear me speak with some familiarity with some of the girls."

Dully, Lord Bellingham said, "So, you really do know Madame Chambon? And her daughter."

"I never knew she had a daughter," Lily replied as they hurried through the smog-ridden streets. "In fact, not until after Dunstable was murdered. Madame managed to keep it secret until she was heard arguing with Lord Dunstable over Evelina's dowry which was when Gracie and Kitty—who had by now been working as Miss Tarot's lady's maid for a couple of weeks—put two and two together."

"Wait!" Lord Bellingham halted and Lily turned to see he'd blanched whiter. "Dear God, are you suggesting—?"

Lily struggled to keep a smile in place as she beckoned to him. "I'm not suggesting anything, Lord Bellingham. However, I do think that at Madame Chambon's, we should be prepared to find answers that will not be what we expect."

Finally, they reached the large four-square dwelling that drew London's aristocracy and those with the funds to pay for one of Madame Chambon's sought-after girls.

At this hour of the morning, the street outside the house was busy with foot traffic. Inside, of course, many of the girls would be sleeping off the excesses of the previous night.

"And now we'll go through the secret back entrance," Archie said.

Then Lily had to hurry to keep up, for she was unfamiliar with this entry to Madame's and Archie was like a fox as he ducked into a nearby doorway, his footsteps in the darkness ahead the only reassurance that the going was clear.

When Lily, bringing up the rear, finally emerged into the drawing room of Madame Chambon's, it was the smell that struck her most forcibly. A cloying mix of perfume and, at this time of morning, carbolic. No doubt Gracie would be hard at work cleaning up after the night before and, indeed, it was she whom they first encountered as she trudged by with a bucket of slops.

"Lordy!" she exclaimed when she registered the fact it was Lily dressed in rags with the two men. She cast an anguished look over her shoulder then whispered, "Madame's lurking about somewhere. Did ye want to see her or not see her?"

"We'll talk to her, Gracie, but I'd prefer to speak to a couple of the girls first."

"Is it about … his dead lordship?" Gracie lowered her voice. "The police inspector has been closeted in the office every day talking to Madame Chambon and they looks grimmer each time. Haven't got a clue who did it, I reckon." She winked at Archie before sending a puzzled look at his companion.

"Gracie, we've brought Lord Bellingham," said Lily, "though don't reveal that to anyone, please. Now, have the police spoken to *all* the girls and all the gentlemen who were here that night?"

"Course. But they ain't goin' to say anyfink though they does answer wot they's asked. Like I said, I reckon the police inspector don't know the right questions." She stopped suddenly as a lovely titian haired young woman in an elegant silk dressing gown decorated with peacocks padded gracefully past them in bare feet.

"Sonia!" she hailed her. "You was drinking whisky with

Lord Dunstable and Captain Blackheath in the drawin' room before LuluBelle took over entertainin'. I'm talkin' the night o' the murder. You was the first to say the police are barking up the wrong tree and these people 'ave questions."

Sonia stopped and when she put her head on one side with a slight frown, Gracie said quickly, "It's orright. Don't you recognize Lady Bradden?"

Sonia's lovely face relaxed into a smile. "I've heard so much about you, Lady Bradden, and would be happy to offer up my suspicions." Her voice was sweet and cultured and Lily wondered how long she'd been working at Madame Chambon's.

Was Sonia just a clever mimic, or was she a girl like Celeste, who Lily suspected really was from more affluent circumstances? But then the sound of heavy, determined footsteps approaching from the gloomy interior had Gracie squeaking, "Follow me so's I can rustle up LuluBelle to talk to yer since she was the last to see Lord Dunstable alive. You can talk to Madame after."

Obediently Lily, Archie and Lord Bellingham followed the girl up the stairs and into an elegant bedroom decorated in the Rococo style, where Gracie left them with promises to return with LuluBelle.

After a disdainful look about him, Lord Bellingham went to the window and stared out into the street while Lily and Archie exchanged looks.

"Lord Bellingham, I promise you that we'll speak to Madame shortly. But I do believe it's important for you to first meet one of the girls who works here because I've come to believe that there might possibly be some connection between the truth of Evelina's background and Lord Dunstable's murder—"

"In what way?" Lord Dunstable swung round and Lily could see by the tightness of his mouth and the pain around his eyes that he was having difficulty coming to terms with the possibility of his new reality.

"I'm not sure, exactly. I want to see if LuluBelle can shed some light on it, so I would simply beg for your forbearance while I question her." Lily glanced at Archie, who nodded, and she went on, "When I lived at Madame Chambon's, I shared a room with a young woman called Celeste. You may recall the murder. It was rather a sensational case eighteen months ago, in which a Russian diplomat was convicted of killing one of the girls here." She waved her arm to encompass the room. "Nothing was—is—known about Celeste other than that name, but I have a strong suspicion that Lord Dunstable returned to the house and began blackmailing Madame Chambon, because he recognized Celeste. Perhaps he knew her in another life." She took a deep breath, then finished, "It has occurred to me that Lord Dunstable *may* have been killed because of what he knew about Celeste."

Lord Bellingham looked unmoved. Bored, even; as if he were determined to disassociate himself from the situation. "What has that got to do with Miss Tarot?"

"For mercy's sake!" Archie burst out at the end of his patience. "Lady Bradden reckons he came here to blackmail Madame Chambon over Celeste, but then he discovered evidence that Madame had a secret daughter bein' educated in Paris: Evelina Tarot. That's when we reckon Dunstable then blackmailed Madame so she'd 'elp lay the ground for Miss Tarot to marry him—before he were done in."

He might have continued had it not become clear to Lily that the news was too forcefully delivered to find sway with his lordship, who said, tightly, "Supposition. Did *you* see evidence that Evelina is Madame's daughter?" he asked Lily.

"No, but that's why *you're* here, Lord Bellingham," she replied. "To ask Madame directly..." She hesitated, adding, "That is, when the time is right and we've spoken to Lulu-

Belle since I don't think Madame would countenance us under her roof a moment longer once she's been tackled with what I suspect is her most closely held secret."

Lord Bellingham raised his eyes, thinking. He finally seemed to reach an acceptance of what Lily and Archie had been trying to tell him, for he said, "I had assumed, like most others, that the man who murdered Dunstable was a rival or adversary. But you, Lady Bradden, are suggesting the motive was very different. Something to do with Evelina, you say? Please explain."

"I think it's possible that whoever killed Dunstable wanted to get him out of the way so that he could profit from the knowledge of Miss Tarot's secret origins," said Lily. "I suspect it was only because Madame was being blackmailed by Dunstable that she agreed to marriage between him and her daughter. And to be fair, Evelina agreed willingly."

"When she had spent less than a week in the capital and knew no better!" Lord Bellingham's voice rose, just as the door opened and a slight young woman entered the room. Her hair was slightly disordered, and she wore a long, loose dressing gown of red and blue patterned silk that highlighted her translucent skin.

LuluBelle looked very lovely and very tired. Even more tired than Lily remembered as she smiled and put out her hand before the girl gasped, "M'lady!" her eyes widening as she took in Lily's disguise before sizing up the two men, relaxing slightly when she saw Archie. "Gracie said there were someone here who wanted to see me especial-like, and she reckoned it would be worth me while, when I argued I needed my rest and were seeing no one else tonight."

"It's just us, LuluBelle," Archie said cheerfully. "Lady Bradden and Lord Bellingham here have some questions about the murder."

LuluBelle seemed suddenly overcome with nervousness

at her audience and Lily, to dispel the awkwardness, invited everyone to sit before realizing the only place other than two spindly chairs, was the bed.

Waving LuluBelle to the chair beside the washstand, Lily sat by the bed while Lord Bellingham and Archie perched on the edge of the pink satin coverlet.

"LuluBelle, please, will you tell us when you first met Lord Dunstable and what your dealings with him were?" asked Lily.

LuluBelle's eyes hardened. "The night he arrived, he requested that he see Celeste again, and when Madame said she was booked that evening, he offered a handsome fee that Madame couldn't resist. Madame can't ever resist the extra blunt the girls bring in." The girl's shoulders slumped, and she stared at the floor.

Lily, who knew all this, wondered suddenly if there really was any new information that would help them understand who might have murdered Dunstable, and why, but continued, "Gracie says you were a particular friend of Celeste's. Do you know if Lord Dunstable was unkind to her?"

Lord Bellingham interrupted. "With all due respect, the murderer of this woman Celeste, has already been convicted!"

Lily pressed her lips together. "Please, let LuLubelle continue, Lord Bellingham. I think it's better if the story reveals itself. LuLubelle, will you please describe Lord Dunstable's visit, and the reason he came here?"

LuLubelle nodded. "Nothin' were strange or different when I saw Celeste after. Dunstable were just like any other customer. But then he came again the next week, askin' for Celeste. He paid well, and he seemed like any o' them high society folks wot come here for a little summat on the side when they's bored with their wives."

Lord Bellingham shifted position but LuLubelle, encouraged by Lily's look, went on, "It were after 'is lordship left the second time that I went to find Celeste. She were cryin' somethin' terrible. Not like her at all. I asked if he were unkind to her and she said no, but that he'd seen her photograph in *Manners and Morals* and said he thought he'd recognized her. Then she put her hand to her mouth and told me she'd said more than enough and would never speak on it again."

Before Lily could answer, the sound of thundering feet on the stairs was truncated by an angry, "What is the meaning of this, LuLubelle?" as Madame Chambon burst into the room.

There was just enough time for Lord Bellingham to disappear behind the Japanese dressing screen while Madame's recognition of Lily made her eyes flash with something indefinable before Lily said mildly, "I am not here to spy on you, Madame, as we wanted to speak to you afterwards. However, now that you are here, would you spare us a few moments to help us with some questions about Lord Dunstable?"

Madame looked cornered as well she might.

"I believe the girls heard Lord Dunstable demanding something of you with regard to Celeste," Lily persisted.

Madame, a striking figure in ruby red silk and lace to match her hair, looked as if she were staring down a predator as she faced Lily and Archie, arms akimbo, in the center of the elegant Aubusson rug. "That is true," she replied. "But, with all due respect, Lady Bradden, what interest—or qualifications—do you have in discovering the identity of Lord Dunstable's killer? And Celeste is of no importance. Her murderer was brought to justice. I have answered Inspector Wild's questions to the best of my ability. I have no idea why you believe you can come here and demand answers to something that happened a long time ago and has no bearing on anything."

"But I believe it does," said Lily. "I believe Lord Dunstable recognized Celeste and came here to blackmail the young woman because he'd found proof of her real identity. When she was murdered, you claimed you had no idea who she really was." Lily was sure Madame looked uncomfortable though it was difficult to gauge her emotional state. Madame, she had found, was always difficult to read as she pretended emotion to suit the moment. Nevertheless, she continued, "I believe you knew LuLubelle had hidden the documents verifying Celeste's identity and that on the night he was murdered, you had gone to demand she release them to you as you'd finally given in to his latest blackmail demands. I'm interested to know what Dunstable might have been blackmailing you with."

Madame Chambon drew back her shoulders. "I have no idea what you're talking about, Lady Bradden."

Archie's voice drifted from the end of the bed. "Word is that you spoke to Dunstable in your study. Then you argued. You were both heard shoutin' before you left to fetch Celeste's identity documents. Then he was murdered."

"All right, I did leave to fetch what Celeste had left behind." Madame Chambon hesitated. "But I didn't hand anything over because ... I found Lord Dunstable dead."

"And there were no sign of a struggle," Lily went on. "The blade of a paperknife had gone straight through his jugular vein cleanly and neatly. He was caught quite by surprise, so that the police have said the murderer could have been either man or woman."

"And you had five girls working in the house, and five gentleman clients—"

"There were another man," LuluBelle said, flashing a quick and guilty look at Madame who turned a telling shade darker.

Interesting, thought Lily, but now Madame was saying

quickly, "You mean Captain Blackheath, I think, LuluBelle. He and Lord Dunstable also argued the night of the murder."

LuluBelle drew herself up, her sweet, tired expression transformed by anger though her words were soft as she said, "*I* was with Captain Blackheath and you know it, Madame. Captain Blackheath visits me every Friday and weren't no different this time."

"Well, he's been cleared because he had an alibi, so enough insolence from you, LuluBelle," muttered Madame. "All five clients and girls have been interviewed and they have been cleared."

"Cept the sixth gentleman," said LuluBelle softly before Madame swung round and said, "Dunstable was a black-mailer, and he was cruel to you, LuLubelle. Yes, I've heard this from another of the girls here, but I haven't told the police as I didn't want them to think *you* had a motive to kill his Lordship."

LuluBelle gasped. "No, Madame! Lots o' the gennelmen are rough, and Lord Dunstable were no rougher. He weren't a real sadist, like, so's there'd be uvvers I'd ha liked to have staked with a paperknife before 'im," she went on before putting her hand to her mouth again for her incautious words. "But I never killed any o' them and I never killed Lord Dunstable and I don't know who did. I reckon only the killer knows that."

"Discovering the killer's motivation in killing Lord Dunstable would go a long way towards discovering his—or her—identity," mused Lily before she asked, "Madame, was anyone other than Lord Dunstable blackmailing you?"

Madame was very still. "The Inspector knows I was not in the vicinity of Lord Dunstable when he was killed," she said, ignoring the question.

So that was it. Lily had spent months living under this roof. She'd honed her ability to read a person's responses through her two years locked away in a lunatic asylum in Brussels. Madame was being blackmailed by someone else, only she wasn't about to admit it.

And, quite possibly, he was the 'sixth' man to whom Lulu-Belle had alluded.

With a nod at Archie, Lily asked, "Please, would you and LuLubelle leave us while I have a few words with Madame, alone?"

When the door had closed behind them, Madame Chambon said viperishly, "So, m'lady, you know the truth about Evelina, but do you now wish to expose her to the world as the daughter of London's most infamous brothel-keeper? Well, I will do anything to preserve the future of the creature I hold dearer to me than any other, and I will not give you the satisfaction of destroying her. Yes, Lord Dunstable was blackmailing me. But you already know that. At first, he blackmailed Celeste, for he'd discovered she was from a good family, whom he intended to blackmail, in turn. I did not know this until he'd established from the general gossip that I had a daughter who was being educated in France."

"A daughter who comes with a handsome dowry so that Dunstable was prepared to overlook her illegitimacy and the fact you are her mother in order to marry her." Lily showed her disdain. "You traded her with Dunstable."

"She agreed to marry him willingly," Madame snarled. "I was never more relieved, for I thought it possible she could make him love her and be kind to her and that he'd be satisfied with the money she brought to the marriage."

"Except you knew he was rotten to the core."

"I also knew he would have no compunction in destroying Evelina if either of us had an objection. What choice did I have?"

"But if Evelina's dowry is so great, she obviously has the

backing of someone who can ensure her reputation is not destroyed; someone who would be glad to know she could enjoy happiness in her choice of marriage partner …rather than be coerced into marrying a blackmailer."

"Her father, of course, though don't think I will reveal his name! But he will never acknowledge her! He is too powerful —" Madame put her hand to her mouth as if she'd said too much, adding more quietly, "Evelina has money…"

"But a background that potentially could damage the reputation or aspirations of the husband brave enough to marry her," finished Lily.

Madame hissed through her teeth. "I don't know what you hoped to accomplish in coming here. LuLubelle knows nothing she hasn't told the police. Everyone who was here that night has been questioned. I suggest you leave me, and my girls, alone. I was good enough not to make of you the demands I could have when you lived here. Now I would thank you to just leave!"

As LILY WALKED with Lord Bellingham through Covent Garden, she asked, "What do you intend to do now, Lord Bellingham? You can't marry Evelina. Not with the risk of discovery of this unpalatable truth so great. You're going to have to let her down gently. That would be kindest."

With quiet and grim determination, he shook his head. "Madame wasn't going to reveal the name of Evelina's father, but I believe if I can learn it, I might persuade him to acknowledge his daughter, at least. You say you think Madame is being blackmailed by someone else and that's the most important piece of information to discover. I believe her father's identity may be at the root of all this." Looking grimly ahead as he wove his way through the streets of

London, a little ahead of Lily, he went on, "Whomever he is, he has money. Perhaps a title. If that were the case, it may be that he is immune from society's opprobrium and Evelina in turn would be accepted and her mother's name could be kept out of it. The marriage can be done quietly. We can make a marriage tour of the continent immediately afterwards—"

"This was just as Lord Dunstable had planned it. Yes, he led Evelina to believe it would be a lavish wedding," said Lily. "And then he pretended to change his mind, though his plan was conceived before he even met Miss Tarot. Later, he either told her, or intimated, he'd organized a special licence or they would elope." Lily glanced at his profile, wishing she'd not visited such pain upon him. She'd misunderstood the depth of his feelings and realized, now, that the couple must have met, and fallen in love, long before their meeting during Lady Gilray's Ball.

"Someone wants to ruin Evelina," muttered Lord Bellingham. "And I need to discover his identity. And discover her father's identity."

"And what if her father is a criminal, languishing in prison, having bestowed his ill-gotten gains on Evelina?"

Lord Bellingham shook his head. "I'll do whatever it takes to protect the woman I love."

"Remember, we are not the only ones who know Madame's secret."

"But it's a secret which must be kept from Evelina." Lord Bellingham swung round to face her. "Lord Dunstable's killer needs to be found before I can safely ask Evelina for her hand in marriage—for that is what I intend to do." As they reached St Paul's Cathedral, the energy seemed to drain from him as he added, softly, "Poor Evelina has no idea of her parentage and I'm not sure how she would survive if the truth were revealed. But if I can find out who her father is, and ensure that he, or at least, his fortune, will protect her, then much of her pain might be mitigated."

Lily drew level as they prepared to go their separate ways. "But what if Lord Dunstable's murderer is not discovered and Evelina is not acknowledged by her father? Would it not be a kindness to her to let her down gently? For you know that the moment your marriage is announced, her background will be closely scrutinized?"

Lord Bellingham regarded her a long moment. "I love her, and I will not live without her. And I will pave the way for her public acceptance. Even if it means crossing the threshold of that ... hellhouse once more to speak to Madame Chambon to demand the answers she would not divulge today. I will do it in order to secure a future with the perfect being who remains blameless and innocent in all this."

CHAPTER 20

Sleep was elusive that night, and it was dawn before he was plunged into merciful, dreamless oblivion.

Later, as he tried to devise how he might secure the information he needed, William was plunged into greater distress.

"Miss LuluBelle Croft?" William repeated the name with even greater disbelief after his valet had relayed it to him while dressing his master for an evening out. No, not with disbelief, but with patent horror.

"Aye, m'lord," replied Sanders. Please raise your arms, so I can put on your shirt. You are expected at Ravenhall Manor within the hour."

William did as he was bid, while he wondered what else he'd missed during the time he'd allowed himself some rest. Exhausted, following the exploits of the previous day, he'd thought he'd never sleep again. "Is that the word around town? That this young woman, Miss LuluBelle Croft, has just been charged with Lord Dunstable's murder? Good Lord, are you sure, Sanders? I've read nothing about it in the newspapers. Where did you hear such a thing?"

Sanders, who had accompanied William during his travel on the Continent, nodded. "News travels fast, my lord. Apparently, she were apprehended this afternoon. I heard it from Lord Newsome's valet, who watched her being marched out of that wicked house with her hands behind her back. Now, your cufflinks, my lord."

Raging at the clear travesty of justice, William submitted to what was necessary to dress him for a dull evening out with some dull gentlemen discussing some dull parliamentary matters.

LuluBelle had been charged with Lord Dunstable's murder?

He recalled the few minutes he'd spent listening to her and to Madame, and knew it couldn't be true.

Meanwhile, his heart pounded with all the other information he was still finding hard to digest.

Chief among this was the confirmation that Evelina was Madame Chambon's daughter. Dear God, how would his poor darling bear up to learning such a thing? William would willingly shoulder whatever burden was required if it meant protecting her from the truth.

But who else knew the truth?

And was willing to kill to expose it?

With a shudder, he thought of pale, delicate LuluBelle, abused and exploited by Dunstable and others like him. Men who thought of nothing but their own pleasure.

Not for a second did he believe she'd murdered Lord Dunstable but it was clear she harbored suspicions who might have, which Madame was reluctant to have aired.

LuluBelle had alluded to a sixth gentlemen present at Madame Chambon's on the night in question, and Madame had immediately named Captain Blackheath whom Lulu-Belle had been quick to defend.

Granted, Blackheath was a cad. William had never liked him. He'd been a swaggart in the army, and his liking of drink and loose women was legendary. But it seemed Lulu-Belle had a soft spot for Blackheath.

While Blackheath had shown a distinct interest in Evelina.

William closed his eyes. Was Blackheath such a black-guard as to murder a man in cold blood so he instead could marry his victim's intended bride? For her money?

During the carriage ride to the dinner to which he was committed, William ran through his options. The police had already apprehended LuluBelle. Hopefully there'd not be enough evidence to convict.

But the police might find a speedy conviction convenient, given the agitation of Lord Dunstable's family; and time was running out. Knowing what he now knew, it was William's moral duty to find something that would exonerate Lulu-Belle's conviction.

Which meant finding the real murderer.

A murderer who had likely killed over what he knew about Evelina's origins.

William could barely attend to his dinner companions as the six of them dined in Lord Ravenhall's lofty dining room at Ravenhall Manor. He had to feign the same relief the other men showed when the earl declared it was fitting that Lord Dunstable's murderer was finally facing justice before poor Dunstable would be laid to rest at Highgate Cemetery that Thursday. And he had to bite his tongue when lovely Lady Ravenhall, whom he'd always known to be an empathetic woman, who ran a school that taught reading and arithmetic to the children of the nearby workhouse, said, "This woman should be locked up forever for the terrible thing she did to poor, blameless Lord Dunstable. And they should throw away the key!"

At which her husband remonstrated, mildly, "She's inno-cent until proven guilty, my love. Are you not the first to preach that vice and crime is more the result of poverty than of an inherently criminal nature? Fortunately, today's justice system will allow her to protest her innocence in court rather than seeing her rot in some windowless cell."

It was counterproductive for William to show his outrage when Lord Ravenhall's lawyer, Mr. Grimshaw, muttered darkly, "No doubt an airless crypt is where she belongs. How often does it prove to be a *woman* who is the root of such evil in what appears now to be nothing more than crime of passion?"

But William knew that Grimshaw had been passed over for an earldom due to his illegitimate birth, for which he held his mother responsible. The man's bitter words blaming a woman were not surprising but they did increase William's determination to discover the identity of Evelina's parentage.

Aristocrats were more likely to acknowledge their male bastards than their illegitimate daughters, but if William could learn the identity of Evelina's father, it was one layer of protection that might smooth her path.

That's if Dunstable's real murderer did not strike first and reveal Evelina's terrible secret to the whole world.

With a great sense of relief, he finally excused himself, following port and cigars.

For it was not yet midnight and, distasteful as he founded it, he would have to return to Madame Chambon's.

For here, he was hopeful he'd find proof that would exonerate LuluBelle.

HE WAS DISAPPOINTED, when he reached the dwelling, to learn that Madame was out that evening.

"Perhaps there's a special young lady with whom you'd like to enjoy the evening, sir?" The young girl assigned to look after him while he waited in the drawing room smiled suggestively. "Does your fancy lend itself to brunettes, perhaps? Or blondes? There are also several redheads—"

"No, please, I need to speak to Madame," William interrupted, sending a desperate look about the room, glad he was the only gentleman waiting. Being peak time for the occupants of the house, several young women in sumptuous clothing reclined on sofas, while gentlemen from society's upper echelons trod the corridors. Some were at pains to disguise themselves, though not all. William, who'd been careful to keep his identity hidden by replacing his white silk scarf, gloves and top hat with a checked cap pulled low, and muffler,

"You look lost and lonely, sir."

William swung round as the soft words purred in his ear seemed to envelope him like her cloying violet perfume, despising himself for the unexpected sensations the young woman's words evoked within him.

"Sonia," he said, recognizing the young woman, embarrassed when she looked at him blankly.

He was not a man who paid for sex, but it had been a long time since he'd had relations with a woman. Not since a brief but highly passionate affair the previous summer during a two-week house party, when he'd been seduced by the wife of a fellow guest whose husband's mistress was their hostess.

The memory reflected well on no one, but that was how physical needs were navigated in the circles in which they moved.

It was why it was so refreshing to feel only the truest, purest love for innocent Evelina.

"I was here with Lady Bradden yesterday. I hoped for a few moments to speak to you," he said to the titian-haired beauty whose two front teeth, he noticed, were slightly crooked, though, surprisingly, this only added to her charm.

He didn't chastise himself for finding the woman attractive. Instead, it bolstered his resolve to be true to Evelina. No one was without flaws and that perfect woman did not exist. When one's heart was engaged by the right levers, pursuing that love determined the caliber of the man.

"Then we shall go upstairs," she replied, hooking her hand in his arm.

He shook his head. "I...I was concerned about what had happened to LuluBelle."

"You are a ... *friend* of LuluBelle?" She dropped her hand, frowning.

William was struck by how beautiful she was. And how beautifully she spoke. Yet her talents were employed in a house like this.

"I was never a friend in that sense, but I don't believe she murdered Lord Dunstable, who was, in fact, an acquaintance of mine," William said. "I came here to speak to someone here who might tell me what they think happened that night."

Sonia looked at him suspiciously, then shrugged. "The police have questioned us all, but they made up their minds as soon as it was convenient to charge LuluBelle, when of course...." She lowered her voice and glanced about her before adding, "Madame would be more likely since it happened in her office. But Madame didn't do it. She was with the police inspector, or as near as makes no difference."

"Do you have any other suspicions... considering no one here appears to have actually witnessed the event?" He hesitated. "Captain Blackheath?"

She was thoughtful. "I did wonder, considering Captain Blackheath was blackmailing Lord Dunstable, and they were bitter enemies. But the captain is a friend of Lulubelle's. He'd not see harm come to her and he'd surely not see her hang for a crime he committed."

William's eyes widened. "His fondness for LuluBelle does not preclude the fact he might have murdered Dunstable if he had a good enough motive. How do you know they were bitter enemies?"

Sonia settled herself on the arm of the sofa when it was clear William did not wish to go to her room. "They came to blows during a conversation I overheard during which Dunstable told the captain to mind his own... business, though in more colorful language than that. It sounded like Blackheath didn't like the idea of Dunstable marrying Madame's—" She put her hand over her mouth. "I've said too much. Madame has spies everywhere and if she knew I'd said half as much, I'd lose my place here. Then where would a girl like me go?"

William's mind was whirring. He understood he couldn't say Evelina's name, though that was what Sonia intimated. So, *Blackheath* had actively sought to dissuade Dunstable from marrying Evelina? "Do you know why he objected to the idea of Dunstable marrying this ... young lady?"

"Did I say that? No, sir. They argued and I have no idea of the cause."

"And there was no one else you recall in the house at the time who might have been motivated to kill Lord Dunstable."

"I cannot speak to anyone's motives, sir, but Captain Blackheath was not the only man here with the opportunity to kill Lord Dunstable."

"Five others have been interviewed and let go," said William. "Was there someone who springs to mind?"

A furrow speared Sonia's brow. "A gentleman I've seen several times over the years, though he does not come here to see the girls. Just to visit Madame, who is always anxious and over-bearing afterwards."

"What is the name of that gentleman?"

Sonia shrugged. "I have no idea. All I recall is that he was an older gentleman, impeccably dressed, and that he carried an unusual cane, carved with two entwined snakes."

William stiffened. "Please, Sonia. Could I speak to you somewhere private?"

Sonia shook her head. "I'd tell you if I knew anything more, if only to save LuluBelle from the gallows. And now, if you'll excuse me, sir, my time is valuable and there is another gentleman across the room who looks like he's in need of comforting."

She was about to leave him, but William detained her with a hand on her arm. "There are other places a woman like you could go, Sonia," he said. "Have you heard of the employment bureau run by Lady Bradden at *Manners and Morals?*"

Sonia smiled at him, almost as if he were dim-witted. "All the girls have heard of it," she said. "And those who can survive on servant's wages to save their souls are clamoring for a position. I am not one of them, for I have a daughter to keep." Her smile was suddenly wistful. "And it costs money to educate her so that she does not end up living this kind of life."

WILLIAM LEFT Madame Chambon's no closer to finding the answers that gnawed at him but determined to seek out Captain Blackheath. Even if Blackheath was innocent in all this, he might be able to shed light on the identity of the man about whom Sonia spoke.

It was nearly two by the time he arrived at his club, where a few enquiries elicited the information that Blackheath had left London to return to his home in Kent.

A few hours' sleep was what he needed, William decided,

and then he'd be up at dawn to make the five-hour journey—depending on the weather and the roads.

In the meantime, he sat down at his desk to write a long and heartfelt letter to Evelina.

In the most artful language, he told her that no obstacle—expected or unexpected, great or small—would stand in his way as long as she returned his feelings, but that a small but urgent matter required his attendance in the country, and he'd be back within a couple of days.

Then he sealed up his heart in a white envelope which he left by the blotter, ready to be dispatched on his way out of his townhouse towards Captain Blackheath's residence.

CHAPTER 21

C heer up, Miss Evelina. Can't you hear the birds singing ever so loud?" Kitty tried to jolly her along as they took a walk through Hyde Park.

"I haven't heard from William in two days, and he said nothing about leaving town. I can't imagine—"

Evelina broke off as she registered the trio advancing towards her: Lady Victoria in company with her sister, Clara, and another young lady.

"My dear Miss Tarot!" cried Clara warmly, hurrying forward. "What a delightful surprise to see you here. Please, let me introduce my friend, Lady Elizabeth Craddock. But, of course, you've already met!"

Evelina's concern regarding the circumstances of that meeting was ameliorated as Lady Elizabeth was clearly not about to allude to the slightly scandalous circumstances: chaperoning Evelina back to the ballroom after she'd left a storeroom cupboard alone with a gentleman.

Fortunately, the young girl seemed blithely unconcerned, saying simply as she dipped her head, "A pleasure to meet you, Miss Tarot."

Clara, who was dancing from one foot to the other, said to her friend, "Miss Tarot is from France. She's visiting the capital for some weeks and was going to wed—" She put her hand to her mouth before finishing with a blush, "the first titled gentleman with one hundred thousand a year who offered." Giving a girlish giggle she went on, "Victoria will never let me put my hair up and my skirts down if I can't learn to temper the first silliness that comes out of my mouth. But didn't I behave with perfect decorum for the two hours I was allowed to attend godmother's ball?"

"I hope you have enjoyed London, Miss Tarot." Ignoring her sister, Lady Victoria spoke more formally but not without kindness, following her sharp look at Clara. "Clara is right. She needs to learn to moderate her impulses if she is to be allowed to attend more adult entertainments. That is why Elizabeth will be going to Lady Jervis's ball tomorrow night and Clara shall not, despite the girls being the same age and having known each other since their school days."

Evelina didn't miss the eye roll Clara sent her sister, which elicited a smile—quickly buttoned up—from Lady Elizabeth.

"If you would only give me the chance to behave like a grown-up, then I would show your faith in me was not misplaced," said Clara in tones that were almost begging. "How can I behave like an adult when you insist on treating me like a child?"

Evelina heard the girl's frustration, though she couldn't understand it. She felt like she'd been forced to become a grownup from the day she'd been packed off to Paris aged six.

"Because you don't understand the dangers of the world, Clara. You have only me to see to your interests and you believe only the best of people. I cannot trust you in the ballroom."

Clara's mouth turned down suddenly. "You say that, Victoria, but do you not think I understand what evil lurks around every corner when I remember what happened to our cousin? Why, barely a week ago, Cousin Dunstable was with Miss Tarot and the two of us were strolling about the zoological gardens. Who could have imagined such a terrible thing would befall him? You certainly would not have spoken so sharply to him had you known, would you, Victoria?"

Evelina saw the young woman's pale skin flame as Victoria replied, "I spoke no more sharply to our cousin than I usually do, Clara. Dunstable can be extremely vexatious, as you know."

"A good thing you didn't marry him, after all," said Clara, blithely, hooking her hand in the crook of Lady Elizabeth's arm and adding, "You will have to tell me all about Lady Jervis's ball, Lizzy, for my destiny is to look at life as if through a glass window for all the fun Victoria intends to allow me."

Evelina was surprised to see the hurt on Victoria's face. "You won't always be seventeen, Clara," she muttered to Clara who, in another change of mood, said happily, "At least I can rub shoulders with London high society when I attend Cousin Dunstable's funeral." She clapped her hand to her mouth again and looked nervously at her sister, saying, "Forgive me, Victoria. I didn't mean to sound as if I didn't care what happened to him. You know how fond I was of Cousin Dunstable, for all that he enjoyed his gaming too much and you were worried he was going to ruin both of us before you gained your majority. But that didn't come to pass, and now he's dead." Pulling out a square of lace, Clare dabbed daintily at her eyes. "Poor Cousin Dunstable. And no one even knows the wicked man who... who... murdered him." Without warning, she broke into loud sobs.

Evelina watched the girl with concern as Lady Victoria

held Clara close and soothed her, the sharpness quite gone from her tone as she whispered, "Hush, Clara, no one thinks ill of you. You act before you think and it's for that reason, I believe you need another year to mature before you are ready for London revels."

Finally, her emotion spent, Clara stepped out of her sister's embrace, wiping her tear-stained cheeks. Offering Evelina and Elizabeth a brave, albeit trembling smile, she said, "I will have to live vicariously through Elizabeth, who is so pretty and kind she'll have a husband before I'm even in long skirts."

Elizabeth laughed, and Clara went on, "Victoria has sworn off nice young men since Dunstable broke her heart, but what about you, Miss Tarot?" she asked. "Have you met a nice young man?"

Evelina stiffened as she prepared to answer, thinking of her mother's opposition to Bellingham and suddenly afraid of declaring her heart engaged when she'd not heard from William in two days. "I have met many nice young men," she said, warily. "London is full of them."

"But perhaps one in particular?" Lady Elizabeth prompted with a speculative smile, obviously recalling the fact that Evelina had emerged from a storeroom alone with him. "Perhaps he will be at Lady Jervis's ball. You are so beautiful you will have all the young men wanting to be your suitor and you won't be able to make up your mind."

"He just needs to be rich," said Clara, but her sister reprimanded her. "He has to be moral and upstanding, too, Clara, and until you can understand that, you will not be putting your hair up and your skirts down. Now, good day to you, Miss Tarot."

"Good day, Miss Tarot," echoed Elizabeth. "No doubt we shall see you at Lord Dunstable's funeral on Thursday."

They were about to move on but stopped, turning in

surprise when Evelina said, "Regrettably, I will not be attending."

The opprobrium on Lady Victoria's face made her squirm. "But… you and my cousin—" She stopped, glancing at Elizabeth and coloring. "I beg your pardon, Miss Tarot, but I thought you would be at Highgate Cemetery. Naturally, I understand if you have other more important matters to attend to that day."

"No, please Lady Victoria, I wanted to attend very much but for some reason my mama is against the idea, though I have no idea why."

Lady Victoria put her head on one side. Flanked by the two younger girls, Evelina felt very much under scrutiny as she continued to defend herself. "My mama insists that I attend a musical afternoon with Mrs. Farnley and her son. Really, she's matchmaking, but I cannot go against her wishes. It is my greatest desire to attend Lord Dunstable's funeral. Indeed, as much as I wish the evil perpetrator of the terrible crime was brought to justice."

Lady Victoria, whose expression had become increasingly sympathetic, now raised her eyebrows at Evelina's last words and said, "But have you not heard? Why, I can't believe we've not mentioned the greatest news of all. The police have found the person who has done this terrible thing to poor cousin Dunstable. Finally! And you'd never believe it, but it was a … woman!"

"A woman? A woman killed Lord Dunstable?"

Lady Victoria lowered her eyes and said in a more chastened tone, "I think that is why we were reluctant to speak of it earlier for it is not very … " She broke off, beginning again with, "Well… it reflects not so well on Dunstable, and I didn't want anyone to be hurt or … think worse of him for it. Not that the truth won't be revealed in good time. So, while it hasn't yet appeared in the newspapers, naturally, being family, Clara and I were among the first to know."

Evelina, whose anxiety to learn the truth had ratcheted up to enormous proportions, finally got a word in edge wise. "A woman? Why, what woman could possibly have done such a thing? How, and why?"

"All I know was that it was a woman by the name of ... LuluBelle," Victoria replied.

EVELINA'S SPIRITS enjoyed no upturn as they continued along the curve of the path. Finally, Kitty said, "You can't tarry any longer. Your ma is waiting for you, and you know how she has things to do. She won't like to be kept waiting."

"Why is she always in such a hurry? It's not as if she has anything better to do than see me for the little time I'm in London." Evelina knew she was whining but went on, "Why can't Mama live like other people do? In a nice house with my father? And why can't she bring along Papa so I can see him after so many years? Is he ashamed of me?"

"I really couldn't say, Miss, except that your ma ain't so easy to live with and I reckon it's hardly no surprise she and your da aren't living together anymore."

"How would you know if she's easy or not to live with, Kitty?" grumbled Evelina. "The way you talk, you know everything about my mother."

"I've worked for her, in a manner o' speaking, so I knows what I'm talking about. She an' Lady Perry are an odd pair, that's for sure. I don't reckon I trust that Lady Perry. Thick as thieves, they used to be, but now it's just a useful service they render each other. Lady Perry likes her blunt, and she'd throw you under a hackney for it. Jest mind what she says and does. Reckon you can do that, Miss Tarot?"

❉

AS KITTY HAD PREDICTED, Evelina's mama was pacing their drawing room while Lady Perry took tea in a corner of the room.

"You do not believe in keeping to time, do you, Evelina?"

"I'm sure you don't need to be anywhere in any great hurry, Mama, said Evelina.

Her mother grunted. "You, young lady, have very little time to do what you came to London to do, and that is find a husband."

"And I've told you I've already found one," Evelina said, sinking down onto the sofa and picking up the magazine lying over the arm in front of Lady Perry. *Manners and Morals.* If Lady Perry had been reading it, Evelina didn't think she'd learned very much. Lady Perry was cold to the point of rudeness. What Kitty said was true. She sent Lady Perry a narrow look as the old woman began conversing in a low voice with her mama.

Clearly, they'd both decided that Evelina's tantrum, as her mama would call it, was going to be ignored.

Evelina flipped open a page to a photograph of a pretty young girl dressed in rags. It was some uplifting moral tale about how a poor milliner named Liza had managed to keep a tidy household with some ridiculous number of brothers and sisters. Evelina peered at the two younger sisters who were wearing stylish little hats at odds with their patched pinafores.

Evelina wouldn't mind wearing a hat like either of those. Vaguely, in the background, she heard the name LuluBelle and realized her mama and Lady Perry were talking about the woman who had killed Lord Dunstable.

It was truly shocking that he'd been murdered by a woman, she thought, knowing she ought to feel more considering that a few weeks later and Lord Dunstable's death would have made her a widow. What would she have felt if she'd learned that a woman had been responsible for his death, then? In truth, as each day passed, Lord Dunstable's memory faded even more. One kiss. No, two. A trip to the zoological gardens, a few dances, and that was the sum of their association. He'd never told her he loved her. Certainly he'd admired her, but that had been more a compliment that indicated she reflected well on him, rather than anything deep and sincerely spoken like Lord Bellingham.

Biting her lip as tears sprang to her eyes, Evelina wondered yet again at Lord Bellingham's lack of communication. Dare she sent him round a note?

To hide her tears, she bent over the magazine to peer at the picture of Liza and her family and decided she ought to do the girls a service and buy a couple of hats. They really were very jaunty.

"Good to see you improving yourself by reading an article like that. You should be grateful for the good fortune that you're not living in the gutter like those poor creatures," Lady Perry said. "Instead, you're living in the lap of luxury and Mr. Farnley and his mother are going to take you to a concert tomorrow. Your dear mama can heave a sigh of relief in a few weeks that she has done her duty, and you are off her hands, married to a solid, respectable and worthy husband."

Evelina assumed she did not mean Lord Bellingham, but she was wise enough to remain silent, so she was surprised when her mama asked, "Has Lord Bellingham called or sent round a note, Evelina? I was harsh with you last night and for that, I am sorry. If he truly loves you, then a lack of dowry, of course, will not stand in his way if he should wish to make you his wife."

Evelina jerked her head up. "What do you mean, Mama?

Papa has made very generous provision for me." She sighed, turning to the next page of the magazine. A group of soberly attired, serious looking men stared up at her. Politicians, all of them. Like Bellingham. Or rather, he had political aspirations, though she wasn't certain what that entailed. She'd imagined being his hostess and organizing lavish dinner parties and grand banquets in between appointments with her dressmaker.

"Not as generous as I had been led to believe, my dear," said her mama. "It was the reason Dunstable took issue with your papa over the contract. Not all that was promised was forthcoming. It's one of the reasons I'm so anxious that you are settled this season. I do not think there will be funds for you to enjoy a second season in London."

Evelina dropped the magazine and sat up straight. "What are you saying, Mama? This is the first I've heard of such a thing. Have I offended Papa? How can I please him if he won't see me?" Her throat felt dry as she added, "Did you tell Lord Bellingham this? That my dowry was not as generous as … as before? What did you say? Oh, Mama, tell me this minute!" Twisting in her chair, she looked at her mother, who turned back from speaking to Lady Perry, her expression implacable.

"That is what was conveyed to him, yes. Now, please don't cry, Evelina. Surely you would not have wanted him if his primary motivation in marrying you was your money? Now, at least, you know the reason he has ceased paying you attention—"

Evelina leaped up with a gasp. "You are cruel, Mama!" she whispered, the tears beginning to fall. "Cruel, cruel, cruel! No wonder Papa no longer wished to live with you. No doubt he believes I am just like you. Maybe that is why he won't see me."

CHAPTER 22

After being directed by the housekeeper of Captain Blackheath's home to the small river that ran behind, William found his quarry sitting contemplatively on a rock by the water, a Panama hat upon his head and a cheroot between his teeth.

Blackheath's eyes widened when he saw William.

"Good lord, is this a fortuitous meeting or have you run me to ground?"

"Run you to ground?" William repeated, taking a seat on a nearby rock. "Isn't that what one does when one is chasing quarry that wishes to evade capture?"

Blackheath shrugged. If he had a guilty conscience, it did not show. "It's also the term used if one feels pursued for any reason. You've not come to challenge me with pistols at dawn because I danced three times with that young lady you've been sniffing after?"

"Miss Evelina Tarot?"

"That's the one." Blackheath's mouth turned up as if he were smirking at her name. William wondered what the man knew. If it was true that Dunstable had been blackmailing Madame Chambon over Evelina's parentage, had Blackheath learned the truth? Could he have been blackmailing Dunstable? Had something gone wrong when the two men had come head to head if Blackheath knew what Dunstable knew?

Even if Blackheath had not murdered Dunstable, it was still possible he might have found the same proof that linked Evelina with Madame Chambon, in which case he had no doubt he'd blackmail William. He had to be careful.

"Caught anything?" William nodded at the fishing rod, its line stirred by the wind.

"Not many fish today, I'm afraid. Still, one doesn't fish purely to reap the rewards of one's efforts," replied Blackheath. "Sometimes it's to enjoy the fresh country air when one needs to escape the noise and dirt of a busy metropolis."

"Escape. Yes, we all need to do that from time to time," William agreed. "That poor girl who's been charged with Dunstable's murder isn't going to escape, though. It's the noose for her, I hear."

"Someone's been charged?" Blackheath showed the first sign of concern. "Who?"

"One of the girls at Madame Chambon's. LuluBelle Croft."

"Good God!"

"Know her, do you?" William asked.

"She's a capital lass. She'd not have done it in a thousand years," Blackheath declared, looking rattled. "When did you hear this? I've not read it in the newspapers."

"My valet told me last night. Said one of the servants who lived opposite had seen her being marched away in handcuffs. Apparently, the girls at Madame Chambon's confirmed the story." He hesitated. "It's also drifted into public discourse that you'd been at the house the night of Dunstable's murder and you were heard arguing with Madame Chambon." William chose his words carefully. "As I was passing this way, anyway, I thought I'd let you know."

"The police took all of that testimony down," Blackheath muttered. Agitated, he flicked his fishing rod, saying with energy, "But they can't convict her if they have no evidence."

William shrugged. "They seem to think they have all the evidence they need. Dunstable's family is agitating for a conviction. They've made their disillusionment with the police quite apparent in the newspapers. You can imagine the reaction of a police inspector, under pressure, knowing that his own conduct does not show him in an admirable light since he was visiting that very house the same evening."

"Dunstable's damn family," Blackheath muttered. "That Miss Victoria has a reputation for being a troublesome female. Never satisfied!"

"You know Miss Victoria?"

Blackheath smirked. "She was once as young and foolish as that sister of hers. At least, she must have been to have fallen for her cousin, Dunstable, who seemed to find it amusing to toy with her feelings. I wonder if she wasn't angling for a rich husband, though, and that it was all an act."

"How do you know so much?" asked William.

"We ran in the same circles, Dunstable and I. And I observed Lady Victoria. But then she inherited a fortune from her aunt, who stipulated that Dunstable keep it in trust until the young lady turned twenty-five. However, he began using it as if it were his own." With a sudden noise of excitement, Blackheath began to reel in his fishing line. "Got something! Patience rewarded!"

Impatiently, William waited as his companion slit the fish's throat before tossing it into an empty bucket. Finally,

Blackheath looked up, his expression surprised. "Still here, are you? You know I've nothing to offer you for dinner, Bellingham. Or any other information you think I might be able to supply you. Sorry, old chap."

CHAPTER 23

The weather was inclement the following morning.

Evelina buried her head in her pillow while the rain beat against the windowpane and her spirits visited the darkest places they'd ever been. There had been no contact from Bellingham for three days and now Evelina's mother had indicated that her father had reneged on funding her beyond the next few weeks.

And Dunstable was dead.

Murdered.

The horror of it seemed suddenly far worse than it ever had.

And Evelina seemed far more alone.

Sometime, long after the sun had risen, Kitty put her head around the door to chivvy her into wakefulness. "You're not sick are you, Miss?" she asked, coming into the room with a tray of tea. "Up with you now. It's going to be midday soon."

"And what do I have to look forward to?" Evelina said, not even opening her eyes. "Lord Dunstable is dead and Mama refuses to let me even attend his funeral. And the man I love has forsaken me. And I have no friends."

Kitty clicked her tongue. "And if you keep up that tone, you will have no friends. Lordy, Miss, I've never seen you like this and it ain't pretty. You remind me of some of my girls when they've had a bad evening and don't have the stomach to go on. Believe me, if you only knew what an easy life you have compared with some o' them things my poor girls have gone through, you'd not be acting like Misery Muggins."

Evelina rolled onto her back to send Kitty a baleful look. "Which of your girls made the grandest match? If you want to make me feel better, tell me I have hope, for right now I have none. Mama told Lord Bellingham Papa has reneged on providing me with the handsome dowry that had been the reason Lord Bellingham wanted to marry me, and now that he knows I have nothing, he has abandoned me."

Kitty made a sound of indignation. "Your mama is the queen of manipulation and will make a girl think anything to get her way. Don't you go believing her over Lord Bellingham. I saw the way he looked at you, and that was definitely like a man in love. Chances are that your mama, or Lady Perry, is keeping his letters from you and that he has a very good reason for going away for a few days but thinks your heart is easy because you knows he loves yer."

Evelina gasped as she bolted upright in bed. "Do you really think that could be true, Kitty?" she cried. "Have you seen any letters from him?"

"Course I haven't else I'd a brought them to you. But Lady Perry and your mama are mighty crafty. They'd a made sure I didn't see any letter wot they don't want you to see."

Feeling far more sanguine than before, Evelina sipped her tea. "Do you really think my mama would do such a terrible thing? How do you know so much about my mama, Kitty?"

"I just do, Miss Evelina. And I worked for many young ladies who were just as sad as you one day, and then the very next, found a man wot made them very happy." Smiling, Kitty patted Evelina's shoulder. "Just like you will be. Your Lord Bellingham is the one for you. I feel it in my bones."

Evelina felt the warmth of her touch as it flooded her with reassurance that all really would be all right.

And when Mary the parlor maid knocked a few hours later to say she had a visitor, Evelina thought her heart would burst with happiness. How much greater was the sweetness of joy when it followed the depths of despair?

But it wasn't Lord Bellingham. However, having gone to pains with her appearance, she did feel much better as she sat in the drawing room across from Lady Victoria and Clara, who had been out walking and who'd decided to look in on her.

Just as if they were old friends.

Evelina hadn't enjoyed intimacy in any of her friendships at the convent school, and her time in London had been brief, but now she experienced a real blossoming in her heart at their concern when she confessed she'd had the blue devils and had only got out of bed just for them.

"When I'm a proper adult, I'm going to indulge in the blue devils whenever my heart is broken," said Clara, daintily picking up a biscuit that had been served with their tea. "Victoria is so bossy, she never lets me be sad for even a moment. Not even when Dunstable died."

"Why, Clara, we are in mourning now and we shed ever so many tears at the terrible news," said Victoria. "You make me out to be a tartar with no heart!"

Clara shrugged. "Well, considering you declared once that Dunstable had broken your heart and it would never recover, I would say your heart is more robust than mine, or Evelina's... or most people's," Clara said between mouthfuls.

"I hadn't realized you and Dunstable once ... had an

understanding," Evelina said, feeling a little awkward as she remembered her fair-weather attitude towards their cousin.

"Oh, I grew up remembering how Victoria said—for years and years—that she and Dunstable were going to wed," Clara replied. "Mama said it, too. But then they had a terrible fight and Victoria said she'd never speak to Dunstable again."

Evelina was surprised that Clara continued her monologue given the dark looks her sister was giving her, though surprisingly, she didn't interrupt after an initial futile attempt but merely looked as if her heart was breaking all over again.

Which made Evelina feel even worse for the way she must have appeared to Victoria at their first meeting at the zoological gardens—goodness barely ten days ago!—clinging to Dunstable's arm with Dunstable all but indicating that he and Evelina were going to make a match.

At the time, that's what Evelina had thought she'd wanted.

"But you made up, and that's what's important," Evelina murmured, thinking now of the fight she'd had with her mama and supposing that some volatile personalities would inevitably clash and make up. Surely her mama wouldn't completely abandon her, and her papa wouldn't leave her without a penny?

Fear once more clawed up her gullet.

Was that the reason for Bellingham's silence?

Or, was her mama lying, and Kitty's suggestion more on the mark and Bellingham had in fact sent her an explanation as to his absence which she hadn't received?

"Yes, we are cousins, and blood is thicker than water," said Victoria, adding more briskly, "But now, we didn't come to talk about that but in fact, to ask you to come to Dunstable's funeral." She sent Evelina a long, level look before adding—just as Evelina began to demur—"Lord Bellingham will be there."

Evelina, who'd started to say that she couldn't possibly defy her mama, who had refused to countenance it, was left with her mouth open and no words.

Victoria and Clara had paid her a visit in order to provide her with the means of seeing Bellingham when Evelina had begun to despair as to when she'd next encounter him?

When she saw the secretive little smile playing about Clara's lips, she burst out, "What wonderful friends you are! I don't know how to thank you—"

"For asking you to our cousin's funeral?" Victoria raised her eyebrows. "You would like to come, then?"

"My mama refused me permission. She wants me to go to a concert with another gentleman but I don't want to."

Biting her lip and looking doubtful, Victoria said, "I daresay it's wrong to defy your mama but I do think it's unreasonable of her to prevent you from showing your respect for a man you—Well, you and my cousin were once very good friends, and I saw how taken he was with you on the dance floor and at the zoological gardens but I admired you for remaining in charity with him after you learned that Dunstable had a dark side so it was a lucky escape for you however—"

"A dark side?" Evelina interrupted her.

"Oh, I thought that's why you rejected him?"

"I...I didn't reject him," Evelina said, realizing too late that now was perhaps a good time to have said nothing if only to perpetuate Victoria's perception, for of course Evelina was inevitably cast into a bad light. She was trying to formulate a way back when Victoria said, with a frown, "So you were engaged to Dunstable when he was killed?"

"No...no!" Evelina shook her head with some energy while Clara leaned in, her eyes large with interest. "I mean, yes, Lord Dunstable had asked me to be his wife and said he planned a grand wedding but then he wasn't happy with the contract my papa was proposing over my dowry and so Dunstable said we'd marry quietly without anyone knowing." Evelina felt herself shrink inside. Why was she telling Victoria this? It was supposed to have been a secret from everybody. "I couldn't understand it and—"

"Dunstable's dark side emerging," Victoria interrupted with a glower, appearing to accept Evelina's words as a valid reason for not having an obligation towards her cousin. "Dunstable said he would look after Clara and me when our mama died, leaving us orphans and with me still with two years before I attained my majority. Then my aunt left me a fortune, charging Dunstable with keeping it in trust until I was twenty-five. Dunstable was our closest male relative, you see." Her forehead furrowed, and she glanced at Clara, whose eyes were like saucers. Victoria put her hand on her sister's and said, "You've not heard it before, but you are nearly grown enough, so you might as well have the explanation now. I learned that Dunstable was spending our money, Clara. Money that our aunt had left us. And he was doing so in the most reprehensible way."

Clara gasped, her shock echoing what Evelina felt as Victoria reddened when Clara demanded an example and her sister whispered savagely, "Gambling and on...on other... females." She put her hands to her face and hunched her shoulders, whispering, "God forgive me for what I'd vowed to keep from your innocent ears forever. But until I learned of this, I truly did want to marry Cousin Dunstable. His betrayal hardened my heart. I vowed never to forgive him."

"But you did," Clara whispered.

"How?" whispered Evelina.

"How did I forgive him?" Victoria asked with a frown.

"How did you manage to salvage your fortune if Dunstable was spending it?" Evelina was feeling more justified by the moment when just minutes earlier, she'd felt guilty of a great betrayal.

"I sought legal advice." Victoria smiled for the first time, and Evelina thought she deserved to feel as proud as she did. Why, a woman...barely more than a young girl, in fact, had had the courage to seek redress for wrongs against her?

"I didn't think that was possible," Evelina said, awed. "You're a female. You can't manage your finances. And Dunstable is your closest male relative. The law is on his side."

"Not when he was contravening the final wishes of our aunt. Mr. Grimshaw was quite in agreement with me on that." She pushed back her shoulders and looked about to rise, but Evelina had questions of her own for a sudden idea had occurred to her.

"So, you understood what was in your aunt's will? Your lawyer explained it to you and then told you when your cousin was ... going against your aunt's wishes ... and then offered to help you?"

"He wasn't my lawyer. No, my lawyer was Dunstable's lawyer, of course—being family— and he was most definitely not a good man. But the lawyer who helped me was the lawyer of our friend, Elizabeth Craddock's papa, and our conversation came about quite by chance which, I suppose, is how so many fortunate things happen in life."

"I can't believe you and Dunstable remained friends after that," Evelina marveled.

A shadow crossed Victoria's face. "I felt I had to make a concession if we weren't to live in a state of enmity. Believe me, Dunstable makes a formidable enemy. He is devious and cruel and... well, I was frightened of him so after Mr. Grimshaw had legally secured Clara's and my fortune so that Dunstable couldn't fritter it away, I gave Dunstable some information about a certain young lady that he'd been wanting for a long time—"

"Miss Evelina! There you are! I thought you were in your bedchamber, still glowering at the ceiling." Kitty's cheerful face appeared round the door. "I just spied your mama's carriage drawing up and thought to warn you, for she doesn't like lie-abeds and she certainly doesn't like misery mugwumps like you've been."

"Well, my heart is less broken than it was this morning, Kitty, since I can believe that I haven't been forsaken. Certainly not by my friends." Beaming at Victoria and Clara as they all rose, she accompanied them to the door, lowering her voice to say hurriedly, "I'll try my best to see you at Dunstable's funeral though I truly don't know how I'll get there with Mama so opposed."

Clara gripped Evelina's wrist, her expression knowing. "We'll stop by in our carriage on the way. In the side lane at midday? And we won't tell your mama, we promise."

And then the door burst open and Mrs. Tarot's statuesque form appeared in the doorway as the two girls offered respectful bobs, saying they were just leaving after paying a call upon Evelina.

Evelina watched them disappear down the garden path as she summoned a dutiful smile for her mama while feeling immensely bolstered by the conversation she'd just had.

Victoria's resourcefulness had given Evelina the courage that she, too, could assert her will without cutting family ties. Somehow, she would discover a way to speak with her father so she could learn the terms of the financial arrangement he'd made to safeguard her future.

Or she'd find a lawyer.

CHAPTER 24

Throw baby's crying, my love."

Lily, who had been staring out across the fields and insensible to anything but her own thoughts, jerked into awareness and bent to stroke the head of the grizzling infant she was pushing in his perambulator along a path by the water's edge.

Hamish gave her shoulders a brief squeeze. "My dear, I hoped that proposing this walk would take your mind off matters, but it seems to have had the opposite effect."

Lily sniffed and bent to pick up the child, although it had settled.

Unlike her own thoughts.

"How can I think of anything other than a terrible miscarriage of justice, Hamish? You, of all people, hate injustice. And I knew LuLubelle better than most, though I know you hate me to mention anything pertaining to—" She broke off, aware she was being unfair. Hamish never reproached her for anything pertaining to her past. With a sigh, she went on, "I saw her every day for months. Fate dealt her a cruel blow when she was sent from the workhouse to a household that exploited and abused her. But she'd kept her brothers and sisters together through the money she earned at Madame Chambon's. And now she's been accused of Lord Dunstable's murder. Charged with his murder. Wrongfully."

"Can you be entirely certain of that, my dear?" Hamish looked quizzically at her. "Of course, you'd champion a friend, but the police must surely have the evidence to back up anything so serious as a murder charge. She may have done it in self-defense and that could save her from the gallows."

Lily shook her head. "LuluBelle doesn't have a temper. She's pliant and yielding and she's been beaten plenty of times without ever raising a finger to defend herself. Believe me, I know."

Hamish squeezed her shoulders again before holding Sebastian in his arms. "Perhaps you could explain to LuLubelle that she'll get a more lenient sentence if she at least confesses with the mitigating circumstances being self-defense?"

His words raised her ire. "Hamish, you may think girls like LuluBelle have no pride or lack morals but that is exactly the reason behind her unyielding attitude," said Lily. "She'll never ever admit to something she didn't do. Even if it'll save her life. If I know LuluBelle, she'd rather die than confess to having murdered Lord Dunstable when she didn't."

"And you don't think Madame Chambon did it?"

Lily shook her head. "I do not."

Hamish gave a frustrated sigh as he began to rock Sebastian who'd started whimpering. "My darling, you are not a detective or a policeman and nor were you at Madame Chambon's the night of the murder. Please be realistic and accept that you cannot do anything to help LuluBelle if the police have charged her with a murder to which she refuses to confess. Clearly, they've interviewed her at length and are satisfied she did it. They would not send an innocent woman to the gallows without compelling evidence, I am sure."

Lily narrowed her eyes. "I have no doubt they would if it made life easier to satisfy the demands of the victim's grieving family to make a conviction quickly and when the person convicted is already morally corrupt as a fallen woman. Why, Hamish, I can't believe—"

"My darling, I think you should lower your voice. People are looking at you. And now I see Lord Bellingham coming this way though I'm not sure if—"

"Why, Mr. McTavish!" Lord Bellingham raised his head at the very moment Lily glanced about her at her husband's exhortation and saw that Bellingham looked as startled as if he'd just been pulled from a reverie as deep as Lily's a few moments earlier.

Lily forced a smile. She had no wish to engage in conversation with Lord Bellingham given the clandestine—no, repugnant--nature of their last meeting. If he mentioned to Hamish that he'd seen Lily in disguise or had gone with her to Madame Chambon's, Hamish would be... well, if not condemnatory, then at least concerned, and disappointed.

Naturally, good manners required Lord Bellingham to stop and pass the time of the day for at least a moment or two since they were the only people gazing at the waters of the pond in the middle of the deserted park.

Hamish tried to jolly the mood, perhaps having been cast down by Lily's low spirits. But clearly, Lord Bellingham was as downcast as Lily had been.

"No doubt you've heard there's been a conviction," her husband said. Most unhelpfully, as far as Lily was concerned.

Lord Bellingham nodded. Evasively—Lily thought—he said, "Yes, a woman by the name of Lulubelle. Not that I believe it," he said. "Why, she—" He broke off suddenly, glanced with confusion at Lily then, fortunately perceiving that they both had a vested interest in keeping their visit to Madame Chambon's from Hamish, said weakly, "Who'd have thought a young girl would have the strength to overpower a man like Dunstable? I hope the police have got the right person."

"I'm sure they've exercised their due diligence," said Hamish. "And I trust you are keeping well, Lord Bellingham?" Though everything about Bellingham was lacklustre, Lily was concerned to note. The shadows beneath his eyes. The tightness to his mouth.

"As well as can be under the circumstances." He looked between Lily and her husband. "You have both done your best to dissuade me of my desire to wed a certain young lady, but you have not succeeded."

Discomfited by the accusation in his tone, she turned to Hamish, whose look was baleful. He'd simply done what Lily had asked of him.

"I…I am sorry if you are angry, Lord Bellingham," Lily said softly. "I had no intention of interfering…in matters of the heart. I just… assumed that it was best you knew—"

"Because you thought I was inconstant enough that I'd cry off the moment there was a sniff of scandal?"

Lily tried to deflect his ire. "You said you intended to discover… her parentage?" She sent a rather desperate glance at Hamish, who was jiggling the baby that had begun to stir. "Have you had any success?"

"None whatsoever." His answer was short.

"Then what do you intend to do?"

Lord Bellingham sent a glance about him, set his mouth, then said grimly, "The only thing I can do, under the circumstances."

"Surely you don't mean to elope, my lord?" Lily gasped.

"If it's the only way for us to be together, then yes. I've just returned from a wild goose chase to Norfolk and back. I truly believed I had located the fellow who could set my mind at rest, or at least supply me with answers."

"And what does Miss Tarot think of all this?" Hamish asked with a frown.

"I hope I'll find a positive answer to my letters when I get back to my townhouse. And I'm only telling you this because it was you who were so determined that I drop my suit. Well, you only succeeded in galvanizing me into action. The police have charged the wrong person, and I'm sorry for it. A woman did not kill Lord Dunstable."

"Then, who do suppose might have, my lord?" Hamish asked mildly.

Lord Bellingham considered the question, then shrugged his shoulders. "I've learned of a fellow who was at the same house Dunstable attended the night of the murder. This man has not been interviewed and it seems that the proprietor is reluctant that he is." He sent Lily a long level look, before adding, "Unfortunately, the only clue as to his identity could be that he carries an intricately carved cane. Apparently two entwined snakes."

"Half of London's gentlemen indulge in such fancies," murmured Hamish. "Why, my cane is also intricately carved."

"With two snakes?" asked Lord Bellingham and Hamish shook his head.

"Then I shall question you no further," Lord Bellingham said with a small smile. "Good day to you."

Lily tucked her hand into the crook of her husband's arm as they watched him depart, Hamish murmuring, "Poor fellow has taken this matter of the heart very hard."

"It's more than just a matter of the heart," said Lily, feeling an even greater clutch of alarm as the young man disappeared around a corner. "It's a matter of life and death." She chewed on her knuckles.

And then the baby began to cry.

CHAPTER 25

T he day of the funeral dawned dark and foreboding, but weak sunlight pierced the storm clouds by midday.

Evelina just hoped her mama did not choose this morning to make one of her unannounced calls.

She'd planned to escape the house with no one the wiser, but decided she'd have to make an ally of Kitty, who could provide excuses on her behalf if Lady Perry or her mother asked after her.

"They're to think I'm ill in bed and that you've made me a sleeping draught, Kitty. Will you tell them that if they ask?" Evelina had just stepped into a stylish mourning gown that she'd had made for her in Paris. Really, she'd covered all contingencies, and she'd not blinked an eyelid at the expense because her father had been so generous.

It's why she'd anticipated that he'd waste no time in seeing her once she established herself in London. And why his abandonment of her felt so painful.

Though not as painful as Lord Bellingham's. Four days and she'd not heard a word from him.

She was afraid of seeing him at the funeral and having her worst fears confirmed, but wondered if his absence would be a greater trial to bear.

Really, she'd never felt like she had during the past ten days. Her emotions had been skittering all over the place, first in relief that she no longer was bound to Dunstable—with the inevitable guilt, of course—followed by the joys of feeling her heart soar, while her pulse quickened at the mere mention or even thought of William.

And then his kisses had transported her to a place she'd never experienced.

If this was what love felt like, then she'd do anything for a return of that euphoric sense of being at one with another human being.

If she only got the chance.

"Are you sure this is a good idea, Miss?" Kitty asked as she tidied the room. "Defying your mama, I mean?" Lowering her voice, she said under her breath, "I've seen other girls do the same thing and it ain't never gone well."

Evelina, though puzzled by her words, ignored them. Kitty was only trying to make her rethink the idea of leaving the house when Evelina had decided that if there was any possibility William was going to be at Dunstable's funeral, then she simply had to be there, too.

"How do I look?"

"Like a young lady dressed for a funeral with no mournful thoughts about the poor murdered man about to be laid to rest, but lots of hopes for a handsome young man who still walks the earth."

Evelina smiled. "My William will be there, and he will say what I've been waiting for him to say. He's only biding his time because it doesn't seem quite right to do it before poor Lord Dunstable is... in the ground," she finished. "At least they found Dunstable's murderer. Now everyone can sleep better, and Lady Victoria can rest easy."

"Cept it weren't the right murderer," Kitty said darkly, causing Evelina to shake her head as she passed her on the way to the door.

"I didn't know you were on the investigation team," Evelina said with a fair degree of sarcasm.

"You know I weren't, but I do know the young girl wot were 'sposed to do it and she wouldn't hurt a fly, much less a man like Dunstable. Nah, the police just found it was easier to charge a fallen woman for a crime wot was done by a man."

Evelina, who had been about to let herself out, turned in surprise. "A fallen woman? You do say the strangest things, Kitty? Do you even know what a fallen woman is? Why, if you'd heard how the nuns described that kind of creature, you'd know you were not applying the term correctly." She glanced across the room to the window. Lady Victoria's carriage was there, so she raised her hand in farewell without waiting for Kitty to reply. Clearly, the girl did not like being put in her place. Her mouth was turned down, her lips buttoned tightly with none of her usual cheer.

"Aren't you going to wish me well?" Evelina asked, her spirits too high to be contained.

"You're going to a funeral, Miss," Kitty reminded her, adding under her breath. "Of the man you was going to be marrying two weeks ago."

Evelina paused. She wanted to march right across the room, put her hand on Kitty's shoulder, and ask her if everything they'd heard of Lord Dunstable's character, in the past two weeks, made him a better husband than Lord Bellingham. Instead, she said, "Kitty, I'm sorry if my behavior upsets you. I don't mean to be heartless. I'm very sorry Lord Dunstable lost his life in such a horrible way, but he did so over a woman. A woman who has now—thankfully—been apprehended. Does that not prove he was likely to make the worst sort of husband and that I'm so lucky to have found a man who is deserving and true?" But, because Kitty's good opinion meant more to her than even her mother's, strangely enough, she did, in fact, cross the room to put her hand on the girl's shoulder.

"I'm sure you're right, Miss," Kitty responded sullenly, but Evelina shook her head.

"No, Kitty, I'm not always right, and you've seen a great deal more of the world than I have. Tell me if you think I'm foolishly losing my head over a worthless man? Or do you think Lord Bellingham is good and true and will make me happy? I want to know what you think. It's important to me."

"It is?" Kitty's head jerked up, and she blinked as if clearing something from her eye. Then she smiled and briefly rested her own hand on Evelina's forearm. "Of all gentlemen I've met, I would choose Lord Bellingham as a husband worthy of you, Miss. He is kind and honorable and brave and I wish you well. My apologies for being a sour puss. I was just aggrieved that the police have charged the wrong person for Dunstable's murder seein' as I knows her. Now, no time for goin' into all that. You go to your funeral and rest assured I'll say all them things to your mama and Lady Perry so's they won't smell a rat." Her smile broadened. "And I hope Lord Bellingham will live up to all them things I jest said about him."

CHAPTER 26

S t Michael's Church, in the heart of the village of Highgate, was a fitting final resting place for an aristocrat.

As Evelina gazed up with awe at its pointed arches, ornate tracery, and decorative stonework, she felt as small and insignificant as the gargoyles grinning down at her from the eaves.

Inside the vast and awe-inspiring interior, flanked by Clara and Lady Victoria, she stared at Lord Dunstable's casket, draped in a rich velvet pall, placed before the altar, surrounded by floral arrangements and candlelight.

As the mournful proceedings began, sunlight streamed through the stained-glass windows, casting ethereal hues of vibrant colors onto the polished marble floors while the minister, dressed in traditional vestments, presided over the service, offering prayers, reading scripture, and delivering his eulogy to commemorate Lord Dunstable's life and legacy.

Evelina hoped her few dances with Lord Dunstable had not aroused suspicions that something as serious as marriage was in the offing.

She was here simply as Miss Tarot, a newcomer with a rich papa whom no one had heard of, recently returned to the capital after being educated in France.

She hoped her presence would not arouse undue interest.

Her interest, of course, was in trying to locate William amongst the congregation.

And to her astonishment, there he was in the pew in front and a little to the right of her, bathed in the soft light of one of the enormous stained-glass windows depicting biblical scenes, which cast colorful rays of light on the pews and the polished marble floors.

He seemed to sense her gaze, for he turned slightly and, catching her eye, smiled; and Evelina smiled back, breathing in the fragrant scent of roses, lilies and other blooms of the magnificent floral arrangements amidst the flickering candlelight while her heartbeat quickened with excitement. Kitty surely must have been right, or he'd not be smiling at her like that.

Finally, the service came to an end, and the casket was carried down the aisle by eight pallbearers.

The three young women joined the slow and solemn procession that stopped as it reached a horse-drawn hearse, and as Evelina bowed her head, she felt the gentle squeeze of her hand and glanced up with a shy smile at Lord Bellingham.

"Did you get my letters?" he asked her softly, the press of such a large crowd offering them the privacy they needed to speak without being overheard.

"No." She shook her head. "I thought you'd forsaken me."

"Never!" He was shocked as he reached for her hand once more. "I had important matters to attend to."

"Clearly more important than me," replied Evelina with a smile to ameliorate the implied censure. But her heart danced with happiness. Kitty had been right. Either her mama or Lady Perry had kept his letters from her.

"Important because they pertained to you and any ... impediments there might be to a marriage between us." William dipped his head, pretending to consult his Order of Service. His voice was low and impassioned. "There are difficulties, Evelina, that you are not aware of, and I wish I could whisk you away this moment."

YES, she knew. Her father was creating difficulties with regard to her dowry, but she wasn't going to tell William she suspected that was because there was something about William of which her father likely disapproved.

"I am navigating my way through certain obstacles, some of which you know about, but some of which you are ignorant. I don't want to alarm you, but if you do not see me for a few days, I want to spare you the soul-searching. My darling, none of this can't be overcome—"

"Is my father refusing to release my dowry?" Fretfully, she gazed at him. "Is there some long-standing enmity between your family and mine that I don't know about? William, for four days I've believed the worst—"

"That I don't love you? Well, that would be the worst, but the fact is, I love you more than life itself. I don't care what obstacles stand in the way of spending the rest of my life with you, Evelina. But it requires a certain delicacy."

Evelina bowed her head. Did the man she loved harbor some dark secret that he was unwilling to reveal to her?

Well, whatever it was, it didn't matter. As long as William loved her, Evelina could live with it.

"You have to go away again?" she asked. "To... to see my father?"

He nodded.

"Then let me come too. I haven't seen my father since I was a baby," she whispered. "He wrote to me in the early years when I was at school. I treasure those letters. But then he stopped, though his generosity never stopped. It made the other girls jealous. Oh, William, please don't go away again."

They'd now reached Highgate Cemetery, the procession following the hearse as it entered the imposing iron gates.

William smiled down at her. "It won't be for more than a day. Two at the most. Bear up, my darling girl. Just a little more patience is all that's needed." He squeezed her hand again. "Trust me, Evelina. I will make everything all right." He clenched his jaw, adding, "And I will find out what happened to my letters."

The mourners had gathered about the casket as it was carefully lowered into the ground with the help of a couple of gravediggers. Prayers were said, the final words of farewell spoken, and as the earth was shoveled onto the casket, Evelina raised her head to see William, but then the crowd surged forward and she was separated from him, and from the two girls.

Slightly panicked, she twisted her head, reassured when she identified Lady Victoria and Clara in the crowd. She began to push her way closer to them, head bowed, arriving beneath the elm tree at the place she'd last seen them. But they'd gone. And, with black bonnets, veils, and top hats everywhere, amidst a sea of mourning, she now could find neither the young ladies nor William.

The crowd began to disperse. Evelina remained where she was, searching her surroundings, listening to the neighs of the nearby horses waiting to bear the carriages back to town, shafts and leather creaking, and the cry of a flock of birds overhead, the soft murmurings of the remaining stragglers.

But she did not recognize a soul.

The last of the mourners were beginning to disperse now, leaving the freshly-dug grave in small groups.

Evelina hung back and watched the gravediggers at their work, the thud of soil hitting the top of the casket sounding like a series of physical blows. Their faces were dirt-streaked and there was something crow-like about their stance as they set to their hard labor in their ragged clothes.

She didn't want to stay here, near these men. They frightened her, and so did her aloneness.

But if she remained by the grave, she would be reclaimed. Lady Victoria and Clara would not forsake her.

William certainly wouldn't. His doubts suggested by his words were troubling, yet his overriding sentiment—of loyalty—warmed her heart.

Patience, he had told her. Well, Evelina had patience in abundance. One didn't survive fourteen years of schooling, most of it in a convent, if one couldn't subsume one's hopes and desires.

But when the mourners became mere specks in the distance, Evelina's patience drained away, and a terrible fear gripped her.

Where were Clara and Lady Victoria? Had they somehow believed Evelina had made an arrangement to return home with someone else?

And how could William have left her like this only moments after declaring his undying devotion?

Dark clouds covered the sun as Evelina finally came to the dreadful conclusion that due to some miscommunication, she was going to have to find her own way home.

With trembling hands, she sought inside her reticule for a few coins that would pay for a hackney cab, but her grasping fingers withdrew only a small lace handkerchief, her dancing card, and a pencil.

"I beg your pardon, Miss, but may I offer you assistance?"

A carriage navigating the rutted road nearby had halted and a middle-aged gentleman with mutton-chop whiskers had put his head out of the window.

Evelina, shaking with cold and anxiety, took a step closer. Her mouth was dry with fear, but she nodded, saying, "I believe my friends thought I'd gone home with someone else and they've left me. Everyone has gone."

Looking concerned, he pushed opened the carriage door and stepped outside. "Mr. Grimshaw," he introduced himself, formally, offering his hand. "Who are your friends... Miss?" He looked enquiringly at her. "Perhaps I know them. London is not such a large place, after all."

Evelina was reassured by his smile. "Lady Victoria and her sister, Miss Clara Jennings. I am their friend, Miss Evelina Tarot."

His lips pressed tight. Evelina registered the shock on his face before his smile returned. "Why, I know Lady Victoria well," he said. "I have advised her on various legal matters, in fact. Won't you step into the carriage, and I will take you to wherever you need to go?"

Evelina clapped her hands. "Indeed, Lady Victoria has spoken to me of you. Mr. Grimshaw, you said your name was?" Then, at his nod as he helped her into the carriage. "She said your assistance was invaluable when she needed help with her financial affairs after—" She stopped suddenly, glancing through the window at the grave of the very man whom Lady Victoria had found vexatious enough to want to employ the services of a lawyer.

Mr. Grimshaw seemed to follow her train of thought.

"Lady Victoria is the late Lord Dunstable's second cousin, that is correct. I gather she has made a confidante of you."

Evelina sat back against the squabs, smiling at him in the gloom of the carriage as the door closed.

"Why, Mr. Grimshaw, this is almost like Divine Providence," she declared. "I had wanted to speak to you—"

"To me?"

She thought she heard a note of alarm in his voice and went on quickly, "My friend Lady Victoria told me that you'd helped insure her affairs from interference in order for her to reach her twenty-fifth birthday which is the date she could manage her own financial affairs. As I am experiencing difficulties with my own, with regard to my father's financial provisioning, I was inspired by Lady Victoria to seek out a... a man of law, but didn't know where to start. And now you have appeared, and I can ask you for help. In a purely professional capacity, of course." When he continued to stare at her, Evelina added with more urgency, "For which I'd pay you, of course."

"Of course." Mr. Grimshaw's dark eyes studied her. He scratched his grizzled gray head. "I don't know how I might do this if I don't know the details of your ... difficulties. But, by all means, there is no time like the present. Do begin."

The surge of hope Evelina had felt when the carriage stopped to assist her flowered into something greater.

But then she hesitated. "You've been kind enough as it is, Mr. Grimshaw, to offer to take me home. I'm not sure I should take further advantage by asking you matters for which you would charge a fee. Not when I am unable to pay it until I have access to my finances."

"My dear Miss Tarot, I am more than happy to dispense free advice for the duration of our carriage ride."

Evelina realized that the carriage had not yet begun its journey, for the horses were standing idle. But at Mr. Grimshaw's encouraging look, she settled herself more comfortably and said, "It's about my dowry. Or rather, finding out there has been a change in the terms of my dowry. I'm not quite sure how to explain it, Mr. Grimshaw, but I know my father has settled a substantial sum upon me, except that it now appears that the original sum promised is being denied to the gentleman who wishes to marry me. At least, that is what I think is the difficulty. I really do not know."

"Can you not ask your father?"

Feeling ashamed, Evelina looked down. "I have not seen my father since I was a baby. Nor do I know how to contact him. But perhaps..." She looked hopefully at him. "Perhaps you, being a lawyer, might seek him out and ask him these questions. I would pay you, as I said. Once I have access to my funds. Please don't think I'd ask you to do this for nothing."

When he looked doubtful, she went on quickly, "Lady Victoria said your assistance changed the course of her life, giving her the independence she needed to look after her sister. I need to find out what the difficulty is regarding the financial contract that my father has made in relation to my future marriage."

"And is there someone in particular you wish to marry? Is this why you are so concerned?"

Evelina toyed with her reticule before answering. "He's a gentleman of some standing. A politician."

"So, you have come to London looking to make a fine marriage, but the gala and fanfare is being denied you because your future husband has found that your father is not so forthcoming as you'd expected when it comes to what you'd thought he was prepared to settle upon you?"

Evelina frowned. "The man I wish to marry is not so concerned with my fortune. He says he will marry me, regardless. But...I am concerned, and I wish I could speak to my father about it."

"Perhaps your father does not approve of the gentleman you wish to marry."

"I cannot imagine that being so. And if he was, why has he not sought me out to speak of it with me, face to face?" She sighed. "I speak rhetorically, of course."

"You speak, rhetorically, Miss Tarot, but in fact, in a quite extraordinary twist of fate, I act for your father. I did not realize it when I first heard your name. But your father is a man of considerable wealth. I can only imagine the matter of your dowry has been neglected due to nothing more than a simple oversight, and the fact he has been for some time abroad. I am sure he has no idea this has been a source of concern."

Evelina gasped. "You act for my father! Then you can tell me where to find him. Is he still in Aberdeenshire? Why, I feel my mother has kept so much from me! Mr. Grimshaw, I can't tell you how much this means to me."

His smile was tinged with sadness. "My poor Miss Tarot. You make yourself out to be friendless and abandoned."

"I feel it, right at this moment."

"And why is that?"

Suddenly, Evelina did feel very forlorn and alone, despite William's bolstering words in the church. But where was he now? And Clara and Lady Victoria? "I've spent most of my life in Paris, but now that I'm here, my mama does not have me to live with her and now my … well, the man who wishes to marry me has gone away for a few days."

"Gone away? Where, Miss Tarot?"

"He's gone to search for my father to ask for his blessing."

Mr. Grimshaw was very still. "Did he tell you where he'd gone?"

Evelina shook her head. "I don't think he knows where to look. But if he'd only not thought I was returning home with someone else and left in other company, he might be with me here and have been in a position to find out the information he is seeking right here! This is good fortune indeed, Mr. Grimshaw. Goodness, I have so many questions to ask you."

"Yes, good fortune indeed. And I'd be very happy to answer your questions. You must be very curious about your family. About your father." He leaned forward, frowning as he tapped his foot on the carriage floor. "In fact, we could do worse than begin setting that to rights, right here."

"Right here?" Puzzled, Evelina put her head on one side.

"Your father's side of the family is all interred in this very cemetery. I could show you your grandparents, your aunts. All your forebears, in fact. I can't believe no one has told you this."

"Mr. Grimshaw, I had no idea I had any other relatives! My mother has told me nothing. And neither has my father. I cannot understand why not, though I suppose it's because they—Well, never mind," she finished abruptly. "I would love to see the family crypt."

Excitement skittered through her veins.

Mr. Grimshaw leaned out of the window to give directions to the coachman before ducking his head back inside. "Well, Miss Tarot," he said, "let us waste no time. I will show you where you belong."

CHAPTER 27

Relief surged through William at the clear delight he'd seen radiating in Evelina's face when she'd unexpectedly beheld him in the church.

No one would look at him like that unless they were clearly in love.

For a moment, he was persuaded to drop everything and simply accept matters as they were. After all, Evelina's love, and their shared future together, would still be possible if William simply whisked her away—eloped—and only returned at a judicious moment when there were other matters to distract the gossips.

If William was happy to accept Evelina as she was, then why twist himself in knots trying to discover the identity of her father?

Or trying to make sense of Dunstable's murder?

But then he thought of LuluBelle.

How could he, in good conscience, refrain from over-turning every stone possible in his attempts to prove her innocent of Dunstable's murder.

The police had not interviewed the one man quite possibly responsible.

A man who owned a walking stick intricately carved with intertwining snakes.

Still, he had done everything he could in that respect.

So, when Evelina had unclasped her hand from his so she could make the requisite mark of respect as she bowed her head during the final words said over Dunstable's casket as it was lowered into the ground, William decided that after a final visit to the police inspector. He needed to furnish him with his suspicions. He'd visit Evelina in the morning and together they'd make secret plans to elope.

One look at her shining face told him she'd accept him.

And wasn't that simply his ultimate objective? He didn't need her money.

He just wanted her love.

Then a chill wind had picked up, sweeping across the cemetery, carrying along with it the icy droplets of water that clung to the branches.

The mourners had shifted position as the gravediggers began their work, and William found himself separated from his sweetheart, just as he glimpsed Lady Victoria and her sister, Miss Clara, who had brought her.

He tried to push his way through the crowd to say his farewells to Evelina and reassure her of his impending visit.

Clearly, she'd not received the two letters he'd written—each of them expressing in heartfelt terms what his hopes were with her for the future.

All she had was his brief reassurance a few minutes ago, which was insufficient, William felt, under the circumstances, for a young woman who felt so very alone—

"Bellingham."

He turned back at the mention of his name and was surprised to see Captain Blackheath, almost invisible in this lake of black, his muffler pulled up high, and hat pulled down low.

"Are you afraid of being recognized?" William asked, indicating his garb. "I must say, you're the last person I thought I'd see here. You had no intention of coming to Dunstable's funeral when last I spoke to you."

Blackheath sent a furtive glance about him and then said in a low tone, "I've been wallowing in a guilty conscience.."

William glanced over his shoulder to where Evelina stood by the graveside, but as he saw Lady Victoria and Clara making their way towards her, he acceded to Blackheath's request and walked by his side through the winding cemetery path.

Was he about to hear Blackheath's confession? He felt both fearful and hopeful, though surprised, too. Blackheath was too much the slippery eel to bare his soul to someone like him for a matter that could see him face conviction.

"I was with LuluBelle for much of the evening in question, so I know she couldn't have stabbed Dunstable in the half an hour after midnight."

William halted. "And she could attest to your innocence? But did you not tell this to the police?"

"I did. But when recounting the details of that night, I made the mistake, under questioning, of saying she left the room for three minutes. She was attending to a request from one of the other girls. The police, however, have decided it suits their purposes to conclude that during those three minutes, she somehow ran through the house to Madame's office, killed Dunstable, then ran back to me."

"Have you argued this with those investigating?" William asked.

"I have, but it's fallen on deaf ears. They're no longer interested in talking to me."

"I also presume that public dissemination of your

frequent visits to LuluBelle was something you wished to keep out of the public domain. Perhaps you didn't press a matter which might point to her innocence sufficiently strongly."

Blackheath wiped his eyes with the back of his hand. "A great many other men in the circles in which we move visited Madame's that night. LuluBelle didn't murder Dunstable. But she tells me the word is that there is one gentleman there that night who was not investigated."

"Who?"

"I did not see him personally. Only his walking stick. It caught my eye for it was propped against the partly open door to Madame's office," said Blackheath. "Usually the lackey collects a gentleman's topper and cane on the way in but this suggested to me that fellow was not a visitor like the rest of us."

The carriages were now lining up at the gate, but the rain had cleared. William indicated the sky before glancing about him, searching for Evelina. It was impossible in this sea of black to identify anyone.

Blackheath's evidence was not new, but Blackheath might well know more. "Will you walk with me?" asked William.

With a nod, his companion fell into step, saying, "I saw that same walking stick amongst the mourners when we gathered around the grave," Blackheath persisted.

William craned his neck as he continued to search for Evelina. But with carriages and black-clad mourners everywhere, it seemed futile. "Did it feature entwined snakes?" he asked. "Oriental in design? There is a craze for the Oriental, you know. It might be unusual, but it doesn't indicate the owner is a murderer."

Blackheath suddenly gripped William's sleeve. "The woman I love is destined for the gallows unless I can come up with evidence that'll make the police realize they've got the wrong person. All right, that is not all I have—"

"You and LuluBelle?" William didn't hide his shock. "You wanted to marry the girl?"

"Course I couldn't do that!" Blackheath snapped. "But I wanted to be with her, take her away from that life and set her up. Protect her. Perhaps you've not felt that urge. Your first marriage was not a love match, so perhaps matters of the heart are nothing to you."

"Good God, if you're about to insult me—"

"No, no! That wasn't what I intended at all. It's just that, five years ago, everyone knew Miss Cooper had other reasons than love for accepting you."

"You mean…that she was in love with another man who jilted her, which was why she accepted me on the rebound," William said, without the bitterness he'd once felt. "True enough, but then, not so long ago, I experienced exactly what she must have felt." William smiled as he thought of Evelina. "Time heals and now I'm determined to find Dunstable's murderer for my own reasons. I think you're clutching at straws when you talk about peculiar walking sticks, though. I'm not discounting the fact the murderer may well own one, but at least ten people at this funeral own one very similar."

"There's something else, as I tried to tell you just now." Blackheath gripped William's wrist and glanced about in the fading afternoon. "I've gone over it a thousand times, thinking I must have misheard. But now I'm convinced that as I looked at that walking stick while passing by Madame's partly open office door, I heard a gentleman say, "Ravenhall will never sanction it.""

CHAPTER 28

"Highgate Cemetery certainly is a very ... ghostly place," Evelina remarked as the horses picked their way past freshly dug graves and vast family crypts. She could barely believe she was soon going to be reunited with what she'd felt was missing her entire life.

She hugged herself against a shiver that ran through her, despite the fact it was summer.

"And my father....? Please tell me about him. How fortuitous we met. As I truly going to see him again after all this time?"

Mr. Grimshaw smiled. He was not an ebullient gentleman, but it was kind of him to take the trouble to first help her out of her predicament and then to take her to her father.

Glancing at his intricately carved cane, she remarked, "Have you perhaps been to India, sir? My Papa visited India when I was twelve and he sent me a wooden box with a very fine carving of two entwined snakes similar to your cane."

A shadow crossed Mr. Grimshaw's hawkish face. "I was sent to India as a young man."

"How very exciting," Evelina said, trying to bolster his spirits.

"I did not think so. My father and then my brother had died unexpectedly in quick succession which meant I had to leave the estate where I'd been born and grown up—" his nostrils flared—"while the executors searched for the new heir. The family thought it was easier to send me away."

"But weren't *you* the new heir?" Evelina asked.

"But for a simple marriage certificate I would have been," Mr. Grimshaw said in a soft bitter tone before adding with a forced smile, "But *your* father is a fine gentleman who loves his children very much."

Evelina was puzzled. "I have brothers and sisters? No, that cannot be."

"Yes, indeed, Evelina. But your father has been especially considerate to *you*. I have been responsible for ensuring a very generous monthly sum goes to your mother for the upkeep of both herself and you. I was responsible for the details of your dowry—"

Evelina interrupted him with a gasp. "So do you know... if my father disapproves of Lord Bellingham?"

Grimshaw considered this. "Your father strives for the peace and happiness of those he loves. He will make great sacrifices to protect those whom he regards as needing and deserving of his protection."

Evelina clasped her hands and leaned forward. "Please, Mr. Grimshaw. I need to see my father, if only to reassure him that no one will look after me better than Lord Bellingham. Only he will make me happy! Perhaps Mama has said something that has set him against Lord Bellingham."

"Your mama and papa have not spoken for many years, Evelina. I act as the intermediary."

"Then you know my mother, too?" She was astonished.

Mr. Grimshaw nodded. "I have known your mother since

you were a child, Evelina. I remember when the decision was made to send you to school in Paris."

"Yet I have never heard your name," Evelina marveled.

"Your mama and papa did not wish their ... estrangement to be made public. They are very private people," said Mr. Grimshaw. "Now, here is the family crypt where all your family members have been interred over the centuries. It's getting a little late and is perhaps a little cold, but if you would like, I do have the key with me, and can show you the resting places of those nearest and dearest to you."

Evelina glanced through the window. The weather did look a little bleak, but she was afraid of squandering this incredible, fortuitous chance to know something of her origins.

If Mr. Grimshaw explained her relationship to some of these people, she wouldn't feel quite so ignorant when she finally went to see her papa.

"It's not too cold, Mr. Grimshaw," she assured him, smoothing her skirts as the carriage came to a standstill.

She let him help her out of the equipage and waited, staring at the enormous lichen covered trees and stones that surrounded them, then at the magnificent family crypt.

"It is one of the largest and finest at Highgate Cemetery," said Mr. Grimshaw, locating an iron key from a large set he had in the leather satchel he carried.

"It's very dark inside," Evelina said as he opened the iron door, stooping to enter and then realizing that Mr. Grimshaw was lighting a flint to illuminate a lantern he held up to illuminate the large space.

"This is my father's family?" Evelina asked, disbelieving. "*My* family?" The crypt was long and cavernous, the floor paved with slate, topped with a row of sarcophagi disappearing into the gloom. It clearly belonged to a very great personage. Why had her mother said nothing?

"This is the final resting place for members of your family, Evelina. You know, when you were born, your father did not know he was to be next in line when his cousin died, leaving him the title and the estate with, of course, all the attendant responsibilities."

"He didn't?" She could barely attend to him as she stepped forward, reverently running her hand over the smooth, cold marble face of an ancestor who'd died the previous century.

"No, you were born when he lived rather a humble life. But if you are patient, I'll introduce you to your forbears while I tell you the story."

Evelina followed him as he explained each of the effigies and marble-topped tombs while she shook her head in disbelief. If she'd only known, she could have held her head up high when the girls at the convent had scorned her for knowing so little about her mama and papa.

Together, they walked the length of the crypt. Ten, fifteen yards of flag-stoned floor with engraved eulogies upon the walls, gloriously colored paintings and stained-glass windows.

"Mr. Grimshaw!" She stopped suddenly, calling out to him as he walked a few yards in front of her."

"Yes, Evelina?" He turned. "It's time I should be returning home. It's growing late and cold."

"Mr. Grimshaw, please bring the light. I think I just saw my namesake."

"Your namesake?"

"Yes, a grave. A sarcophagus. I see it belongs to a young girl called Evelina. She died when she was a child, but I cannot see what year she was born unless you bring me the light."

"Ah, you have found Evelina."

Mr. Grimshaw hovered near the doorway.

"I have. Please, bring the lantern so I can quickly look and then I will be ready to leave. Then you said you'd take me to my father? Does that mean he doesn't live far?"

"No, he doesn't live far away at all, Evelina. In fact, he lives at Ravenhall Manor just ten minutes away by carriage." Mr. Grimshaw raised the lantern high and for a moment, the light illuminated far more than just where he stood.

"Ravenhall Manor?" Evelina repeated in confusion as she bent close and saw that the girl had only lived to the age of five though she couldn't quite see the year she'd been born.

"Then why has Mama hidden the truth from me? I've been trying to locate him ever since I came to London."

A strange, gnawing unease churned in her breast. *Ravenhall Manor? The estate of the 5th Earl of Ravenhall?* It didn't make sense. Her father lived so close? And now the child named Evelina. So many questions, she didn't know which to ask first.

Agitated, she ran her hand over the gold-chiseled letters in the aged marble. "Mr. Grimshaw, I think there must be a repeat of family names unless two daughters named Evelina were born to my father."

"Only one, Evelina," came Mr. Grimshaw's distant reply.

Evelina glanced up, frowning as she puzzled over the wording.

"Mr Grimshaw—" She drew her hand away and ran towards the sliver of light, quickly snuffed out.

But not before his final words resonated throughout the silent, empty chamber as she heard the sound of the iron key turning. "And you are that one."

CHAPTER 29

"Archie, these are wonderful!" Lily exclaimed as she looked at each photograph on her desk. There were five of them showing the little flower seller in various poses or at different times of the day. "I do like the one where she's standing in the doorway selling her violets. Her expression is most appealing and goes well juxtaposed with the one where she's in the field picking the flowers where we can see the spire of St. Pauls in the distance. It highlights how far she has to travel each day to sell her wares for such a pittance. Hamish, just look at these!" she said as her husband put his head through the door on his way to his office.

Hamish came to the table and stood by her side, his admiration clearly echoing his wife's. "It's been a week of good works," he said, standing up. "Not only have you found another position for a young girl who'd been dismissed with no character reference for breaking her mistress's teapot—"

"But Lord Bellingham has eloped with Miss Tarot," Archie broke in with a grin. He gave a nod to emphasize the claim. "Yes, Maisie said Kitty was all a-fluster at finding her mistress's bed empty last night but then she found a letter from his lordship tellin' her to be ready at an instant's notice cos he didn't care about the money and if that were the problem then he'd whisk 'em away from all o' that."

Archie began to gather up the photographs but Hamish stopped him, hesitation in his voice. "Bellingham, you say? Why, I saw Bellingham at my club last night. I stopped for a chat, but I did not gain the impression he was a man about to stage an elopement that very night."

Lily glanced between him and Archie, who frowned, saying, "Well, apparently that were what Kitty said must have 'appened for there weren't no uvver way to explain why her mistress had scarpered in the night."

After a moment of clear concern, Hamish's expression lightened as he clarified, "No doubt this was backed up by finding Miss Tarot's essentials were missing."

Archie shook his head slowly. "No, they weren't missing, which was, at first, why Kitty thought it odd. And so did Lady Perry, who made enquiries with the young ladies who had taken Miss Tarot to Lord Dunstable's funeral yesterday. 'Parently the Madam had forbidden Miss Tarot to go but Lady Perry had given the say-so. Lady Victoria and Miss Clara fetched her, secret-like, in their carriage, yesterday afternoon."

"And?" asked Lily. "What light did the young ladies throw on all this?"

"Miss Victoria said she and her sister had seen Miss Tarot talkin' to Lord Bellingham during the funeral and when they went to fetch her to return home, they couldn't find her but then they saw her in the far distance steppin' into a carriage, so they reckoned she was goin' with Lord Bellingham, after all."

Lily saw her husband frowning as he repeated, "I really didn't gain the impression from Bellingham last night that he had Miss Tarot secreted away somewhere preparing for a dash to the border or, however, they were planning to elope."

Lily tried to puzzle it out. "Lord Dunstable's funeral would have seen Miss Tarot back at Lord Bellingham's or on the road by late afternoon. Lord Bellingham was at his club at—what time did you say?"

"It was close to midnight," said Hamish, putting his hand on Lily's wrist and adding, with a sigh, "I'm sure we shouldn't interfere. Not again. I'm sure there must be some perfectly good explanation, for I hardly think Miss Tarot has mysteriously gone missing or been kidnapped."

Lily nodded. "Of course, you're right. There has to be a good reason. But I do feel a little concerned. Especially in view of what's happened lately. I mean, Lord Dunstable's murder—"

"Which was perfectly adequately explained by the apprehension of that young woman—"

"Hamish! She's not guilty," Lily exclaimed, while Archie nodded fiercely.

"But this young woman admitted that she'd been unkindly treated by Dunstable. She has the motive," Hamish defended himself.

"She had the motive, but not the strength or the opportunity. The police have got it wrong," Lily declared. "But we're not talking about that right now. We're talking about Miss Tarot, and I'm worried about her. Please, will you see if you can find Lord Bellingham, just to put my mind at rest?"

Hamish nodded. "I have a meeting with my father in an hour. I promise I will go afterwards."

"In that case, I think I will go, myself," said Lily. "Archie, will you come with me?"

WITH HAMISH SHAKING his head as he clearly believed his wife was overreacting, Lily made her way to Lord Bellingham's townhouse where, to her consternation, she found him taking an early lunch while reading the newspaper.

Apologizing for the intrusion, Lily said, "I was hoping to find Miss Tarot here, Lord Bellingham."

"Unless the pair of you've eloped, m'lord," said Archie boldly.

"I intend to meet her this afternoon." Coloring slightly, Bellingham stirred his tea. "I thought an elopement was a little extreme. But we are going to make arrangements to get married with as little fanfare as possible, and far away from London."

"Very admirable, my lord," said Lily, tempering her growing concern, "but it would appear Miss Tarot has gone missing. Her maid said she did not sleep in her bed last night."

Lord Bellingham raised his eyebrows and then shifted forwards as he clearly tried to establish a reason for this. Lily could see he was trying to hide his alarm. "Perhaps she spent the night with Lady Victoria and her sister," he said. "They drove her back from the funeral. She might have stayed for some reason." But his frown deepened as Lily shook her head.

"Lady Perry has already visited the young ladies to ask if they know where Miss Tarot might be. They said they thought she went home with you since they saw her stepping into a carriage at the funeral. But no one has seen her since the funeral."

"What?" Bellingham's voice rose as, clearly rattled, he stepped out from behind the table, raking both hands through his hair. "Miss Tarot has been missing since yesterday afternoon and no one knows where she is?"

Lily nodded, glancing at Archie, who said, "My sweetheart's friend, Kitty, wot's maid to Miss Tarot, thought she might 'ave eloped with you, m'lord. Letters pertaining to such a possibility were found in her room."

Lily interrupted. "But my husband said he'd seen you at his club last night, so that's why I'm here. To set my mind at rest." She nibbled at her lower lip, adding, "But it's not at rest."

"No, because I clearly have not eloped with Miss Tarot, who is not where she should be and not with the only friends, I believe she has in London." Lord Bellingham looked wildly at Lily. "Where else could she be? At her mother's house?" He shuddered as he obviously recalled where that was and Lily said, "I think it's the next obvious place to check."

Archie sent her a sidelong look. "I'll go wiv yer, m'lord, as I don't fink you want to be havin' a cosy chat wiv Madame on your own."

"And I'll go, too," Lily said decisively. She looked down at her fashionable gown of cerise but before she could speak, Archie said, "I don't reckon there's time to change, wiv all due respect, Lady Bradden. But we'll go the secret way. No one'll see yer. And you can pull down yer veil once you's inside the house."

FIFTEEN MINUTES LATER, Lily and Lord Bellingham faced Madame Chambon across her desk while Archie waited outside the door in the corridor.

The shock on the face of the proprietor of Madame Chambon's when she beheld his Lordship in her office would have amused Lily if the matter had not been so serious. Madame rarely allowed herself to appear at a disadvantage. And this was even before they relayed their fears.

"Evelina has gone missing?" she repeated, fiddling in agitation with the keys on her chatelain, her mulberry-stained lips puckered in her heavily powdered face. "Since when? Why has no one told me this before? Nothing is more important than Evelina! Yet you've been making trouble over Dunstable's murder--"

"Madame, listen, please!" Lord Bellingham remonstrated. "I've only just been relayed Lady Bradden's fears after she learned that Evelina hasn't been seen since Lord Dunstable's funeral yesterday."

"I strictly forbade her from attending his funeral. What is the meaning of this?"

Lily's fears were hardly assuaged by learning that Madame Chambon also had no idea where Evelina had gone. "Lady Perry tells us that Evelina went with Lady Victoria and her sister to Lord Dunstable's funeral, but that they did not bring her home."

"So, my own daughter defied me?"

"Please, Madame, that should be the least of your concerns." Lily tried to speak calmly. "Your daughter is miss-ing. Lady Perry visited her young friends this morning, and they surmised that Miss Tarot had eloped with Lord Bellingham because they saw her stepping into a carriage in the distance at Lord Dunstable's funeral yesterday."

Lord Bellingham spoke. "Furthermore, none of her clothes or belongings are missing, and she is with none of her friends. And she has left no note. It's as if she's disap-peared into thin air." He made a gesture of helplessness. "The only place I can image she has sought refuge is with her father."

"Perhaps she discovered where he lived," Lily interrupted. "When I last spoke to her, she said there'd been a difficulty with her dowry payment." Lily watched Madame carefully, but the woman was very still; almost as if in shock. She hurried on. "Evelina thought it was the reason Lord Dunstable mentioned eloping rather than have the elaborate wedding he'd initially proposed."

Then Archie thrust open the door saying, "I just bin havin' a chat with Gracie. She wonders if it's possible that Miss Tarot has discovered where her father lives. Sorry Madame, but some things are more important than others and if you want to be assured your daughter ain't in harm's way, then perhaps you'd better let us know the identity of the man wot's her father. Cos likely it was findin' that information wot brought Dunstable to his last moment. If you knows what I mean. And I think you does."

Madame passed a shaking hand across her brow. She came out from behind her desk, her dark green polonaise gown a contrast with her fiery red hair. Her powdered cheeks looked deathly white beneath two spots of high colour. With shaking hands, she encircled her throat as she whispered, "I was told I was never to contact Evelina's father if I wanted --" she began, then stopped abruptly.

"If you wanted what?" Lily prompted.

"If I wanted to continue to be paid my ... very generous ... monthly allowance... plus Evelina's."

"Well, if Evelina is missing, there won't be a monthly allowance for her and you can pocket the lot," Archie said with false cheer. "I'm thinkin' that maybe you had as good a reason as anyone for poor Miss Tarot to just go missin' without trace."

"How dare you?" spat Madame as she began to pace in front of the fireplace. Hissing in a breath between her lips, she began to mutter, first unintelligibly, before she said with more clarity, "Yes, it's true that Lord Dunstable was black-mailing me," she said. "He found evidence that Evelina's father was a man of some means and that I've been paid handsomely for many years. I rely on that money to keep

Evelina in the style to which a young lady of her … station should expect, Lord Bellingham. You can rest assured that my daughter is an innocent whose life experience encompasses only learning and the domestic arts. She has never been to this house. She would, in fact, be repulsed. I have gained the feeling that she is repulsed by me, too. But… you're right. I will send a note to her father."

"And will he respond immediately?" Lord Bellingham asked, his voice tight. "I would like to remind you that I believe we have something of an emergency on our hands."

Madame Chambon stopped beneath a large portrait of herself in her younger days. If it was true to life, she had been a beauty. Now she looked raddled, and her expression was bleak. "He has never contacted me directly. I deal only through his lawyer, a man who has made it very clear that if I breach the stipulation of the contact, then my payments will cease."

Lily moved in front of her, forcing her to meet her eye. "If this man has been so generous as to continue these payments, he must have some affection for you, or at least Evelina. He would surely be concerned that she has gone missing. Can we not approach him discreetly?" Running her hands the length of her fashionable gown, she added, "In fact, I'm confident he would see Lady Bradden if she made an unexpected call upon him. And Lord Bellingham, too, of course. Please, Madame, who is Evelina's father?"

Madame Chambon stared at her for a long moment as if weighing up whether to divulge this information. Finally, she relented. "Lord Ravenhall," she said softly, and the others gasped.

"The Earl of Ravenswood?" gasped Lily and Lord Bellingham in unison. "He is Evelina's father?" asked Lily.

"And he continues to maintain both of you?" asked Lord Bellingham. "Or, to some extent, otherwise you would not need to continue this work, I suppose. Dear Lord, I dined with Lord Ravenhall only this week."

Madame gave a short laugh. "And I have not seen him for nearly twenty years, but I continue this work as my insurance that I will always be able to provide for my daughter as befits the station of a lady. There is no guarantee the payments will continue."

Lily waited, and when Madame didn't move, she prompted, "Then we will go to see Lord Ravenhall. Right now."

Still, Madame remained rooted to the spot, her face trained on her once beautiful face in the portrait. "My poor Evelina," she whispered. Then, swinging round, she said with more energy, as if she were reassuring herself, "Evelina is safe. This has nothing to do with Lord Dunstable's murder. I have done everything that was asked of me and fulfilled every stipulation. I cannot be held accountable."

"No one is holding you accountable, Madame Chambon," said Lily, as she exchanged a concerned glance with Lord Bellingham who stepped forward to open the door.

But Madame shook her head, saying, "I cannot possibly go. If I break my promise and make myself known to Evelina's father then all payments will cease. Evelina will have nothing!"

Lily hesitated. "Then you will go in disguise. Archie!" She beckoned to her friend, saying, "Tell Maisie to find something demure and appropriate for Madame to wear for a visit to nobility. And perhaps a hat with a concealing veil." Then, when he'd gone to expedite her request, Lily patted Madame on the arm saying reassuringly, "I'm sure our fears will prove groundless, Madame. We will find Evelina at Ravenhall Manor where, would you believe, she has a friend in Lady Elizabeth Craddock, the Earl of Ravenhall's only daughter?"

But it was only as she said the words that she and Lord Bellingham realized the enormity of this statement.

Evelina was the illegitimate half-sister of Lady Elizabeth.

Archie returned, and after Madame had been helped into her new clothes while the gentlemen stepped out, Lily said, "Madame Chambon, I shall introduce you as my friend, Mrs. Tennant. Come, Lord Bellingham, let us pay a call on Lord and Lady Ravenhall and be prepared for what we find."

CHAPTER 30

The three of them—Lily, Lord Bellingham, and Madame Chambon—were soon in the carriage, Madame Chambon wearing a modest afternoon dress with a hat and veil. Lily had never seen her so nervous and wondered how she'd retained for so many years, the loyalty of an old lover who could have discarded her at any time.

But perhaps the man had a soft spot for his daughter, thought Lily, until she was disabused of this notion when Madame said, "Lord Ravenhall hasn't seen Evelina since she was an infant."

When the carriage drew up in front of Ravenswood Hall, Lily was dumbstruck. Her father, Lord Lambton, lived in a grand home, but it was nothing like this.

Manicured gardens fronted an imposing façade dominated by towering classical Greek columns. However, later additions incorporated both Georgian and the Gothic revival. For such a strange amalgamation, the result was both whimsical and charming. It also made clear that this was an estate that had been in the family for many centuries.

Lily sent Madame Chambon a dubious look and saw that the brothel madame was looking distinctly awed.

Ravenswood Hall belonged to Lord Arthur Edward Craddock, the 5th Earl of Ravenswood.

What kind of man would he prove to be? And would the earl really feel any serious concern over the unexplained disappearance of his former mistress's daughter—a child he hadn't seen for nearly twenty years. Would he even remember Evelina? Aristocrats were not known for their morality.

Furthermore, what would be their reception? Of course, Bellingham was known to the family. They'd be surprised, but if they were home, they would receive them. It was some consolation.

They were greeted with no surprise by the butler, who led them into the drawing room. A short while later, a parlor maid said his lordship would see them.

Instead, it was Lady Ravenhall who appeared, in company with her daughter, Lady Elizabeth and Lady Elizabeth's friend Miss Clara who greeted Lord Bellingham with a surprised, "How nice that you should call, my lord! Why, are you here to tell us you and Miss Tarot —?" She clapped her hand to her mouth at a surreptitious dig in the ribs from her friend.

Lady Ravenhall, an attractive woman with light brown hair and a sweet smile, sat down on a pale blue sofa opposite Lily. The two girls took a seat at right angles. "I'm pleased to meet you, Lady Bradden," said their hostess. "I'm a great admirer of the work you do and the column you write in *Morals and Manners*. I look forward to each week's story on the worthy person who has bettered themselves through their own endeavors. In fact, I had contemplated whether to contact you regarding how I might add my support. You see,

I run a small school for the workhouse girls on reading and arithmetic."

Lily sent her a surprised smile as she went on, "My daughter Elizabeth and her friend Clara know Lord Bellingham and when they heard he'd called, insisted we all come through." Lady Ravenhall nodded at Lord Bellingham. "I believe you spent the day together at the zoological gardens several weeks ago."

"Yes, with Miss Tarot," said Clara with a frown. "In fact, I thought perhaps you'd come here to pass on some happy news about Miss Tarot. Lady Perry was asking after her this morning, but we suspected she'd—" She broke off as she sent a confused and worried look in Lord Bellingham's direction.

Lord Bellingham shook his head. "I wish that were so, but I'm here because we don't know what has happened to Miss Tarot. Pardon me, Lady Ravenhall—" He broke off, clearly agitated, as he frowned at the three ladies. "The reason we're here is that we're trying to locate Miss Tarot. Lady Perry says you saw her stepping into a carriage at the funeral yesterday. But it was not mine." The strain in his voice was evident, "Can you describe it?"

Shocked, Clara and Elizabeth exchanged looks, Clara saying, "Evelina has gone missing? My goodness, what a terrible thing! But a carriage?" She frowned, trying to recall. "I'm sure my sister could describe what she saw better than I. Victoria notices that sort of thing. All I can tell you is that it looked like any other navy blue, nondescript carriage."

"And you didn't see who was in it? Why would she get into a stranger's carriage? Why did you not convey her home if she'd come with you?"

Clara put her hands to her mouth and gave a sob while Elizabeth and her mother looked on, concern etched into their smooth, lovely faces. "Lord Bellingham, I'm so sorry,"

Clara said on a hiccup. "We were both so sure it was you who was conveying her away."

"What's this now?" came a genial voice as a tall, fine featured youth with light curling hair entered the room in company with a man whom he greatly resembled in terms of charm and mobility of expression.

"Oh, Rupert! You'll never believe what's happened!" Elizabeth twisted in her seat, her face a picture of distress as she gestured for the young man to join her. "Miss Tarot has gone missing."

Lady Ravenhall waved her arm towards the newcomers whom she introduced as her husband and son, frowning at everyone while, to Lily's surprise, Lord Ravenhall gave nothing away as he took a seat beside Elizabeth and Rupert settled on the arm of his mother's sofa.

Madame Chambon, still veiled, remained silent, but Lily could see the tenseness of her clasped hands, the knuckles white. As Lily had pre-arranged, she'd been introduced as Mrs. Tennant, a visiting friend of Lily's, and little attention had been paid her. Clearly, she was too overcome to interrupt.

"And who is this young lady...this Miss Tarot of whom you speak?" Lord Ravenhall finally asked. "You mentioned your friend earlier, Elizabeth. You said you'd seen her—Miss Tarot, did you say? - at the opera that night we took you with Mr. Grimshaw. I saw her vaguely out of the corner of my eye. And now you say she has gone missing?"

Lord Bellingham rested his elbows on his knees, hunched forward, his voice shaking as his eyes bored into Lord Ravenswood. "I wish to marry the young lady."

Lord Ravenhall's smile was a little blank, Lily thought; a little uncomprehending. As if he truly didn't know whom they were discussing. Or perhaps he was very adept at subterfuge. She wondered suddenly if Madame Chambon had been hallucinating earlier and had now lost her nerve.

Carefully, Lord Ravenswood said, "Congratulations, Bellingham." Then, with a frown, "But you say the young lady has gone missing?"

"We are all very worried about her," Lily said, twisting the fabric of her skirts between trembling fingers. Madame Chambon had sent them all here asserting that Lord Raven-hall had been paying her hundreds a month to support her and Evelina, and yet he didn't seem to know his own daughter.

"Miss Tarot was at Lord Dunstable's funeral yesterday?" clarified the youth. "Bad business that. I was sorry to hear it. And to think that a woman did it."

"Rupert!" cried his mother. "You ought to know nothing of all this. I told you not to say it in Elizabeth's hearing."

"I read the papers, Mama." Rupert rolled his eyes before his father ruffled his hair and said fondly, "I told you, my dear, the boy is too young to be wrapped up in cotton wool." Then the frown returned as he turned to Lily and Lord Bellingham. "I'm sorry we can't help. I do hope you find the answers you are looking for. Or, hopefully, that Miss Tarot is found, safe and sound, by the time you return home."

They all rose, having earlier declined tea.

Lily felt her desperation rise as Lord and Lady Ravenhall prepared to quit the room. "My lord, I wonder if I might ask you a question—in confidence—on behalf of my father, Lord Lambton," she said. Then, when he sent a questioning look at his wife, she added, "It would take only a moment of your time. And Lord Bellingham might also benefit." She smiled, trying to dress up her request in the guise of something light-hearted.

Nodding approbation, Lady Ravenhall departed with

their two children, and Clara, while Lily and Lord Bellingham trailed behind.

At the door, he waited obligingly for whatever Lily might have to say, but as there was a parlormaid hovering nearby, Lily nodded into the garden. "In fact, it is about your roses, my lord. Yours are particularly fine specimens and my father is most fond of roses."

"But I am not the horticulturist in the family, Lady Bradden. I think you would be better served asking my wife," he said with a smile and a look that suggested he might call after her.

But Lily took his arm and ushered him through the open doors to the front portico.

Putting up no resistance, but his surprise evident, Lord Ravenhall strolled into the garden with Lily. Lord Bellingham and Madame followed a few feet behind, leaving Lily feeling foolish and with a growing anger towards Madame who had clearly fabricated this entire debacle.

What had Lord Ravenhall to do with this? Madame had simply sucked a name out of her thumb.

It was mid-afternoon now, nearly a full 24-hours since Lord Dunstable's funeral and the last time Evelina had been seen.

"What is it you wished to ask me, Lady Bradden?"

To her surprise, Lord Ravenhall hid his understandable irritation. He was smiling at her as if he had all the time in the world, although he did glance at his timepiece and murmur that his wife would be waiting for him for their afternoon drinks.

Lily got the impression he was uncommonly fond of his wife. She'd noted the easy way they'd smiled at one another, and his companionableness with his son and daughter. She hesitated. "The truth is, Lord Ravenswood, we really had hoped to find some clue to the disappearance of Lord

Bellingham's fiancée– or rather, soon-to-be fiancée—Evelina Tarot. Are you sure you've heard nothing?"

For the first time, his brow furrowed. "Evelina," he repeated, as if thinking. "It is an unusual name. I'm sorry she's missing, and I hope you find her." His smile was now tinged with sadness. "I once had a daughter called Evelina." He hesitated. "She died when she was an infant… and then I married my dear wife, Elsie, and was blessed with the twins."

"You lie!" Madame Chambon spoke for the first time, stepping forward and raising her veil, almost ripping it from her hat. "How can you stand there and claim that Evelina is dead? When you've been paying for her upkeep for more than twenty years?"

Lord Ravenhall looked as if he'd been struck. Drawing back his shoulders, he raked Madame with a scornful gaze, dismissing her as if she truly were a madwoman. "With all due respect, I have no idea who you are, Mrs. Tennant, but I find your claim absurd in the extreme." He looked at Lily as if she might usher the clearly raving acquaintance back to their carriage, which was waiting a short distance away. But then, glancing once more at Madame, a flicker of recognition gave him away.

He did know her.

Though, clearly, he was only realizing this for the first time, for suddenly it looked as if he might crumple on the spot. "Dear God, it's you, Catherine." The color completely left his face as he faltered. "You're … alive?"

CHAPTER 31

O f course, I'm alive," she all but shouted. "You've been paying me a handsome allowance with the occasional communication for nearly twenty years. And I've been true to my word and kept my silence in order for those payments to keep coming." Her voice had roughened, but she made another attempt at refining her tones as she went on, "I've never contacted you until now, on account of your threat to cut Evelina and me off with nothing if we did. But now Evelina is missing." There was a catch in her voice before she went on, "I thought she might have discovered the truth that you were her father. I hoped that was the case and that I'd find her here. Please, don't punish me, Arthur. If she is with you, please put me out of my misery. I promise I won't trouble you and your family again. I don't want anything from you other than ... well, the money you've been paying me, of course, since it's what's ensured Evelina was brought up the fine young lady she deserved to be ... in view of the fact of who she is: an earl's *legitimate* daughter."

Lily heard Lord Bellingham's soft exhalation beside her.

Madame Chambon was clearly a madwoman. Lord Ravenhall was going to make this quite clear, and they'd have to take her away without being any closer to knowing what had happened to Evelina.

But Lord Ravenhall said nothing. His mouth was slightly open, and he was still staring at Madame Chambon as if he'd seen a ghost. He sent a nervous glance towards the house then said, softly, "I don't know what you're talking about, Catherine. I… I was led to believe you were dead. After you left me, taking Evelina with you, I heard nothing. Nothing for three years and then—"

"When Evelina was five years old, I heard you'd unexpectedly inherited the earldom," Madame interrupted. "And all this." She encompassed their surroundings with a sweep of her arm. Of course, I was going to contact you, being your legal wife an' all."

Again, the earl shook his head. "But you didn't contact me. I had my lawyer spare no expense in searching for you. He told me he'd had confirmation that you and Evelina had died. Why, I even put marker in the family crypt to mark my darling Evelina's life and death.

"Who did you say told you we had died?" Madame demanded angrily.

"My lawyer, Nathaniel Grimshaw. Grimshaw has been my solicitor since I inherited from my cousin. He was my cousin's solicitor, too, and in fact he lived at Ravenhall until he was a young man. He knows everything there is to know about this family." Lord Ravenhall looked a little wild as he raked his hands through his hair. "As soon as I learned I was the new Earl of Ravenswood, I told him I'd married you, Catherine Canning, an actress I'd met in my youth. I told him everything. That you'd abandoned me to be with your new lover, taking Evelina with you. He promised he'd investigate and then he reported to me that—"

"That we were dead? Lord, no!" Madame put her hands on her hips and thrust out her bosom. "Grimshaw's been paying me an allowance for years! He paid for Evelina to go to school. And he was paying a handsome dowry for her, which is why Lord Dunstable was so keen to marry her—

"Dunstable? The man who was murdered?"

"Murdered, yes. So, you knew all about that, but you say you knew nothing about us? You sent letters to Evelina when she was at school. Why, Grimshaw passed on the occasional birthday greeting from you to Evelina, though she cried, often as not, that you'd forgotten her birthday. But Grimshaw said you'd stipulated that the money would *only* continue if we remained silent because that would be a better deal for me than declaring to the world the truth about me —" She took an audible breath, adding, "He said society would never accept me in view of my profession and that with your resources, you would find a way to declare our marriage null and void—"

Lily could see how difficult it was for Lord Ravenhall to keep up. The horror in his expression as he gazed upon Madame Chambon with her patently dyed hair and her raddled skin had not abated, but now he interrupted to ask, "What profession? What are you telling me, Catherine? The last communication I had with you was ... acrimonious ... as you announced you were leaving me and taking our daughter with you... when you knew little Evelina meant the world to me!"

Madame Chambon heaved in a breath. "I thought I was doing the right thing for both of us. For all of us. At least, at the time, I did. Yes, I ran away with Evelina for a better life because I had a better offer and you had nothing. You could barely put food on the table, Arthur! How was I to know you were next in line to inherit this—?" She flung her arm about her, adding fiercely, "But then it was my turn to be abandoned. For a couple of years, I did what I could to put food on the table. I pulled tricks so that Evelina and I could survive. But I still had my beauty and a rich protector set me up. Madame Chambon's? That's my legacy! Perhaps you know of the establishment?"

Lily thought Lord Ravenhall was about to faint. "Madame Chambon's?" The speed of his response and the disgust with which he uttered the name made it clear that he had very much heard of Madame Chambon's. He raked Catherine with another horrified look. "You--?"

"Yes, that's what Mr. Grimshaw said would be the reception from everyone. You see, when I discovered the shocking news that my Arthur was now the 5th Earl of Ravenswood, I went looking for you. A woman like me, however, doesn't get to see a great man like you—even though I was your wife. Your *legal* wife! I was introduced to Mr. Grimshaw. He took over all negotiations and refused to allow me to speak to you in person. But I was given a great deal of money. He said that if I was silent, then you were prepared to continue to pay me a very handsome allowance to keep my mouth shut. And I was silent. And Evelina does know nothing! Oh, she's asked many a time about her father, but she believes you are quiet, retiring Mr. Tarot who lives in Aberdeenshire separate from me. It was Mr. Grimshaw who said it must be this way because—"

Madame stopped abruptly, staring at Lily as if suddenly aware she'd gone too far and that they were speaking of matters that should not be heard in a stranger's presence.

Lily did not miss the inference. "Lord Ravenhall, I'm sorry we are hearing this. I swear it shall go no further. We are here because we fear Evelina is in great danger. Not for any other reason. But, hearing Madame speak, and what you've been told, I now believe there's a connection between Lord Dunstable's death and Evelina's disappearance."

"In fact, it's highly possible her disappearance is linked to Dunstable's murder." Lord Bellingham's voice cracked. "We think Dunstable was blackmailing someone who then murdered him on account of what he knew." He looked at Madame and entreated her, "If you know anything you haven't told us, will you please reveal it?"

Lord Ravenhall gave one slow nod. There was a lot to take in.

Meanwhile, Madame sent a panicked look at Lily and Lord Bellingham before glancing up at the mullioned windows of the large house. She appeared to be considering whether to reveal more. Finally, she returned her gaze to his face and continued, softly. "One day, when I was away from my office, Lord Dunstable, who was visiting one of my… young ladies, was discovered searching my drawers. It transpired that he was looking for evidence to the identity of a young lady who worked for me. A beautiful young woman called Celeste. You may recall her? The young woman murdered by the Russian a little over a year ago?"

Lily interjected. "Her name was Celeste, and she tried to warn me of the danger this Russian posed. Tragically, she paid with her own life. But that is not related to Evelina's disappearance." She nodded at Madame, who continued.

"During his search, however, Dunstable discovered some communication between Mr. Grimshaw and me that hinted at my real identity. He then found confirmation in the church records to prove we were legally married, Arthur, and so he blackmailed me. He wanted Evelina's dowry, and Evelina agreed to marry him. I didn't coerce her into agreeing," she added defensively. "But Dunstable was charming, and Evelina was naïve. He flattered her and when she agreed to marry him, of course, I was relieved."

Lily heard Lord Bellingham's intake of breath. He'd turned a little gray, but he said softly, "Nothing was official.

Evelina was targeted by the first man who asked her to dance when she arrived in London because Dunstable had a secret agenda. Yes, I see how it could be so if Dunstable had discovered the truth: that you, Lord Ravenhall, were legally married to Evelina's mother. For Dunstable was murdered barely two days later."

Lord Ravenhall's frown deepened. "You were prepared to let our daughter marry a blackmailer?"

"I thought if Dunstable got what he wanted—Evelina's money — then he would be satisfied," Madame defended herself. "Dunstable agreed to say nothing because, of course, Evelina is just a girl and would not inherit the estate. And my scandalous background hardly equips me to be accepted as a countess, as I've said," Madame added with a bitter laugh. "So, Dunstable agreed that as long as her dowry was handsome enough, it was in all our interests to remain silent."

"Oh, Catherine..." Lord Ravenswood continued to shake his head. "I was told you were dead. I believed you were dead. But now you are here and..."

"What's this, now?"

They all turned at the cheerful greeting of a gray-haired gentleman appearing from the shrubbery by the side of the house. Clearly, the newcomer had not heard the gist of the conversation, for he greeted Lord Ravenswood with easy familiarity, saying, "Your son bested me in tennis this afternoon. I shall have to return for my revenge. And whom do I have the pleasure of addressing? Ah, Bellingham. We meet again!"

He was a dapper little gentleman in a perfectly pressed suit, his grizzled hair neatly parted in the center, and a pert little mouth in contrast to handsome mutton-chop whiskers.

Madame had now pulled down her veil and was standing, head bowed, close to Lord Bellingham. Lord Ravenhall introduced them. He was tense, though clearly striving to appear relaxed as he used Madame's nom de plume, Mrs. Tanner.

Mr. Grimshaw appeared not to notice her, though his smile for Lord Bellingham and Lily was charming.

"Well, I thought I would offer my greetings since I was passing, but now I have business to which I must attend." Doffing his hat, he offered a small bow and then continued along the path towards where his carriage waited in the circular drive.

When he'd stepped inside and closed the door, Lord Bellingham gave a slow, audible sigh as the four bay horses set their course for the front gates.

"I couldn't help noticing Mr. Grimshaw's walking stick," he remarked. "It's very distinct from its entwined carved snakes. Oriental in design, I believe?"

They looked at him, eyebrows raised.

"Very much like the walking stick that caught Captain Blackheath's eye the night he was at Madame Chambon's. The night Dunstable was murdered."

CHAPTER 32

H ad she really managed to sleep?

Evelina slowly regained consciousness, shivering as she breathed in the musty scent of dampness that rose from the stone floor and cold stone walls. Confusion and fear gripped her as she blinked open her eyes. All was darkness, though not as dark as it had been, for she was now aware of a high, small window above her that proclaimed it was daylight.

Not that it made any difference since she might spend an eternity here.

Or not be found until the next Ravenswood family member was interred.

All night and for much of the day she'd lain on the small sarcophagus belonging to her namesake Evelina, tucked between two larger final resting places for deceased members of the great family.

And then finally, a flock of chattering birds flew overhead, their sudden silence replaced by the distant crunch of gravel—a carriage pulled by four horses—and her heart raced, pounding against her chest, while fear and hope flooded her mind.

Dragging herself upright to move towards the entrance, she pushed against the heavy door, her muscles weak and fatigued from her long captivity.

But as before, her efforts were futile. The only man who could save her was the man who had the key for this ancient, massive metal door.

And that was the man who'd locked her up.

Who was he, this Mr. Grimshaw?

A lawyer? Her *father's* lawyer?

She'd spent hours trying to puzzle out from his few cryptic sentences why he'd done this.

Why he'd wanted her dead.

Because her father wanted her dead?

The thought was almost as painful as was the thought that William would not find her before it was too late.

Her beloved William, with whom she wanted to spend the rest of her life.

Too late. Happiness was brief. She'd felt love, and that is what she must cling on to during these final hours.

Her throat was dry. Thirst was raging in her, worse than any hunger.

"Help me! Please help me!"

To her astonishment, footsteps now crunched on the gravel that led to the heavy door. Someone had come. Someone was going to rescue her.

The turning of the key was like the elixir of hope. She'd not think the worst. Nothing could be worse than remaining in the dark, breathing in the cold, dank, dusty air that smelled of death and decay.

The door opened, and the sudden glare made her put her hands to her eyes. She staggered forward, tripping on her black bombazine skirts, squinting in the painful light as she sought for features of the man she loved.

Dear Lord, please let it be William come to rescue her, not...

But the arms that went round her waist, whisking her up and carrying her swiftly to the carriage, were wiry and the smell of him was of whisky and fear.

This could not be happening, she raged internally as he laid her across the seat.

Safety? Release? They were not to be hers, after all?

She'd been incarcerated for so long, and was so thirsty, Evelina was nearly beside herself. "Water," she croaked. "Please...give me water." Her head was spinning. She was barely aware of her surroundings until her arms were wrenched behind her and she felt the harsh bindings pulled taut, pinioning her wrists behind her.

"Final wish granted," came the same urbane tones she recognized from yesterday while, thankfully, a flask was put to her lips and she felt the rush of liquid down her throat, bubbling up over her cheeks and chin as she coughed on the burn of brandy.

Nevertheless, it was some relief, though she wept from fear as the carriage door slammed and her jailer settled himself in beside her.

"Blessed relief if I could have left you there, Evelina, but time is of the essence, and I must find somewhere safer to put you. I can't risk that they'd put two and two together and find you there."

"Somewhere safe?" she whispered. "I don't know what you mean. Why are you doing this to me? What have I done? Who are you?"

"As I told you, I am your father's lawyer, and he does not wish to be troubled by you, my dear. A confluence of unfortunate events forced my hand when I never thought it would come to this. I blame the man you were to marry. Never trust a man who claims to love you, Evelina." He gave a wry chuckle as the carriage rocked slowly over the gravel. "Ultimately, everyone is driven by self-interest. It's a sad reflection, but it's true."

"William? William loves me! He does!"

"I'm not talking about Bellingham. He's far too diligent. That's why I have to move you. There he was at Ravenhall Manor today, looking for you, making enquiries. No, I was talking about Dunstable."

"William was trying to find me?" Evelina felt another spark of hope. At the funeral, he'd said to expect him any time. He'd not forsake her, regardless of her position, wealth or lack of it, he'd said.

"Sticking his nose into business that has nothing to do with him, and visiting your father with questions the poor man has no need to be troubled by."

"Questions about me? William spoke to my father? Lord...Ravenhall?" She barely dared say his name, though she'd whispered it in confusion half the night.

"Lord Ravenhall is my father? He is, isn't he? Why will you not take me to him? Please, Mr. Grimshaw?" If she asked nicely enough, appealed to his compassion and integrity, might he not change his mind about wherever he was taking her? For she greatly feared it was a place no better than the family crypt.

The family crypt where she had slept on the sarcophagus of the child who bore her name and who had been born the same day Evelina had but whose life had been cut short when she was a child.

"My duty towards your father is the same as my duty towards all the earls of Ravenswood: to ensure the continuation of the Ravenswood line and that the family assets are not dispersed. For nearly twenty years, your father, the 5th

Earl of Ravenswood, has been comfortably of the belief that you were no more, Evelina. That you and your mother were blessedly no more. Dead, my girl, so that he was free to marry the woman he really loved who would bear him the son that a man in your father's position requires if the family name is to continue direct, and the family estate and wealth not pass over to the next male heir—in your father's case, a distance, feeble-minded cousin. I've served your father, the 5th earl of Ravenswood, for nearly twenty years and I served his cousin, the 4th earl, before that. I have dedicated my life to serving the Ravenswood family and I will not let the worthless offspring of an immoral woman derail five centuries of greatness. Your father's family depends on the next heir being your half-brother, Rupert. My godson. My blood, impure though mine is. And, for that to happen, you needed to have died at six years old, Evelina. Just like your father thought you had." A note of savagery crept into his tone as he added, "For your blood is as impure as mine, my girl, only God chose to bless you...but I will not have it!"

Evelina struggled to comprehend, but she vaguely understood now that this man had kept her existence a secret from her father. Just as he was keeping her existence secret from all those who were looking for her.

The cords that bound her chafed at her wrists, and she whimpered. "I knew none of this," she whispered. "I never sought wealth or greatness. All I want is to marry William. Please let me go. We were planning to elope. He doesn't care about my dowry, if that was the sticking point. Please just release me, Mr. Grimshaw, and all this can be forgotten."

"Ah, but what is said cannot be unheard. What is seen cannot be unseen." Mr. Grimshaw clicked his tongue. "That interfering Lord Dunstable learned that to his cost."

"You killed him?" Gasping, Evelina sat up, opening her eyes to stare at the monster before her. Though the brandy made her head swim, at least her throat was no longer so parched.

Mr. Grimshaw nodded. "He left me with no choice. The man became greedy. He learned the truth about you, Evelina."

"The truth about me? I have no secrets!"

He threw back his head and laughed. "Your entire life is one dark secret, Evelina. Your father is Lord Ravenhall, 5th Earl of Ravenswood. Your mother is an immoral whore!"

Evelina jerked back as if he'd struck her, gasping as she stared, horrified, at the spittle that dusted his neat mutton-chop whiskers.

"Nevertheless," he went on, "your mother knows that to rock the boat threatens a delicate livelihood. She also knew that, established in her profession, she could never be accepted by polite society. So, she made a strategic decision to accept the money I paid her in return for her silence. And for nearly twenty years, there was no issue, no difficulty. I should have known that a pretty, headstrong daughter would rock the boat. There you were, falling in love without a care, asking questions, scratching at the truth. To lose your heart to Dunstable was a big mistake."

"I never lost my heart to Dunstable!" Evelina objected fiercely, pushing up against the door of the carriage, her hands behind her, seeking for the door handle. "My mama did her best to persuade me he would make a good husband and, since I'd not lost my heart to anyone at the time and was so desperate to please her, I was prepared to be obedient."

Grimshaw sighed. "But Dunstable was venal and avaricious. A blackmailer once will forever be a threat."

"Lord Dunstable *blackmailed* my mother? Is that why you killed him? I don't understand. How could my mother have information that was valuable to Lord Dunstable?" Evelina managed to push herself up into a sitting position, her eyes widening as she saw the carriage was slowing by a large, freshly dug grave. She no longer cared about the answer, though Grimshaw seemed happy to oblige her.

"You really don't know what your mama does for a living, do you, poor Evelina?"

But Evelina was more concerned by the scene before her. The grave was in a remote part of the cemetery, shrouded by high, moss-covered trees that blocked out the sun. She twisted wildly but movement was painful and restricted with her wrists tightly bound and Mr. Grimshaw so close in the closed carriage.

"Well, I shall tell you, Evelina, as the last piece of the puzzle," he said. "For it will help you understand why my duty towards one of England's greatest families forces me to carry out this unpalatable task. You see, your mama is London's most notorious brothel-keeper, Madame Chambon. Yes, you are right to gasp, and I am glad to see the surprise on your face, though your disgust saddens me for it seems you really are an innocent victim. I would much rather be doing this to your mother than to you, Evelina; though in time—and sooner rather than later—I will have to find a way to prevent your mama from continuing to pose the threat she does. Money, however, might keep her mouth shut, since she is very aware of the dangers of exposing too much. You, however, in your innocence, have presented more of a threat. Certainly, the men who love you—or, rather, who love your money—are inclined to ask far too many questions about your lineage to make me easy. But with you gone, so is the danger you pose. Your mama, now that I think of it, will have to be next, though that shouldn't be so difficult. Nor as painful as this is to me. Now, up we sit. Let's smooth out those skirts of yours, and I'll straighten your bonnet. You're as pretty as a picture, Evelina. I should have known you would be since your mama was quite the beauty in her day when she married your papa. An actress on the stage with a string of lovers before penniless Mr. Arthur Fairchild took up with her and sealed your fate by making their union legal just before you were born." Mr. Grimshaw sighed. "If he hadn't been so noble, and if you were simply a bastard, there'd be no need for all this. But then your mama tired of the fact that her new husband was penniless and unable to pander to her excesses so she abandoned him and took you with her. Then he unexpectedly inherited the earldom and became Lord Ravenswood, You should never have existed, Evelina. Not as a legitimate child. I was a bastard though much more loved than my father's rightful heir, the 4th Earl of Ravenswood. But a bastard is nothing! Only... you weren't a bastard. And if the Ravenswood estate was to continue through the male line, you were suddenly more than just an inconvenience."

It was becoming clear. Though the haze of terror was enmeshing her, Evelina did have the cognizance to understand what he was telling her. She was the legitimate daughter of the Earl of Ravenswood, who did not know of her existence, and who had married again and had a son.

"But if my father's second marriage is bigamous and his son will not inherit because I am the legitimate child, I don't stand to gain because I am simply a girl. Neither the estate nor title will pass to me, but rather to the next male. I am no threat—"

"Bravo, Evelina. You really can think fast in a tight spot," Mr. Grimshaw congratulated her as he opened the carriage door from the other side and stood over her. "And in fact, that was why I was prepared to let you live. Perhaps, if your worthless mother had given birth to a son, I might have found a way to have disposed of him twenty years ago. But as a girl, you are no direct threat to the line. However, you know the truth." He scooped her up, panting a little, for he was not a young man and he'd already exerted himself. "You know too much. You know that Rupert is not the real earl in waiting. He and his sister are not even Lord Rupert and Lady Elizabeth Craddock. They are bastards and always will be. You have the power to destroy their destinies and I will not let that happen to Rupert, who is dearer to me than if I'd had my own son. I lived much of my life at Ravenswood Manor and Rupert has asked for my return. No, I will not see the Ravenswood name dragged through the mud because of you!"

"Elizabeth Craddock is my sister?" Evelina asked, her voice rising, the scream bursting from her as she struggled in Mr. Grimshaw's arms by the edge of the large, cavernous hole.

"Your half-sister. And with that final piece of the puzzle illuminated to you, it'll make it easier for you to accept what you are, Evelina. Your continued existence is too much a threat to this great family," said the man who, she now saw, intended to throw her into the large unmarked grave. "But here it will end. A pauper's grave. You will join the bodies at the bottom of this pit: the final resting place of those too insignificant to warrant a proper burial. You will be covered by dirt and no one will ever find you because no one will ever know where to look."

Evelina squirmed and twisted and screamed. "The coachman knows! You will not get away with this!"

"The coachman is deaf, and he knows what's good for him. Silence can be bought, Evelina, especially when one knows the price of disobedience. Your mother knew that. But you—" Sadly, he shook his head. "You had to rock the boat. And, regrettably, you now have to pay the price."

CHAPTER 33

William tried to hold the rising panic at bay as Lord Ravenswood put up his hand. "I need to follow him but so he doesn't realize he's being followed!"

"I've known Grimshaw for twenty years," protested Lord Ravenhall "He's my son's godfather. And though it was wrong of him to keep something so profound from my ears, he is not a murderer. If he really was prepared to go to such lengths to ensure the estate went to my son, he'd have acted long ago—with all due respect, Catherine."

William could understand the difficulty the Earl of Ravenswood, would have in accepting such a possibility. Acceptance was a gradual process. Poor Ravenswood had learned in the space of only a few minutes that his marriage was bigamous, that the son he believed would succeed him was now a bastard, and that the wife and daughter he'd thought dead for twenty years, were alive.

At least, his wife was.

And now it was up to William to do whatever was in his power to ensure that Evelina was rescued from whatever ghastly situation she was in. His stomach clenched. Would she still be alive?

Was she locked up somewhere?

He sought for inspiration, his mind going over the possibilities. Could it have been an opportunistic kidnapping?

If Grimshaw *were* the perpetrator, where would he have taken Evelina if had picked her up at Highgate Cemetery?

With rising fear, he watched Grimshaw's carriage disappear out of the front gates and onto the road.

"Lord Ravenhall, allow me the use of a horse. I beg of you."

"I do not believe Grimshaw capable of such a thing," the earl persisted, his genial face contorting.

"And I need to find Evelina," William insisted, turning on his heel, shouting over his shoulder with sudden inspiration, "Lord Ravenswood, you said your child was buried in the family crypt? That is where I'm going now. And, with your permission, I'll ask one more time for the loan of a horse."

But this time he didn't wait to be granted the request, although he heard it as he ran towards the stables, wasting no time as he shouted orders to a stable hand.

The road was curved, winding through a lightly wooded area which afforded William the cover he needed in case he rounded a bend and unwittingly came upon Grimshaw's carriage.

It had taken a good ten minutes to reach the stables and saddle up a horse, once Ravenswood had agreed, so all William could do was base his direction on that in which he'd seen Grimshaw disappear. The closer he got to London, the more opportunity there was of making a wrong turn.

Except that William was becoming increasingly certain that his hunch was right. He would find that Grimshaw had gone to Highgate Cemetery.

And he would find Evelina there.

Anger spurred him towards the evil perpetrator, and love for Evelina enabled him to keep up the wicked pace as he tried not to think of the fear she must be enduring.

So, now the truth had been revealed.

Evelina—or Lady Evelina as she should be known—had been targeted for her high birth. For the fact she was legitimate, not a bastard as he, and Lady Bradden, had thought.

And Grimshaw was prepared to kill her for disrupting the succession of whom he saw as Lord Ravenhall's rightful heir—and, Mr. Grimshaw's godson—Rupert.

Catching his breath, he decided to set his course for Highgate Cemetery rather than try to locate Grimshaw.

Something his lordship had said kept niggling. Highgate Cemetery was, as Lord Ravenswood had said, the final resting place of all members of the Ravenswood family.

Of the daughter he'd believed dead. Evelina.

And if Evelina had stepped into Grimshaw's carriage yesterday at Highgate Cemetery, it would be the easiest place for Grimshaw to dispose of her.

The sun was low on the horizon by the time William crested the hill and saw the village of Highgate below him.

The large iron gates loomed up before him and he urged his horse through, not knowing where to turn until a gravedigger stabbed his finger in the direction of a copse of moss-covered trees, telling him with a lop-sided grin that it was where the Ravenswoods were buried.

He was breathing heavily as he dismounted outside, noticing the freshly churned gravel indentations just outside the heavy door to what he now realized was the family crypt. Someone had been here not too long before.

And it hadn't been the earl himself. The crypt was not on the main pathway, so whoever had visited had made a special detour.

"Evelina!" he shouted as he pounded upon the thick iron

door before realizing with dismay that no one inside would hear him

Nevertheless, he had to try. "Evelina!" he shouted again, louder, as he pounded more insistently, his disappointment acute when he received no response.

Desperately, he looked about him and spied in the far distance a couple of gravediggers shoveling dirt into a large pit.

He leaped astride his mount once more and spurred it over the uneven ground. "Have you seen anyone in this area at all today? Or yesterday?" he shouted when he was within hearing.

The closer man raised his head, focusing on him with a myopic stare but not answering as he scratched his grizzled thatch of salt and pepper.

William knew he must look wild and odd. He was not dressed for riding and his fine London coat was spattered with mud. "A man, perhaps? A carriage, even? Did anyone visit that crypt over there?" He pointed at the crypt. If he was correct and Evelina had been incarcerated there since the funeral, she might be unconscious from the cold, or lack of food and water.

"See anything, Bert?" the one gravedigger asked his companion, who put down his shovel, his interest sparking when William fished in his pockets for some coins. "Ah, now, I think me memory serves me better. Yes, there were a carriage there a day or two ago. Were it yesterday?"

"After Lord Dunstable's funeral?"

"For the cove wot were done in?" surmised Bert, and William nodded.

"Aye, there were a carriage. Didn't fink too much about it, but there were a carriage indeed." He sent a contemplative look in the direction of the crypt. "Not there now, is it?" he remarked.

"No, but maybe it came back. Did a man in a carriage return to the cemetery today?"

The two men exchanged glances, then swiveled their heads about them. "We get carriages that come by and we don't take note. Maybe there was, and maybe there wasn't. What do you reckon, Tom?"

His companion chewed his lip and screwed up his forehead. "I'm thinking perhaps I saw a carriage at the Ravenswood crypt this morning," he said, then stopped, staring meaningfully at William's coat pocket.

William had given away his smaller coins and had only a gold sovereign. If it really would buy the information he needed, he'd pay a small fortune. Though of course the man might be stringing him along.

Still, of course, he'd take that chance.

"Saw a carriage heading in that direction, guvnor only this morning," Tom said, stabbing his thumb towards some trees in the distance. "But that be where the paupers get put and his were a fine carriage. We be fillin' it in next."

"Did the carriage return?" William wheeled his horse around, looking over his shoulder for an answer.

"Don't rightly recall, guvnor." Tom shrugged, then added thoughtfully, "Don't reckon it did, now you come to mention it."

William barely heard the last of his words. He was urging the horse in the direction of the paupers' grave on a slight chance and not expecting to see a carriage of any sort.

And certainly not expecting to see the dark blue carriage he'd seen earlier on Lord Ravenswood's driveway.

A screening of trees obscured much of the large open grave from view and the pathway was rutted. Despite his mount's reluctance, William did not hurry it. He needed the element of surprise on his side.

"Mr. Grimshaw!" He greeted the man as if he had

happened upon a vague acquaintance. It would not do to alarm the man who was now stepping back into his carriage. To William's great disappointment, Mr. Grimshaw was alone.

The lawyer raised his head and stared at William enquiringly.

"Mr. Grimshaw, we met a little earlier at Lord Ravenswood. Have you forgotten me already? Might I ask why you are here? And if you are alone?"

The smile he received was genial. "As a member of the board of Highgate Cemetery, my responsibility involves supervising the upkeep and preservation of various areas within the cemetery grounds, including paupers' graves." He tipped his hat. "Good day to you."

The gaping open grave separated them. William sent a desperate glance into the pit and then at Grimshaw. He didn't want to let him go. He couldn't.

Desperate to detain him, he tried again. "Sir, I am interested in perusing the Ravenswood Family crypt. I believe you are in a position to help? Lord Ravenswood indicated you had the key."

Was he imagining it, or did Mr. Grimshaw blanch? Nevertheless, his tone was calm as he inclined his head. "By all means, follow me. Take care, for the path is uneven. I see we are being observed by three ravens." He chuckled as he pointed overhead at the three glossy birds who perched on an overhanging branch.

He was being manipulated, surely, yet William couldn't help himself.

But as his gaze swept upwards, a movement in his peripheral vision alerted him to something abnormal far down in the depths of the mud-filled grave where the unidentified dead covered in their coarse burlap shrouds lay shoulder to shoulder.

He jerked his head back downwards, squinting to see if the movement had been merely a figment of his imagination. The open grave was filled with several feet of mud, bodies piled on top of one another on one side, while on the other side the muddy water would be the welcome for the next tranche of bodies tossed in.

William's stomach churned with disgust. Despite the chill in the air, the smell was nearly overpowering.

"This way, sir!" Mr. Grimshaw hailed him. He'd opened his carriage door and was about to step inside.

And William was about to go after him.

But a faint splash of movement caused him to glance up to see if one of the ravens had dislodged something or dropped a morsel into the waters below. The birds, however, remained still, watching him.

And watching the ripple of movement far below in the muddy grave water.

A movement that filled William with revolted horror when he thought he saw one of the bodies move; though when he opened his eyes wider and saw a pale hand twitch, he thought he was losing his mind.

Before realizing that if he didn't act swiftly, he would soon lose the woman he loved.

Evelina!" he bellowed, leaping off his horse, then sliding down the side of the pit with no thought for how deep it might be or what he would confront.

He could distinguish one body from another. There were sacks of them: bodies piled upon other bodies. But, sliding off the last one, half in the water, he could just make out a splash of white lace: an expensive trimming of a lady's petticoat peeking from beneath her black skirts, the rest of her covered in mud.

"Evelina!" he shouted again, wading through thick muck past his knees, gripping whatever was in front of him to gain traction to reach that painfully vulnerable sliver of lace, the only sign that this was not a pauper like the rest; praying Evelina was still alive.

He reached her in a few seconds, sliding his arms beneath her armpits and heaving her upwards so that her head lolled forward.

"Wake up, Evelina, wake up!" he cried, shaking her gently at first; then more vigorously after he'd untied her bindings.

But she was heavy and unresponsive, her lush mulberry lips slightly parted, her dark hair cascading over her shoulders.

With a wail, he held her close, stinking water up to his knees, and the dearest thing in his life, limp across his chest.

"Please don't leave me, Evelina! I love you!"

And at that her eyelashes swept upwards, and she gazed at him, her look vacant for a split second before her eyes filled with disbelief.

And then joy when she rasped, "I thought you were going to be too late."

"Thank God I wasn't. Oh Evelina, I can't believe I found you." He glanced about them, stumbling as he floundered through the dead bodies, looking desperately at the top of the grave, its sides too high for her to manage in her weakened state and with her cumbersome skirts.

He was about to shout for help, but then the ravens rose in a flurry of indignantly flapping wings as a carriage drew up.

He tensed, his first reaction to protect from another evil assault if it was Grimshaw.

Instead, Lord Ravenswood, Lady Bradden, and Madame Chambon appeared above them.

He felt weak with relief, then buoyed up by renewed joy as he shouted, "I've found Evelina. But I need help to bring her up."

Lord Ravenswood shouted something over his shoulder and a short while later, the two grave diggers emerged, their eyes widening in their grimy faces as they beheld the scene.

But they were fast and efficient, one of them sliding down the side of the grave while the other sent down a rope which William wrapped around his waist; so that within a few minutes, they were all at safely at the top, Madame kneeling by her daughter who lay, shivering, covered in mud and barely recognizable as William covered her in his coat, and then a traveling rug fetched from the earl's carriage.

"We need to get her warm quickly," said William, looking at the earl, adding quickly, "There's an inn barely a minute from here."

For although Ravenswood Manor was where she belonged, now was not the time to take her there.

Nevertheless, when William crouched beside Evelina to ask if she could bear to take another carriage drive so she could be made warm and comfortable, she put out her hand to touch his cheek.

Smiling weakly, and barely able to keep her eyes open, she just whispered, "Take me anywhere you like, William. As long as you stay with me."

EPILOGUE

ONE MONTH LATER

"Miss, there's someone 'ere to see yer!"

Evelina raised her head from the pillow as Kitty hurried in and began rummaging through her wardrobe, turning to brandish Evelina's nicest tea gown, a loose floral shimmering confection.

"You mean it's William? He's returned?" Evelina's heart fluttered wildly as Kitty helped her into her gown.

"Now, Miss," Kitty admonished her when she tried to stand. "You jest sit right back down for your ankle is not quite healed—"

"But the cuts on my face are, and that's all that's important to me right now. Oh, Kitty, I've missed him. Has he said anything about—?"

"That's for him to say and, might I add, that I never saw a more handsome feller than your Lord Bellingham wot's bearing the biggest bunch of roses you ever did see."

"Roses and wondrous news!" William declared, entering the room at that moment and thrusting the bouquet into

Kitty's hands with a smile and nod of dismissal before sweeping Evelina into his arms.

"Then your abandonment of me has not been in vain?" Evelina asked, rising to hug him tightly before resting her head upon his shoulder as the door closed behind her maid. "Do you know how hard it was for me to subdue my jealous need to have you by my side every minute of every day rather than see you depart for London even though I knew how important this trial was? But now, don't keep me in suspense. What is the verdict?"

William set her away from him, gently helping her to the window seat, then sitting beside her, before he declared with a broad grin, "Innocent! As you could only expect when you had such excellent testimonies from Lady Bradden, her husband and others, and—" William executed a small, flourishing bow—"of course, me! LuluBelle Croft was released and allowed to return ... home." Then he sobered, sending a worried sidelong glance at Evelina. "But, of course, justice was not fully served since Dunstable's murderer will now never be made accountable for his crimes."

Evelina leaned her head against the window and closed her eyes. "Unless he's accounting for them in the fiery furnace of hell," she muttered. She shivered at the memory, then, opening her eyes, reached for William's hand.

"But I think you feel the injustice more than I do, William. Mr. Grimshaw's decision to take his own life has enabled me the anonymity needed to lead the life that I believe will make us happy."

"But, darling, your rightful inheritance continues to be denied you." William looked troubled. "Your father sought me out after the trial. He's a good man, Evelina. He wants to do what's right. He always has, I believe."

"I believe it, too. That's part of his legacy: to do what's right," Evelina said. She gazed past his shoulder at the same comfortably appointed bedchamber she'd occupied since arriving in London to stay with Lady Perry.

"Soon I will leave this place to become your wife, William. And as your wife, *all* my dreams will come true. What purpose does it serve to expose a truth that would ruin the lives of my half-sister Elizabeth and, more importantly, poor Rupert?"

She was sure that William felt the same and that he'd be secretly relieved.

But this was Evelina's life and legacy.

It was Evelina's decision. Alone.

"Besides, I cannot inherit the title or estate because I'm a girl," she went on. "Why should I deny Rupert what he's grown up believing is rightly his? It would break my father's heart to see Ravenswood go to a distant cousin with little connection to the family, which would happen if I claimed my birthright and therefore disinherited Rupert." She shook her head. "Surely, my father never thought I'd trade what I have with you, just so I could tell the world I'm his *only* legitimate child...with all the heartache that would bring?"

William brought her hand to his lips, then stroked her cheek. "Well, it doesn't sound like there's much more to be said on the matter."

"No, there isn't. What's much more important," said Evelina, "is the matter of our wedding. I've thought long and hard about dates, and ... the guest list."

"Ah."

"Yes, I don't see how I can live with myself if I don't invite Mama." Evelina grimaced. "I thought she could come in disguise and pretend she didn't know me, but that sounds so cruel."

Willliam clearly didn't know what to say, so she went on brightly, "And while you've been gone, I've had endless visits from Clara and Victoria and Elizabeth—"

"Do they still think your injuries are the consequence of a tumble into the Serpentine?

"Of course! And they always will!" Evelina frowned. "I hope *you* can keep a secret, William."

"I'll have to since I'll be living with one for the rest of our lives."

"That's better than living with one for a lifetime without even knowing it," Evelina reminded him before she brightened again. "Anyway, Elizabeth and I had the most jolly time looking at hotels for the reception. We'll have the service at St Margaret's, of course—" Then she put her hand to her mouth and whispered, "But how can I when my birth certificate will reveal all?"

"We can get around that, my darling. We can manage to hide the truth, if that's what you really want. But it'll mean forgoing the pomp and ceremony when I know that's what you really had wanted."

Suddenly, none of it was important.

Evelina threw her arms around William's neck. "Let's elope," she whispered. "Let's scandalize everyone by getting married without anyone knowing, then disappearing to the Continent for three months. Much as I love London, I love you more than anything! All I want is to escape to our new world together, without worrying about whether Mama will disgrace herself, or if something of the horror of the past month will unexpectedly reveal itself." Evelina cupped his face and said with even greater excitement, "Let me show you Paris, darling! It truly is a city for lovers and it's *my* city! Will you elope with me to Paris? Tomorrow?"

William laughed, caught up in her enthusiasm, removing her hands so he could more properly kiss her lips.

"Paris it is!" he declared. "But not tomorrow, my darling, though I do love your spontaneity. Let's elope in a week so that I can be comfortably prepared for every contingency and can rest assured you'll be in the best of hands."

"I already am," Evelina said, snuggling more closely into him. "But if that's what you want, I'll compromise. Paris in a week!"

And together, they sealed their future with a kiss.

THE END

MURDER AT MADAME CHAMBON's follows the previous book in the *London Ladies in Peril Mystery series:* A Fatal Rendezvous in Mayfair.

A FATAL RENDEZVOUS IN
MAYFAIR

A Fatal Rendezvous in Mayfair is Book 1 in the *London Ladies in Peril Mystery* series.

Mayfair, 1878

The scandal-soaked historical mystery that will keep you turning pages deep into the night...

A murdered courtesan. A clairvoyant's desperate deception. And a crusading editor who could expose everything — if only his heart would let him!

When one of Madame Chambon's most sought-after "Fallen Angels" is found dead in Mayfair, Lily, Lady Bradden, knows her own precarious sanctuary at the pleasure house hangs by a thread.

Forced to play the part of a spirit medium to survive, she's already treading a dangerous line between deception and discovery. Now she must find a killer before she becomes the next victim.

Hamish McTavish, the righteous editor of *Manners & Morals*, has made his career exposing London's frauds and charlatans. The mysterious Lady Bradden should be just another story—if only he could ignore the magnetic pull she has on his heart.

When their paths collide over a murder investigation, Hamish must decide: pursue the truth, or protect the woman who's awakened feelings he thought long buried.

But as Russian diplomats circle, a vengeful husband closes in, and more bodies appear, Lily and Hamish discover that in a world of secrets and lies, trust may be the deadliest gamble of all.

A Fatal Rendezvous in Mayfair is Book 1 in the exciting London Ladies in Peril Mystery series where danger and desire walk hand in hand.

Get it at all retailers in eBook, audio, and paperback.

Or buy direct from the author's website at www.beverleysbooks.com

READING LIST ORDER

Daughters of Sin series

BUY DIRECT

Two nobly born debutantes and their illegitimate half-sisters—an actress and a governess—unite to bring a dangerous (handsome!) traitor to justice.

"These books are the best-written timepieces I've ever read." ~ **Goodreads.**

1. Her Gilded Prison

2. Dangerous Gentlemen

3. The Mysterious Governess

4. Beyond Rubies

5. Lady Unveiled: The Cuckold Conspiracy

6. Prequel: The Scandal of the Season

Fair Cyprians of London

BUY DIRECT

Ruined vicar's daughters and kidnapped countesses are amongst the courtesans feted by the aristocrats who frequent Madame Chambon's Pleasure House.

But each woman has one desire in common: revenge...and their own "happy ever after".

1. Saving Grace

2. Forsaking Hope

3. Keeping Faith

4. Wedding Violet

5. Christmas Charity

6. Loving Lily

7. Murder at Madame Chambon's

Hearts in Hiding series

(Read in Kindle Unlimited)

Heroines who must hide their identity for the protection of their hearts - or their lives.

1. The Duchess and the Highwayman (steamy suspense)

2. The Bluestocking and the Rake (sweet suspense)

3. Duchess of Seduction (steamy second chance love)

4. The Countess and the Cavalier (steamy suspense)

Scandalous Miss Brightwells series

(Read in Kindle Unlimited)

A series of delightful romantic comedies!

Two daring sisters cause scandal and mayhem as they storm London's Regency ballrooms in search of husbands to please their mama.

Once successful, they are keen to put their husband-hunting skills to good use as they set about matchmaking—with hilarious results!

1. Rake's Honour

2. Rogue's Kiss

3. The Wedding Wager

4. The Accidental Elopement

5. The Honourable Fortune Hunter

6. The Courtship Caper

7. The Wilful Widow

(Box sets available: Books 1-3 and Books 1-4)

Books 4-7)

Georgian Mystery/Romance series
BUY DIRECT

1. Wicked Wager

2. Her Valentine's Secret

Scandalous: Three Daring Charades
BUY DIRECT

1. Lady Olivia's Butterfly

2. Lady Sarah's Redemption

3. Lady Rose's Secret

The Governess and Lowly Companion series

BUY DIRECT

Three Regency-set Cinderella retellings

1. The Governess's Secret Love

2. Hazard's Mistress

3. A Scandalous Reunion

Dutiful Wives

BUY DIRECT

1. The Reluctant Bride

2. An Unsuitable Alliance

3. Passion Fever

Wings over Africa series (writing as B. G. Nettelton)

BUY DIRECT

(Prequel novella) Twilight over the Okavango

Shadows over the Delta

Diamond Mountain

Botswana-set novella

Okavango Angel

DAUGHTERS OF SIN SERIES

THE DAUGHTERS OF SIN SERIES

Two nobly born sisters and their illegitimate half-sister — an actress and a governess — compete for love as they bring to justice a dangerous (but very charismatic villain) during several London Seasons.

With Hetty and Araminta both falling for men on opposing sides of a dastardly plot that is being investigated by Stephen Cranborne, a secret agent in the Foreign Office, there's lashings of skullduggery and intrigue bound up in the central romance.

What Readers are Saying About the Series

"...lies, misdeeds, treachery, and romance. What an

impressive story! Ms. Oakley has a unique way of telling her stories, bringing unknown heroes/ heroines into the spotlight, as they navigate a world of espionage, and intrigue, all while trying to survive and find their HEA. Magnificent and mesmerizing!" ~ **Kindle Reader**

"Full of secrets, murders, intrigues and you feel you know the characters and want to strangle some of them, especially Araminta!!! I have since read all in the series and can't wait for Book 5... This is a series I will read again and again." ~ **Kindle Reader**

Below is the order of the books:

Her Gilded Prison (Book #1)
Dangerous Gentlemen (Book #2)
The Mysterious Governess (Book #3)
Beyond Rubies (Book #4)
Lady Unveiled: The Cuckold's Conspiracy (Book #5)
Prequel: Scandal of the Season

DAUGHTERS OF SIN ~ BOOKS 1-3

Read now

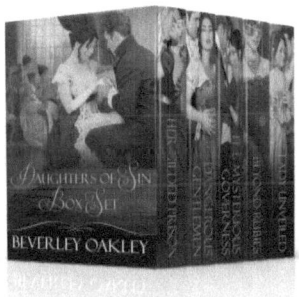

Or read the entire Boxed Set and save even more.

OR, THE BEST IDEA! - YOU CAN BUY DIRECT FROM THE AUTHOR

When you buy books directly from the author's Shopify store, you support them more fully while also receiving a personalized experience, exclusive offers, and the satisfaction of a direct connection with the creator of the works you love.
Buy the series Direct Here.

Visit Beverley's Bookstore and website at www.beverleys-books.com

ABOUT THE AUTHOR

Beverley Oakley is an Australian author of more than 30 Regency romps, and Victorian and Georgian-set romances laced with mystery and intrigue.

Under her other pen names - Beverley Eikli and B.G. Nettelton - she writes Africa-set romantic suspense and Women's Fiction.

Born in the African mountain kingdom of Lesotho, Beverley married the handsome Norwegian bush pilot she met in Botswana's beautiful Okavango Delta while managing a safari lodge.

She began her writing career as a journalist, but it was during long aerial survey contracts around the world—often as the sole woman on the crew—that she began to write romance novels as an escape from the isolation.

Beverley lives just north of Melbourne with the same wonderful husband she whisked away from Botswana thirty years ago, together with their youngest daughter (the oldest lives in Norway), and a gorgeous, dopey Rhodesian Ridge-back who weighs more than she does.

When she's not writing, she runs a bed & breakfast & Farmstay business (called *Wuthering Heights*) in South Australia's beautiful wine growing Clare Valley with her two sisters, and teaches Writing.

Visit Beverley's website and Shopify store:
www.beverleysbooks.com

Join Beverley's reader group on Facebook

Follow Beverley
On Bookbub
On Goodreads
On Facebook